LOGAN

BLUE HALO SERIES BOOK ONE

NYSSA KATHRYN

D1452899

An NW Partners Book
Cover by L.J. Anderson at Mayhem Cover Creations
Edited by Kelli Collins
Proofread by Marla Esposito and Jen Katemi

Her scars are invisible, to everyone but him.

Grace Castle lived through hell, and she's never fully recovered. Nor may she ever. But she's better than she was, and now devotes her time and energy to helping other women...until someone connects her old life to her new one. Suddenly, she's forced to do something that goes against her conscience, her moral compass... her heart.

In the aftermath, her only choice is to seek redemption.

Former special forces soldier Logan Snyder is intimately familiar with captivity. He was taken, kept from loved ones, irrevocably changed. Now finally free, all his enemies dead, Logan is operating a security business with his team. Just as he's moving on with his life, the world learns his incredible story.

And one woman is to blame.

When Grace appears in Cradle Mountain, Logan isn't certain he can offer the absolution she seeks. As the couple attempts to build trust and overcome past hurts, Grace is unexpectedly in jeopardy when old demons cause new threats.

Danger has a way of putting everything in perspective. Logan can forgive the woman he's coming to love...but it might be too little, too late.

ACKNOWLEDGMENTS

Thank you to everyone who helped bring this book to life—Kelli, Marla and Jen, you guys are superstars.

Thank you to my ARC team for reading this book before anyone else, giving me your honest and constructive feedback before taking the time leave a review.

Thank you to my readers—you are amazing, and you are the reason the next book gets published.

And lastly, thank you to my husband, Will. You and Sophia are my world and none of this would be possible without your love and support.

PROLOGUE

E*ight years ago*

HIGH-PITCHED BEEPING DRUMMED through the room. The steady, even tone obliterated every other sound. Washing them out like white noise.

It was kind of soothing. A thin connection to the environment where she felt otherwise so disconnected. It took her attention off the other stuff. Off the ugly. The terrifying. The black fog that tried to hedge her vision.

At least there was no pain, though. Not physical, anyway. A numbness had seeped into her limbs, one she was certain had something to do with the liquid flowing from the bag into her arm.

The woman in white had connected it. The same woman currently trying to talk to her, smile at her. The one whose mouth moved, but words never made it to her ears.

All she heard was the beeping. It was like a hammer. Loud and clear. Demanding every little bit of her attention.

The lady's smile faltered at her silence.

She didn't want to see the woman's disappointment. So she looked away and found a small black dot on a wall, so faint it was almost invisible.

It wasn't invisible to her. She saw it, and she didn't let go. She watched the dot as if it was part of her. Like if she looked away, the fog would disintegrate and reality would ravage her mind.

For a while, voices continued to sound around her. The words were static in her ears. But even if they weren't, would they even make sense to her?

Probably not. A lot of the world had stopped making sense over the last week. For a while, she'd been thrust into a darkness so black that she could have sworn she'd never see again. So many times, she'd wished for freedom. Was this freedom? A little white room with a bag of liquid to take away the pain?

She didn't feel free. She'd dragged herself out of the depths of hell, yet every thought was still soul-destroying. Every breath a battle.

She felt just as trapped as she had in that basement.

The woman leaned over and touched the bandage on her chest, adjusting it. There was another bandage on her thigh. Scars were forever, weren't they? So she'd carry these scars for a lifetime. An eternal reminder of her suffering.

They were nothing compared to the internal wounds. Invisible scars that no one could see but her.

Maybe she shouldn't have wished for freedom in that basement. Maybe she should have wished for something more final.

The fog tried to clear again, the pain attempting to creep through the cracks. She tugged the fog back, keeping it there by sheer will and desperation. Focusing on the beeping, she allowed its predictable rhythm to soothe the frayed parts of her soul.

Endless minutes passed like that, until someone stood in front of the dot and her vision blurred. The calm foundation she'd built in this small room rocked. Threatened to crumble.

It was a chest. A man's chest. Not the man she'd been forced to look at for the last week, the one who had shattered her very existence.

No. This was a different man. His chest was wider. And somewhat familiar. She could see it moving, like he was talking. But the beeping still decimated all other sounds, including his.

The chest started to get bigger. Closer. The man was coming toward her.

No. She didn't want him closer. She didn't want *any* man close, ever again.

Her heart began to hammer in her chest. The beeping doubled, the steady rhythm that had become so familiar altering.

It wasn't until his chest was right in front of her, touching distance, that it paused.

She wanted to scream. Cry at him to step back. But her voice felt broken. It was a brokenness that matched the rest of her. One she'd become intimately familiar with over the last week.

He was still speaking, his chest still rising and falling in uneven waves.

She tried to block him out, *did* block him out for a moment... but suddenly, something disturbed her fog. A scent. One that overpowered the smell of ammonia and antiseptic that had filled the air since she'd woken. It was a mixture of Scotch and Old Spice.

Scents of her childhood.

The smell was so familiar, she forced her eyes up. First to his shoulders. Then to his neck. When she reached his face, she saw the tears. Then she saw the eyes. *Her* eyes. Or at least, eyes very similar to her own.

His mouth was still moving, but she didn't need his words to know the emotions he was expressing. He wore them on his face like a mask.

Pain. Frustration. An anger that ran so deep it would probably never be soothed.

And just like that, the fog cleared. Her chest cracked open as she watched her father cry for the daughter he'd lost. The daughter who'd been taken. Tortured. Brutalized. The daughter who was gone forever.

CHAPTER 1

 *resent Day*

LOGAN THREW a hard punch at the leather bag. He'd thrown so many that his arms should be trembling. Sweat should be beading his forehead, dripping down his arms and shoulders.

He'd been at this for over an hour. So long that the building had quieted and the window darkened.

There was no tremble in his limbs. No sweat. Because his body didn't have an off-switch. He could go at this for hours and probably never feel the weight of exhaustion.

He landed another punch. This time harder.

The bag shuddered at the ferocity of the impact. At the weight of his frustration. No, not just frustration. Anger. Rage.

He should be free. Wasn't that how it worked? Destroy your enemies and become a free man?

He was hardly free when reporters were in his face every damn day. When the world suddenly knew his story and wanted to hear a version from the man himself.

All thanks to that goddamned article.

Was it not enough that he'd been kidnapped and held against his will for *two years*? Routinely drugged, forced to train, turned into something other than normal? Faster and stronger than he should be. Able to hear the impossible. Hear things that no normal man should be able to hear.

Two additional punches. Each time the bag flew more violently.

His gaze shot to his phone, silent finally. It was only over the last few days that the calls had decreased. Reporters on the other end. And celebrity talk show hosts trying to outbid each other to book appearances with him and his brothers. Writers and actors begging for the rights to their story. Hell, even foreign leaders desperate to learn how the Americans managed a "successful super-soldier drug".

The calls hadn't stopped entirely. Probably wouldn't for a while.

The worst had been the call from his parents.

His insides rebelled and a new round of frustration rocked him at the memory. He hadn't told them the truth after he'd escaped. He couldn't. He'd made up some bullshit story about being sent away on a mission. He'd been a special operations soldier, so it was believable enough.

Now they knew the truth he'd tried to protect them from.

He aimed a ferocious kick at the bag. The impact was so loud it could probably be heard on the street.

The sound of footsteps penetrated his anger, footsteps that a normal man wouldn't be able to hear. Logan paused, already knowing who was about to walk in.

The door creaked behind him. "You gonna punch that bag all night?"

Dropping his arms, Logan turned toward his friend and business partner, Jason. One of *seven* business partners. All of whom had been through the hell of Project Arma. "Nah, it wouldn't last that long."

Jason chuckled. "You're not wrong. Man, we're gonna be replacing them left, right, and center." Some of the humor left his face. "Anything you want to get off your chest?"

Logan almost laughed. That's what he was doing here in the workout room. He just wasn't using words. "You mean like the fact that we've been fending off a dozen strangers a day for the last two weeks? Or how half of Cradle Mountain's residents look at us like we've got two heads?"

Jason lifted a shoulder. "It's kind of like being a celebrity, isn't it?"

This time he *did* chuckle. Trust Jason to try to find the positive.

His friend stepped further into the room. "Seriously though, it'll die off."

He knew that, but *when* would it die off? *Soldiers Given Experimental Drugs Become More Than Human* was a pretty sticky headline. "I know. But patience doesn't seem to come as easily to me as it used to."

And it was in particularly low supply when people followed him home. Or camped outside the Blue Halo office, waiting to bombard him with questions.

The team had opened Blue Halo Security a little over a month ago. As a security company, it offered whatever their clients required, whether that was private or corporate protection agents, consultation on personal security, or self-defense education.

They also completed off-the-books missions for the government. Missions that normal men could seldom accomplish.

"Did it really *ever* come easily to you?"

His lips tilted up. *Asshole.* "Probably not."

The smile slipped from Jason's face. "You thinking about that therapist, too?"

Logan's muscles bunched at the mention of the woman. Grace Castle. She'd broken her therapist-patient confidentiality when she'd exposed everything the women in Marble Falls had told her.

Spoke volumes about her ethics.

"I just don't get why she did it," Jason continued.

Logan scoffed. "Doesn't matter. The point is she did." He was lying. It *did* matter to him. He wanted to know what motivated a woman to disregard her professional ethos.

Jason sighed, no doubt hearing the lie, but not pulling him up on it. He started to turn, then stopped. "Any word from the guys?"

Callum, Flynn, Tyler, and Liam were in Celaya, Mexico, completing one of those off-the-books missions, attempting to shut down a sex trafficking ring.

"Flynn contacted me earlier today. They're making progress, still haven't found the exact location of the operation, but they don't think it'll take long."

Jason nodded. "Looking forward to them catching the scum and shutting the organization down."

"Shutting it down for good," Logan agreed.

By killing every last asshole involved. Less evil in the world was always a good thing, as far as he was concerned. Apparently, this trafficking ring had been in existence for nearly a decade. Ten years of American women being kidnapped, kept in a guarded compound. Used. Sold like fucking property.

"They will."

They were supposed to capture and bring the guys in. But if they were "required" to protect themselves...well, they'd do whatever was necessary, even if that involved dead scumbags.

"Anyway, I'm gonna head home." Jason tapped the doorframe. "I'll see you tomorrow, brother."

Giving his friend a nod, Logan turned back to the bag, tightening the boxing gloves around his wrists. This time when he hit the bag, he imagined he was hitting the assholes in Mexico.

He knew what it was like to be a prisoner. To be held against his will, his body no longer his own. But while he'd been fed well, remained predominantly uninjured and was provided with decent accommodations, he knew that wasn't the case for the women.

He hit the bag again and again. His fists never slowed.

Freedom was an illusion. He'd come to understand that very quickly over the last few years. People thought they were free—but was it really freedom if it could be snatched away in a split second?

Punch, punch, kick.

Logan had thought he was safe three years ago when he'd returned home from a mission and gone to bed in his apartment. Then he'd been snatched away. Separated from his life and thrust into a new one.

Punch, punch, kick.

And now the entire world knew. Not his pain; they couldn't know that unless they'd lived it. But they knew the basics.

His next punch was so hard that the bag flew up, hitting the ceiling. The bang echoed through the room, almost sounding like a gunshot.

When it fell, he grabbed it with both hands and pressed his head against the surface, trying to calm himself.

The people who had taken him were dead. And now, his team would work to rid the world of other criminals, starting with those assholes running the trafficking ring.

Yanking his gloves off his hands, he tossed them in his gym bag before heading down the hall to the shower. The full bathroom was an addition to Blue Halo Security that wasn't necessary but was definitely well used and appreciated.

He stripped and jumped into the shower, closing his eyes as the warm water beat down on his back. Would there be reporters waiting outside? By his car? Would they attempt to follow him to his house again?

He'd just continue telling them the same thing he'd *been* telling them…to go to hell.

Logan was about to turn off the water when a noise skittered from another room. He stilled.

A door opening and closing. Then footsteps.

Last man out at night was normally the person who locked the office doors, since they were fully capable of protecting themselves and fending off intruders, so the unlocked door wasn't a surprise. The intruder on the other hand…he wasn't expecting company. It was past closing time. Was it someone looking to hire their services? Or was it another overstepping, lowlife reporter wanting a story?

His fists clenched.

He left the water running, not wanting to tip off whoever was out there that he'd heard them. He stepped out of the shower quietly. Drying himself quickly, he threw on a pair of shorts before moving silently down the hall.

When he neared the entrance of the foyer, he didn't walk through the doorway, instead remaining just behind, standing in the shadows.

A short brunette with her hair tied up in a bun faced the desk, but her head was turned, like she was looking back at the door. The hallway he stood in was perpendicular to the entrance she'd just come through, giving him the perfect view of her while remaining unseen.

The woman wore blue jeans that hugged her generous hips and a tight beige T-shirt that accentuated her waist.

He watched as she took a step closer to the desk. When she turned her head, Logan got his first good look at her face. The room was dark, but just like his teammates, he had enhanced vision and could see perfectly. Her eyes were a light brown, almost topaz.

Reaching out, she lifted a framed photo. It was a picture of his team, from the first day they'd opened Blue Halo last month.

The woman studied the image closely.

Did she plan to take it for an article? Snap a picture of it and go?

She didn't do either of those things, instead placing it back down on the desk.

Her head swiveled toward the exit again. Was she going to leave?

Go, sweetheart. Don't do something you shouldn't.

She took a step toward it but stopped.

His gut clenched. She wasn't going to leave. Not just yet anyway.

As if she'd heard his words, she turned back toward the desk. Only this time, she moved around it, opening the top drawer.

That's when Logan came out of hiding.

He was across the room in under a second. Positioning himself behind her, arms trapping her to the desk, hands going to her wrists, stopping her mid-search.

There was a sharp intake of breath, quickly followed by an acceleration of her heartbeat.

Yeah, you're not taking anything, sweetheart. Not today.

CHAPTER 2

*T*he cool evening air of Cradle Mountain, Idaho, brushed across Grace Castle's skin, chilling her, causing tiny goose bumps to pebble over her arms.

She should have pulled on a sweater before leaving her motel. Actually, she should have pulled one on the moment she'd stepped off the plane. Idaho was far cooler than Texas. She'd known that. But her mind had been elsewhere.

Here. At Blue Halo Security.

Reaching out, she tried the door. Unlocked. The business looked closed, but maybe someone was still here?

She was about to push inside but paused, knowing she should wait until morning. It was six o'clock on a Friday evening, hardly the time to introduce herself to men she'd wronged. Apologize in an attempt to lift some of the unbearable weight of guilt off her chest.

But she'd barely dropped off her bags before leaving the motel again. Her body had a mind of its own. Because she was suffocating. *Would* be suffocating until she made amends. Or at least tried to.

Sucking in a shaky breath that did nothing to calm her, Grace stepped inside. There was a staircase to the left, with a sign for Blue Halo Security pointing to the second floor.

Every step she took on the stairs felt heavier as anxiety crawled up her throat.

When she reached the top, there was another door, this time with Blue Halo Security painted on the surface.

She took a moment to breathe.

The men would be angry. Christ, they'd probably look at her the same way the guys in Marble Falls had—like she was the enemy they hadn't seen coming.

And they were right. She'd hurt them.

When she'd apologized, she'd told them that she'd been threatened. That she hadn't had a choice but to give the reporter, Phillip Barret, the information he'd asked for. They could detect a lie, so they'd known she was telling the truth.

But when they'd pushed for more information—asked why she hadn't opened up to them sooner or asked for their protection—her throat had closed in fear. She couldn't share the truth with them. She couldn't share it with anyone.

Then there was the way Evie and Samantha had looked at her. Two women who had trusted her with their secrets. Their pain. The expressions on their faces were ones she would never forget.

Shock. Hurt. Betrayal.

She was on a mission now. Once she apologized to everyone in Cradle Mountain, she'd leave, but she wouldn't be returning to Marble Falls. She didn't know where she was going. It didn't really matter. Just…somewhere else.

If only she could at least tell Evie and Samantha the truth. But she couldn't. Not if she wanted to protect her father.

Taking a deep breath, Grace pushed through the door into a dark reception area. The evening light coming through the windows to her right cast a soft glow throughout the room.

Silence. Silent apart from a distant sound of…running water?

Was someone showering? Grace wrapped her arms around

her waist, debating over what to do next. Leave? The office was clearly closed, even if the door had been unlocked.

It would be the smart thing to do.

The problem was, if she went back to her motel, there was a chance she'd lose the courage to return. That was why she'd driven here without overthinking it.

She looked around the room, debating what to do next, when her gaze caught on something. A picture. It sat on the large desk. It was almost *all* that sat on the surface.

Stepping closer, Grace lifted the frame and studied the photo.

Eight sets of intense eyes stared back at her. Eight men who had gone through the unthinkable and were now able to do the unimaginable. Run faster than humanly possible. Lift things that should require ten men. See through darkness, heal quickly... The list was long.

They were victims who were now reclaiming their freedom. And she'd taken their anonymity from them.

Her breath stuttered at the thought. They'd hate her. How could they not?

Thank God no one was here. She hadn't thought of what she was going to say if she *did* find someone in the office. Hadn't planned beyond the pathetic "I'm sorry" that had been barely a whisper to the men in Marble Falls a couple of weeks ago. She was just being driven by this suffocating guilt.

Placing the photo down on the empty desk, she took a quick step toward the exit—but forced herself to stop, locking her knees.

She had to do something to ensure she'd come back. Leave a note, maybe? Tell them where she was so they could pay her a visit if they chose?

Maybe she could find paper and a pen...

Moving behind the desk, she opened the top drawer. She'd just placed a hand in when heat suddenly pressed against her back. Arms, thickly corded with muscle, came around either side of her, and hands took hold of her wrists in a firm grip.

For a moment, Grace couldn't breathe. The air lodged in her lungs and it almost felt like her throat was sealed shut.

Memories she worked so hard to keep buried tried to snake their way to the surface. Blur her vision and fog her mind.

"I wouldn't do that if I were you."

His deep voice vibrated through her back, right down her body. She opened her mouth, but his close proximity made it almost impossible to think or speak.

She'd done a lot of work over the years. Work to stop the panic attacks. To heal from the trauma. But physical contact with men was something that still triggered her to this day. It was impossible to think beyond the rush of panic in her ears.

Silence. Thick, heavy seconds of it stretched into eternity. The man behind her remained still, not moving from his position against her back. Not removing the hands that held her wrists in place, acting as manacles.

Deep breath in. Hold. Deep breath out.

"I don't know what you're looking for," his breath skimmed across her neck, heating her limbs but cooling her blood, "but knowing what you do about us, I'm surprised at your attempt to steal from here."

His voice snuck through the haze of her panicked mind.

Steal? Oh, God, he thought she was robbing him?

It took her three tries to get words out, and even then, they were quiet and shaky. "I-I'm not."

"You're not what? Looking for something to use for your story?"

Story...the guy thought she was a reporter. She wasn't. But she almost wished she was. Swallowing, Grace shook her head. "I'm not a reporter."

Another beat of silence. Another breath of courage.

"Then what are you doing?"

Lord, it was hard to think with his large body surrounding her. Caging her. She was certain he felt her trembling. She couldn't stop it.

Deep breath in. Hold. Deep breath out.

"I'm looking for a pen and paper to leave you a note. Then I was going to leave."

More silence.

Finally, he stepped back.

Grace almost sagged against the desk, legs threatening to buckle beneath her. She only remained on her feet by locking her knees and holding the desk.

After a few seconds of reminding herself that she was safe after all, she turned slowly. Then she looked up, way up, to find a shirtless man with guarded brown eyes and short brown hair staring down at her.

Dangerous. That's what he looked. And so damn big.

There wasn't a lot of light in the room, but he was standing so close she could see most of his features, right down to the lines beside his narrowed eyes. He was angry. But then, she'd known that from the edge in his voice.

She tried to keep her fear of the stranger at bay. Now that he was no longer touching her, she could finally catch her breath.

"Who are you?" His voice had softened a fraction. It in no way tempered the threat he emitted, but at least she didn't feel like *she* was in danger.

Her throat suddenly felt dry. God, is this how she'd have to apologize? Here, under the cloak of near darkness, after almost having her first panic attack in years?

"I was hoping to talk to you and your team. Is anyone else here?"

She wasn't sure if she was hoping he said yes or no. Would more men in this dark office make her feel safer? Unlikely. But at least they'd probably turn on the light.

As if he heard her thoughts, the man moved to the wall and

flicked a light switch. For a second, she was blinded. Three blinks, then her eyes adjusted.

When she looked at him again, she almost took a step back. If possible, in the light, he seemed even bigger than he had before. Tougher.

She knew he was ex-special forces. Knew what he'd been through. And he looked every little bit the deadly killer.

He stalked back toward her slowly but, possibly sensing her unease, stopped a few feet away, studying her. "My team's gone home. My name's Logan Snyder and I'm part owner of this company. Are you looking to hire Blue Halo Security? Do you need help?"

That was almost laughable. She was past the point of needing help. And the one time she'd had external help, it hadn't ended well. These days, she just kept her head down. Well, *had been* keeping her head down, until a few months ago.

"I need to apologize."

His brows rose. "What do you need to apologize for?"

God, she wished the guy would take a seat. Or at least put on a shirt. Anything to make him look...*less*.

Wetting her lips, she took a moment before saying the words she knew would wipe away any softness he was showing her. "I'm Grace Castle."

The change in him was immediate. The gentleness of seconds before disappeared. Disbelief mixed with confusion mixed with anger in his expression. "Grace Castle? As in, 'the therapist from Marble Falls who spoke to the reporter about us' Grace Castle?"

Yep. That was the one.

She wrapped her arms around her waist, the reality of her vulnerability suddenly making her want to flee the room. She hadn't known the men in Marble Falls, not really, but still, she'd trusted them not to hurt her. Maybe because Evie and Samantha had spoken so well of them.

Logan, though…she didn't know him at all. Hadn't heard a single thing about his integrity.

"Yes. That Grace. I came here to apologize. For what I did."

He took a small step forward, shrinking the space between them. "You traveled across the country to apologize for exposing us to the media?"

"Yes." Did he have any idea that what she'd done was eating away at her? That her job was her life, and breaking patient-therapist confidentiality had torn her in two? "I feel terrible about what I did. I'm so, so sorry. And I need you to know that before I leave."

He lifted a brow. "Before you leave?"

"Yes. I'm not returning to Texas."

He almost looked like he was going to laugh. "So, you've been run out of Marble Falls, and now you stop here to seek redemption for your sins so you can start your new life with a clear conscience."

Redemption? No, she hadn't been that optimistic. And she doubted her conscience would ever be clean again. "I just wanted you to hear me say the words in person."

Because that made it more meaningful, didn't it? More real…

He took another step closer. She wanted to back away, but with the desk behind her, it was impossible.

"Why did you do it?"

She swallowed, giving the same vague reason she'd given to Wyatt's team. "Phillip Barret threatened me." The reporter had blackmailed her into telling him everything she knew about Project Arma. The man was now dead, but the story had still been published by his coworker.

"What did he threaten you with?"

"He threatened to hurt me." Which was true. It just wasn't the *whole* truth. He hadn't threatened her with bodily harm. But if he'd done what he'd said he would, the bodily pain would have come. And so much more.

Logan frowned. "What were his exact words?"

Grace shot a look toward the door, then back to Logan. "I don't remember."

He tilted his head. "You're lying."

Of course. He was a human lie detector. They all were. But she didn't have a truth for that question that she was willing to share. "It's getting late. I need to go."

She tried to walk around him, but as she passed, fingers wrapped around her arm. Her heartbeat picked up. Her breath once more caught in her throat, cutting off her air.

He gave a quick frown before clearing his features. "Three of my teammates will be back here in the office tomorrow morning. The other four are out of town at the moment." When she remained silent, he tilted his head again. "Didn't you want to apologize to everyone?"

Yes. But, God, she was a coward. Just *this* had been unbelievably hard.

The hand on her arm was stealing her breath again. But she forced words out. "I did." She shook her head. "I do. I'll come back tomorrow."

His fingers didn't immediately loosen. Maybe he heard the way her voice trembled. Could you hear a *possible* lie? Because the truth was, she wasn't entirely sure she would have the courage to come back tomorrow.

"I'll see you tomorrow, Ms. Castle."

She gave a small nod, her voice stuck. When his fingers fell from her arm, Grace pushed through the door and walked down the stairs on shaky legs.

It wasn't until she reached her rental car and sank into the seat that tears pressed against the back of her eyes. She blinked them away quickly.

She hated that she was still so affected by what had happened to her.

As a therapist, she'd counseled dozens of women on how to

recover from trauma. Yet, here she was, eight years after the most traumatic experience of her life, still triggered by something as simple as a man's touch.

The damaged therapist who sold out her patients. Yeah, she was doing an outstanding job at life.

Shaking her head, she drove toward her motel. What she needed was a good night's sleep. Then tomorrow, she'd hopefully return and apologize to those men before leaving town for good.

CHAPTER 3

*L*ogan saw everything. The way her eyes pinched at the corners. The way her fingers of one hand wrapped around the other so tightly, her knuckles were as white as clouds.

She was nervous. And for some reason, that tugged at Logan's conscience. It didn't fit into the perfectly constructed bio of the unethical villain he'd created in his mind. The therapist who'd heartlessly sold out her patients.

"So Barret threatened you with bodily harm if you didn't give him the information you had on us and the guys in Marble Falls?"

She squirmed at Aidan's question. She clearly didn't want to answer it. But then, she hadn't wanted to answer similar questions of Logan's the previous night. Why? What was she trying to hide?

She wet her lips, gaze shooting around the Blue Halo conference room table, brushing over him, Blake and Jason, before landing on Aidan. "My life would have been endangered if I didn't give him the information he requested."

Interesting. She'd rephrased the question, answering it in a way, but also not completely. Why? Because he *hadn't* threatened her with bodily harm?

Blake rubbed at his temple. "I have a daughter, Grace. She's almost five, and reporters have been taking pictures of her. Scaring her. Scaring her mother."

Grace paled. Again, there was that same tugging at Logan's conscience.

He gave himself a mental shake.

"I'm sorry," she said quietly.

Logan didn't need to be trained in detecting a lie to know that wasn't one. Remorse all but bled out of her. The woman was making it hard to maintain his anger.

The mere fact that she'd stepped back into Blue Halo this morning surprised him. Last night, she'd seemed scared. Vulnerable. Like she wanted to be anywhere but here.

He hadn't been expecting her to return. He'd expected the woman to have hightailed it out of town at the crack of dawn.

Jason leaned forward. He'd always been the calm one in the group, and today was no exception. He spoke to her like he'd talk to any other person. "Why didn't you speak to Samantha's partner, Kye, or anyone else from his team? You knew what they could do. That they would have protected you."

There was a slight shake of her head. "It's not that simple."

Really? Because it sounded pretty damn simple to Logan. "Why not?"

Pain flashed across her face. It was so fleeting that he almost missed it. "I'm sorry, I…I have a plane to catch. I should go."

She pushed to her feet quickly, and Logan, Blake, Jason, and Aidan all followed. She paused when she looked up at them, her nervous energy bouncing around the room. Logan had no doubt they were an intimidating sight. All well over six feet tall and muscular.

"I need to go," she repeated, eyeing the door. "I just…I had to apologize in person. I'm truly sorry."

She gave them all a quick, wonky-as-hell smile before turning and all but fleeing the room.

They remained where they were as they heard the entrance door open and close, then the distant pattering of her moving down the stairs.

Aidan sighed. "Well, that was unexpected."

Jason dropped back into his seat. "What isn't she telling us?"

"A lot," Logan muttered.

The idea of her leaving town, and him never learning her truth, left him...uncomfortable. She didn't seem like a terrible person, which meant she'd likely been backed into a corner. Why? How? What kind of force was used?

Pulling his phone from his pocket, Logan called Wyatt in Marble Falls. Not only was the man a former SEAL, he was also a whiz with technology.

Wyatt answered on the second ring. "Logan, what can I do for you, buddy?"

"Hey. We've just had an interesting visit from Grace Castle."

There was a beat of silence. "She flew out to Idaho?"

"Yeah, we were surprised, too. Just wondering what you know about her. Background? Family?"

"Her parents are retired, father was a real estate agent, mother a receptionist. They live in Fort Valley, Georgia, where she grew up. She acquired a Bachelor of Psychology from Capella University, which she studied online. She then did her masters before moving to Marble Falls."

It all sounded incredibly normal. "If you didn't know she was coming to Idaho, I'm guessing you don't know where she's heading next?"

"No. We've been focused on dodging media right, left, and center. It's been a nightmare."

Aidan grunted. "For us, too."

"I can keep an eye on the airlines," Wyatt offered. "Let you know where she's headed?"

Logan tapped his fingers on the desk. "I'd appreciate it."

"You got it. And for what it's worth, I *do* think she's sorry. And I also think there's a lot more to the story than she's willing to share."

He wasn't surprised the guys from Marble Protection saw what they saw—secrets. "Thanks, Wyatt."

When Logan hung up, Blake shook his head before standing. "What a mess."

Jason lifted his shoulder, a half-smile on his face. "At least we're getting plenty of business from this media fiasco."

He wasn't wrong. The phone had been ringing off the hook with people wanting the "super-soldiers" as their security.

The rest of the guys began to exit the room, while Logan remained where he was. Jason was the last to leave, but he paused at the door, turning. "She's staying at The Apollo Inn."

Logan raised a brow. "And you know this how?"

"Saw the room card when she took her phone out of her pocket." He tapped the door frame. "You're welcome."

GRACE GRABBED her items from the bathroom counter, placing them into her toiletry bag.

Bob Dylan's "Handle with Care" played in the background. It was pretty fitting really, given how fragile she felt at the moment.

Music had been playing since she got back to the motel. But then, music of some sort usually played in the background of her life. It was her escape. Her place of peace.

She still had no idea where she was going. Iowa, maybe? Des Moines was supposed to be one of the quietest cities in the US. She could use some quiet right now because her mind was loud.

And if not Iowa, then maybe Florida. She'd been looking at pictures of Anna Maria Island. Gazing at its beaches. It looked peaceful. A perfect escape from the world.

Sighing, she zipped the small bag, returning to the room and popping it into her suitcase.

Right now, she just needed to get out of Cradle Mountain. There was too much media here. No one had discovered she was Grace Castle, the main source of information on the Project Arma piece. But if she stayed too long, it was entirely possible they would. She'd successfully avoided bringing attention to herself for eight years. She needed to reclaim that anonymity. If she didn't...

She couldn't think about that right now. All it would take was one headshot of her, and he could see.

She shivered as she slid the closet door open, taking out the four dresses she'd hung up just yesterday. Coming here had been a risk. One her father had strongly advised against. But her need for absolution had been stronger than her fear. She hadn't been able to apologize to the entire team, but half was better than none.

Zipping up her bag, she was just about to lift it onto her shoulder when a knock sounded.

Grace paused, moving to the door without opening it. "Who is it?"

"My name's Nicole Fleece. I saw you leaving Blue Halo Security and I'd like to talk to you about what you know about the owners for an article I'm writing."

She froze. Did the woman know who she was? No, she couldn't. She hadn't even booked this room under Grace Castle. "Sorry, I'm not interested."

"Are you engaging their services? I would love to know the nature of your relationship with them."

And *she* would love the woman to go away. Had she followed her all the way from Blue Halo to here? She'd said more than enough to Phillip Barret. She was done answering questions.

"Please leave."

Grace blocked out whatever the woman said next, instead

focusing on checking the room for any last items. It took about five minutes before the woman's voice silenced. And another two before Grace heard the clicking of her heels as she left.

Good. Grace shot a quick glance to her phone, almost willing it to ring. Her father called once a month. Always a call, never a text. And the calls were kept short.

God, she missed him.

For the first two years after her hospitalization, she'd barely seen him. Then, as time went on and she started to feel safer, he began to take "vacations" to visit her. He was good at being careful and stealthy. Not seeing each other wasn't an option. Not when he was the only family she had.

She was about to lift her bag yet again when another knock sounded on the door.

A long, frustrated breath released from her chest. Could the woman not take a hint? "I said no."

"Grace?"

At the deep familiar voice, Grace's breath froze in her lungs.

"Logan?" She said his name under her breath. No regular man would have been able to hear. Of course, he did.

"Yeah, it's me. Can we talk?"

Did he want another apology? She felt pretty depleted of them.

It took a moment for her to snap out of her frozen shock and move across the room. When she tugged open the door, she saw him standing there, looking as tall, dark, and dangerous as he had that morning.

Why did the man have to be so good-looking? Good-looking and dangerous, a lethal combination. It was the dangerous part that had every guarded part of her screaming to stay away though.

He stared back, unsmiling. "Can I come in?"

"Ah...sure."

Stepping back, she watched him enter, taking up all the space, making the tiny room feel even smaller.

Christ, his head almost touched the ceiling.

Closing the door, Grace wet her dry lips. "Sorry. There was a reporter here a few minutes ago asking for information. Not because she knew I was Grace Castle, but because she saw me leave Blue Halo. She must have followed me back."

Anger flashed through his eyes and his jaw ticked. He shoved his hands into his jean pockets, biceps straining the fabric of his shirt. "Yeah, they're a bunch of overstepping jerks." He cast a quick look at her suitcase. "What time's your flight?"

"I haven't actually booked anything yet." Still, she'd returned to her room and started blindly packing like a mad woman. "But I'm on my way to the airport now. If you'd come a minute later, you'd probably have missed me. How did you know I was here?"

"Jason saw your motel card at the back of your phone." He studied her eyes far too closely, as if seeing way more than she wanted him to. "You didn't book this room under your name."

She hadn't. Which begged the question—

"I described what you looked like, and they sent me here." Even though he said the words with the same smooth, give-nothing-away voice, she could see the tinge of annoyance in his eyes. Despite being the one asking about her, he didn't like her privacy being broken any more than she did.

For some reason, that small detail heated her insides.

"Lucky I'm leaving then. Do you need something?"

He crossed his arms over his massive chest, and if possible, the guy looked even bigger. "I'd like you to stay until the rest of my team gets back. Apologize to them, too."

Her heart skidded in her chest. He wanted her to stay? In this media-infested town where her obscurity was about as fragile as glass in the hands of a toddler?

"I don't know if I can do that, Logan."

Well, she could. But it wasn't safe for her. And safety had to come first. It always did.

Logan took a small step forward, his granite jaw so hard it could have been carved from stone. "Didn't you say you wanted to apologize to everyone?"

"Yes. But…"

But I can't?

But if I stay and someone discovers what Phillip Barret discovered, I'm in danger?

But if the media gets a picture of me and shares it across news channels, I'm as good as dead?

She nibbled her lip. "When will they be back?"

"A week, maybe two."

A beat of silence passed as her mind battled her conscience. Even if he was right, she *did* want to apologize to every man she'd hurt in person, she could say no. But…

"Okay." The second the word was out of her mouth, she wanted to snatch it back. Too late.

"Great."

"Just one week, though." She'd simply have to keep her head down.

For the first time since she'd met Logan, he smiled, his granite jaw relaxing. Her heart did a funny kick.

Suddenly, he looked less intimidating, less threatening, and a whole lot more human. She could almost convince herself she was safe with him.

CHAPTER 4

*G*race tugged the jacket tighter around her shoulders. She'd been in Cradle Mountain three days but didn't feel any closer to acclimatizing to the cooler weather.

She moved her feet faster in a weak attempt to chase off the chill of the morning breeze. The coffee shop shouldn't be much further, not if the directions the guy at the motel had given her were correct. When she got there, she intended to ask for her coffee extra-extra-hot. Like, burn-the-tongue-level hot.

Grace felt warmer just thinking about it.

The place was called The Grind. It was supposed to be the best coffee in Cradle Mountain, if the reviews were to be believed. And boy did she need a good coffee. She'd tried some at the motel, but the lukewarm sludge just didn't cut it.

A couple passed Grace, smiling at her. She smiled back.

The few times she'd left the motel, she'd received at least a dozen of those smiles. Waves and greetings as well. To say people here were friendly was an understatement. And it wasn't just that the people were nice; the town was gorgeous. Nestled right beside Ketchum with a perfect view of Cradle Mountain itself from her motel window.

She'd debated venturing out and exploring the rivers at the base of the mountain in the afternoon. They were supposed to be spectacular.

Grace came to a stop in front of a very colorful shop. A smile she couldn't stop stretched across her face. The outside of the store was painted a warm honey-yellow shade, and all the window trimmings, as well as the door, were bright red. And then there was the big pink sign that read "The Grind".

The place was a rainbow of colors. A shop that would be difficult to walk past and *not* notice.

Pushing inside, Grace shuddered at the warmth, her chilled muscles finally relaxing. Soft music played through the speakers, adding to the inviting feel of the place.

David Bowie, "Life on Mars". A favorite of hers.

Making her way to the front, Grace took a seat at the counter. A dozen tables were scattered around the shop, along with a couple of booths by the windows. Each table and booth was a different color.

She wouldn't say the place was busy, but it wasn't empty, either. A young man with short brown hair and glasses was taking coffee out to a table, while a lady stood behind the counter serving someone a few stools over. She had long blonde hair pulled up in a hair band, and deep red lips. Her hair had bright pink highlights along the sides, and her eyes were spectacular. Two different shades, one green and one the lightest of browns.

Her smile was almost as wide as her face as she turned to look at Grace. "Hi there. I'm Courtney."

She returned the smile. "Grace."

"Nice to meet you, Grace. What can I get for you today?"

"Coffee, please. Extra hot if possible."

Courtney dipped her head. "You got it. Not used to the cold weather?"

"Did I give myself away?"

She lifted a shoulder. "Girl, all I need to see is your face to know you're an out-of-towner. Cradle Mountain is small." Turning, she grabbed a mug and started working on the coffee.

"Is this your shop?" Grace asked, looking around once again.

"Sure is. My baby. My pride and joy. My second home." She turned her head back. "So if you tell me you don't like something, I may cry."

Uh, no, she doubted that would happen. "If you have heating and hot coffee, I will worship you *and* the ground you stand on."

"*Those*, I can provide. Want anything else with the coffee? These amazing sesame cakes arrived this morning." She lowered her voice. "Don't tell anyone, but I've had three."

Grace chuckled. "Not for me, thanks. I'm allergic to sesame seeds."

The woman's eyes widened. "Oh, wow. Okay, forget what I just said, the cakes are terrible. You definitely don't want one."

Grace laughed again. It felt rusty, but good.

"So, what brings you to Cradle Mountain?"

Guilt? "Uh, I came to see the guys from Blue Halo Security."

Courtney paused midway through heating milk, the smile leaving her face and a much less pleased expression replacing it. "Are you a reporter?"

"Oh, no. No, definitely not. I'm about as far from being a reporter as possible." Rather than seeking people out, seeking stories out, she was quite happy sticking to herself.

Courtney's shoulders visibly relaxed. "Sorry. They've just been so dang invasive. They come in here, pretending to want coffee, when what they really want is answers to a hundred and one questions about the guys that are none of their business." She shook her head, turning back to the machine. "And if that's not bad enough, they'll then wait for one of the guys to come in here and pester the crap out of them. It's despicable. I've started refusing them service."

It didn't surprise Grace. Particularly not after that Nicole woman had followed her back to her motel yesterday.

"The men deserve peace," Grace said quietly.

"You're not wrong."

When Courtney started pouring the heated milk into the mug, Grace almost salivated on the spot. After days of bad coffees, to say she was excited for a good one was an understatement. And she had a feeling this would be a good one.

On the side of the mug, Grace noticed writing. She squinted, reading. "Every time I hear that dirty word 'exercise' I wash my mouth out with chocolate!"

She threw back her head and laughed. If any mug was going to speak to her, it was this one. "I like the mug."

Courtney's brows rose. "Oh, if you like this one, you'll love some of the others. No two mugs are the same at The Grind. I've got quite the collection. The quirkier the better."

Quirky. That was the perfect word to not only describe this woman, but also her shop.

Courtney placed the mug in front of her. "Tell me, Grace, what are your plans while in town?"

She wrapped her hand around the mug, almost sighing out loud. So. Dang. Warm. "Today I was thinking I'd go and explore a bit. I'd love to check out the walking trails around the base of Cradle Mountain. And the rivers." Along with music, nature was something else that had helped a lot in her recovery. It was grounding. And something she often recommended to her patients.

"By yourself?"

Grace took a small sip of her coffee and, sure enough, it was the best damn cup she'd ever tasted. "Ah, yeah. Why? You don't think it's a good idea?"

Courtney studied her jacket. "Do you have anything warmer?"

"I can chuck some more long-sleeved tops on. Add some layers. And I'll stay on the move once I'm there."

The bell by the door rung and Courtney swung her gaze up.

Her smile immediately widened. "Well, if it isn't two of the most handsome men in town."

Handsome. She had to be talking about…

A figure came to stand beside Grace and an oddly familiar scent penetrated the air. A woodsy, masculine scent.

She didn't need to look up to know it was him. Still, she did.

Logan and Aidan stood at the counter. Logan was so close, his heat just about pierced her side.

"*Two* of the most?" Aidan asked. "Courtney, we all know these Muppets don't hold a candle to me."

Courtney laughed as Logan cast his gaze down to her. "Hi, Grace."

Her chest tingled at his quiet words. At the way he looked at her so closely. She was almost certain her cheeks flushed.

It was strange, reacting to a man like that. Or in *any* way. She hadn't been attracted to a guy in…well, a long time.

"Hi."

Courtney leaned on the counter. "Logan, please let Grace know that her jacket is nowhere near warm enough for a hike around the mountain."

Logan frowned. "You're exploring Cradle Mountain?" he asked in the same are-you-out-of-your-mind kind of way that Courtney had.

"Well, I was thinking about it."

He studied her clothes. "Do you have a warmer jacket?"

"Told you so," Courtney sang as she turned back to the coffee machine.

"No. But I'll layer." Christ, she felt like a broken record. "And I'm sure it will be physically taxing enough to keep me from freezing."

If possible, his frown deepened. If the man scowled any harder it would probably be etched on his face for life. "I don't think that's a smart idea."

For some reason, her defenses rose at that. "Well, lucky for me, I didn't ask for your opinion on the matter."

Aidan chuckled from the other side of Logan. Nothing about Logan's expression changed. She almost wanted to squirm as he continued to stare at her. Study her. Like he was waiting for her to cave and say she wasn't going on a hike.

"Here you go, boys, your regulars." Courtney put two cups of coffee to go in front of them.

When Logan finally looked away, Grace sucked in a deep breath, only just realizing that she hadn't for a while. Tightening her fingers around the warm mug, she took a sip of her coffee, again loving the way it heated her insides.

Aidan straightened, swiping his coffee. "Thanks, Court."

"You got it."

Grace waited silently for Logan to move away. He didn't. Instead, he reached into his back pocket and took out his phone. A second later, he was sliding it back into his pocket. "I just sent you a pin to a meeting location. It's at the walking trail that borders Big Wood River. I'll bring you a warmer jacket to wear."

Wait—what? "You're joining me? And how do you have my number?"

But then she remembered…

"That motel really isn't good with privacy. See you around midday."

Before she could stop him, Logan was gone, moving through the shop and out the door within the span of a few seconds.

LOGAN STEPPED OUTSIDE, ignoring Aidan's pointed look. He was sure if he gave his friend a moment, he'd—

"Hiking?"

There you go. "Yeah, so the woman doesn't get lost and freeze her ass off. Why, you got a problem with that?"

Aidan lifted his coffee to his lips as they walked, taking a sip. "Nope. Just find it interesting."

Yeah, it was interesting to Logan, too. He should hate the woman. Instead, he was planning to hike with her. Most sane people would wonder what the hell was wrong with him.

Logan sipped his own coffee. "She may not be our friend but that doesn't mean I want harm to come to her. Besides, might be a good opportunity for me to dig deeper and find out the finer details of what happened back in Marble Falls."

He wasn't holding his breath, but a slim shot was better than none.

"The reason behind what she did won't change anything." Aidan swung a quick look Logan's way. "Even if she does have big doe eyes you can get lost in."

Ha. It wasn't just her eyes that Logan could get lost in. But that wasn't the point; she called to Logan's protective instincts. "She flew across the country to apologize to us. That has to count for something." He wasn't saying she could be trusted, but most people wouldn't have gone to the effort.

"That's true."

Logan took another sip of his drink. Courtney's coffee never disappointed, and this one was no different. "Anyway, like I said, helping her today is purely about keeping her safe until she leaves Cradle Mountain, and hopefully learning something about whatever it is she's not telling us."

"Mm-hm."

Shaking his head, Logan rounded the corner and immediately cursed under his breath. He didn't miss Aidan's groan.

Nicole Fleece headed their way. The woman was in her early thirties, of average height—and she was the most frustratingly persistent reporter out of the lot of them. Logan had lost count of how many times she'd approached him asking for an exclusive.

She swept her brown hair over her shoulder, a small smile

curving her lips. She stopped in front of them. "Good morning, boys, how are you both today?"

Aidan rolled his eyes. "There're only so many times we can say no."

They both stepped around the woman and continued down the street. It didn't surprise Logan when he heard the clack of her heels on the pavement as she hurried to catch up.

"Then don't. One interview, that's all I want. An exclusive on what it was like being held by that deranged man, John Hylar. Trained by his soldiers. Drugged."

Well, as fun as that sounded... "Not gonna happen."

"Come on, people already know anyway. I can give you a voice. A platform."

"How about you listen to my *actual* voice and get the hell out of town?" Aidan called over his shoulder.

"Sure. After the interview."

Should have seen that coming.

The woman continued to talk all the way down the street, only stopping when they reached Blue Halo Security. When she tried to follow them inside the building, Logan blocked her way.

"You need to leave, Nicole." She opened her mouth, but he cut her off before she could get a word in. "If you're waiting for us to talk to you, you'll be waiting a very long time." *Forever kind of long.* "All you're doing is wasting energy that could be spent chasing a story that will actually get written. Do yourself a favor and leave."

Logan stepped inside, closing the door behind him. Moving up the stairs, he half expected to hear the door open and the light pitter-patter of her heels on the stairs.

He didn't.

Good. Maybe she was finally getting the picture.

Stepping inside Blue Halo, Logan went straight to his office, placing his coffee and phone on the desk. It was a Sunday, but with the business still being new, they were open every day. Luckily, they were a big team, so days off were still possible.

But not today. A full morning of phone calls awaited him, most of them discussing commercial security. And in between, he needed to touch base with his team to see how the mission was going.

The thought had barely flashed through his mind when his phone started to ring, Flynn's name on the screen.

Lifting it, he answered the call. "Flynn, how's it going down there?"

"We found them." Heavy wind sounded in the background. "They've got a compound on the outskirts of Celaya. We're finalizing details on the best way to get in and out without any of the women getting hurt. We're going to infiltrate tomorrow."

Thank God. "Need anything from us?"

"When we've got it all worked out, we'll make contact with Steve, make sure the evacuation plan is rock solid." The light shuffle of feet sounded, telling Logan his friend was on the move. "If they can only get one evacuation flight, there's a chance the victims might be temporarily taken to Cradle Mountain. Might need you to check how resourced the town is for that."

Resourced as in medical staff. He wasn't in a position to hire more, of course, but Steve might have some pull to make something happen. "I'll look into it."

"Thanks."

"And, Flynn, when you catch this ringleader, Ice...make sure he suffers."

The guy didn't deserve an easy death, and he knew his team wouldn't grant him one.

"Already planning on it."

Logan hung up, relieved his friends were finally going to shut this organization down.

They didn't know a lot about Ice, just that he'd taken over the running of the organization after the old boss died. They didn't know what he looked like...hell, they didn't even have a real name. But when the team got in there, they planned to find out, one way or the other.

They believed he was a US citizen because of his easy access and movements in the US. They also knew he had no problem instructing his men to take women away from their homes and loved ones. Treat them like property. And allow unthinkable things to happen.

The guy was the scum of the earth, and he didn't deserve the air he breathed. Tomorrow, when he breathed his last breath, the world wouldn't bat an eye.

CHAPTER 5

$\mathcal{G}$race shot another look at her phone as she drove to the river. She'd missed two calls from her father that morning. Two! Once when she'd been in the grocery store and again while in the shower. He never called twice. And it made her nervous.

Usually, if she missed a call, he'd call the next day. Two calls almost in a row had to mean something was wrong, didn't it? And if there was something wrong, was it wrong on her end or his?

Her gut clenched at the thought of her father being in trouble. She would put herself in danger over him in a second.

She'd tried calling him back each time, but both calls had just gone to voicemail.

Taking a steadying breath, Grace paused at an intersection before turning left. The further she drove, the fewer buildings she saw and the more trees. She was now surrounded by nature. The trees swayed beyond her windows, exposing the heavy wind.

"Beautiful," she said quietly under her breath.

A few miles later, Grace slowed the car, pulling onto a short dirt road before parking at the end in a small clearing.

Climbing out, she was immediately greeted by the sound of water flowing in the river. Of birds chirping in the sky and the rustle of leaves on the ground. Sure, it was cold. Really cold. But there were no car horns. No construction sounds. Just the tranquility of nature.

Closing her eyes for a moment, Grace sighed. It was peaceful. Something she could definitely use more of.

After locking her car, Grace briefly scanned the area, quickly noticing hers was the only vehicle. Logan hadn't arrived yet.

Fine with her. She had a few moments to take it all in on her own.

Moving toward the water, she wrapped her arms around her waist. Was Logan's offer to join her today a small step toward forgiveness? Lord, she hoped so. When she looked at him, she saw anger, frustration...but not cruelty. Which made what she'd done to the men seem even worse.

When the breeze rushed over her skin, her body gave an involuntary shudder. Okay, she was starting to understand why everyone had looked at her like she was crazy for hiking without the appropriate clothing. It was proper cold. And she doubted any amount of layers or walking would keep her warm without a thicker jacket.

Rookie error.

Stopping at the water's edge, Grace admired the daylight reflecting off the surface. So dang beautiful. Maybe one day she'd build a home in the middle of a forest. No neighbors. No car engines passing her house. Just her and the trees.

She almost laughed out loud. Maybe not. Wasn't that how most horror movies went? Woman alone in the woods gets skinned alive by axe murderer?

At the feel of her phone vibrating in her pocket, she couldn't get the thing out quick enough. "Dad?"

Crackling sounded over the phone, the line cutting in and

out. Her father's muffled voice sounded between strings of silence.

Dammit.

"Dad? Can you hear me?"

More crackling and broken voice.

Pulling the phone away from her ear, she groaned out loud. A single bar of signal.

Dang it to hell.

"Dad, hang on, I'm going to move around and see if it helps. Please don't hang up." She knew if she took too long, he would.

Walking up the river, she kept one eye on the path in front of her and the other on the phone, begging the signal bars to increase.

When that didn't work, she raised her arm, and for the first time, an extra bar came up. *Yes!* Height. That's what she needed.

Her gaze shot around the area, landing on some large boulders bordering the river. If she could climb up there, would that give her the signal boost she needed? Worth a shot.

"Hang on a sec, Dad." She had no idea if he could hear her. He probably heard what she did, bits and pieces broken up by the line cutting out.

Pushing her phone into her pocket, Grace ran over to the boulders and began to climb. Even though there were plenty of edges to grab, the rock itself was slightly damp, and her cold fingers did nothing to help the situation. But, dang it, she was determined.

When she got to the top of the boulders, she steadied herself before pulling the phone from her pocket. She sighed in relief when she saw that not only was her father still on the line, but she had another full bar of signal.

"Dad?"

"Gracie, are you okay?"

The line wasn't completely clear, but she could hear him. He sounded anxious.

"I'm fine, Dad. What's wrong?"

"Kieran's fingerprints were found."

Her breath caught in her throat. Over the last eight years, there hadn't been a single sign of the guy. He'd just disappeared.

"Where?"

"Phoenix, Arizona."

The air eased out of her chest. So, not close to her.

"It was a few days ago. He attempted to abduct a woman. She managed to fight him off and, in the process, one of his gloves came off. When she grabbed her gun, he fled, but touched her doorknob. That's how his prints were lifted."

Grace gnawed at her bottom lip. "But she was okay?"

"She's safe, Gracie. I just wanted you to know so you can be careful."

The man had disappeared without a trace eight years ago. This was the first piece of evidence confirming he was still very much alive...and still hurting women.

The idea had Grace's chest hurting. A small part of her had hoped Kieran hadn't been found because he was dead.

"I will. Thanks, Dad."

"Have you left Cradle Mountain?"

She scrunched her eyes shut. Should she lie? No. She couldn't. Not to him. "I haven't, but I'm safe. I'm keeping my head down and the reporters haven't identified me as Grace Castle. Or as anyone else."

"You need to disappear, Gracie. All it takes is one reporter to snap a photo."

She knew that. She also knew she shouldn't have come. "I will, Dad. I love you."

"Love you too, baby. Stay safe."

Safe. Something her father *wasn't* because of her. Because of how he'd helped her. His danger was different to hers though. It wasn't the physical kind. It was the lose-everything-you-have kind.

A pang of guilt snaked its way up her spine as she hung up the phone. She'd told her father why she'd spoken to the reporter in Marble Falls. He knew she hadn't had a choice. Not if she wanted both her and her father to stay off Kieran's radar.

Grace was stowing her phone when she heard the voice.

"What the hell?"

The booming question had her spinning around so fast, her back foot slipped from beneath her on the damp boulder.

Pain radiated through her skull when it collided with rock before she tumbled toward the ground. She scrunched her eyes, expecting to feel the pain of hitting hard-packed dirt.

Instead, she landed in strong, warm arms. She didn't have a chance to feel fear from his touch because he immediately eased her to the ground.

"Are you okay?" His deep gravelly voice penetrated the gray specks trying to hedge her vision.

"My head." She touched it, eyes shuttering, feeling liquid on her fingers.

Logan cursed under his breath.

At his touch in her hair, her eyes snapped open. That's when her focus involuntarily shifted. From the ache in her skull to the way he hovered over her. Crowding her.

A familiar panic bubbled to the surface. A panic that had nothing to do with hitting her head against a rock and falling from almost ten feet high.

Her heart rate increased, breaths shortening.

Logan frowned. "Grace? What is it?"

She swallowed, attempting to push herself up.

Logan's hands went to her shoulders. "Whoa, I think you need to give yourself a second."

His touch made it worse. So much worse. It convinced her mind that he was holding her down rather than helping. Dread crawled up her throat, stealing her breath. "I need—I need to sit up!"

And she needed him to not touch her while she was beneath him.

His brows drew together, his brown eyes darkening in their intensity. Just as black dots began to hedge her vision, his hands shifted behind her, urging her into a seated position.

The second she was upright, his hands dropped. And finally she could breathe again.

Closing her eyes, she let the soothing sounds of nature bring her back to the moment. Back to reality, rather than the ugliness that her mind tried to recreate.

When she finally looked up at Logan, it was to see the intense look on his face remained. Had he seen more than she wanted him to? Did he see all the old cracks inside that she'd worked so hard to seal?

"Sorry. I panicked." She didn't offer any more than that. She couldn't.

Logan's eyes held hers for a beat longer before they rose to her hair. "Can I check out your head?"

The dull throb radiating through her skull was still there. Not only that, but nausea was starting to build in her stomach.

Nodding slowly, she remained still as Logan parted her hair. She barely felt his touch.

He swore softly under his breath. "We need to get you to the hospital. I'm pretty sure you'll need stitches."

Great. That was just what she needed.

Logan rose, moving a few feet away before returning and handing something to her.

Oh, crap. Her phone.

She took it lightly from his fingers and tried pressing some keys. Nothing happened. Sighing, she pushed it into her pocket and was about to get to her feet when Logan's hand went to her arm. His touch was so light that she easily could have broken away from him.

"I think I should carry you to the car, Grace. I'm pretty sure you have a mild concussion. Your head's bleeding and it doesn't look good."

Her heart tried to drum in her chest, but she took steadying breaths to calm herself. She just needed to remind herself that she was safe with Logan.

As if reading her thoughts, he lowered his voice. "You're safe with me."

Something shifted in her chest. She wasn't sure if it was because of the look on his face or the calm in his tone, but suddenly, she wanted to trust him. And trust *herself* to feel safe with him.

Maybe that's why she nodded. Why she didn't stop to question why he'd felt the need to say those words so gently.

Logan wrapped one arm around her back and the other under her knees. Then he stood, lifting her as if she weighed nothing and carrying her toward the car.

Panic almost bubbled to the surface again, but she reminded herself that she was safe about a dozen times in her head. Focused on the calming sounds around her and the warmth of his chest. Heat just about radiated off him.

When a gust of wind blew past, Grace curled toward him, not thinking about anything but hiding from the icy breeze. She didn't miss how Logan hunched his body around hers, shielding her from the worst of it.

When they reached the cars, Logan walked straight past hers, instead depositing her into his truck. "I can get one of the guys to drive your car back to your motel," he said.

He hesitated, and for a second she wondered what he was doing. Then, slowly, he reached across her body, and connected her seat belt.

Her breath caught in her throat—but this time it had nothing to do with her past.

Straightening, Logan closed her door and moved around the car.

God, the man must think she was a shipwreck. Falling off the rocks. Panicking at his touch.

Over the last few years, she'd barely spared a thought to the way a man's touch still sent her into a fit of fear. Mostly because she'd gotten good at not putting herself in a position where she'd need to. Avoiding the touch of a man had become second nature.

Until Logan.

CHAPTER 6

*C*hrist, he was stupid. Yelling at Grace while she'd been at the top of a goddamn pile of boulders? What the hell had he been thinking?

Actually, he knew what he'd been thinking. That the woman was in a precarious position. It had scared the crap out of him, and yelling had been a reflex.

When her foot slipped and her head collided with the rock... Logan's muscles tensed again just thinking about it.

"So how long have you two been dating?" the nurse asked conversationally as she continued to work on the stitches.

Grace's brows rose so high they almost went into her hair line. "Oh, no. No, we're not dating. We barely know each other."

"Oh, sorry. I just assumed because he stayed with you..." She trailed off.

"It was my fault she fell," Logan said quietly from his seat in the corner, hating how true that was.

Grace frowned. "No, it wasn't. I was the one who climbed to the top of the rocks."

Yeah, to take a call from her father. He'd only heard the tail end of that conversation, but he was sure it was one that could have waited for later.

"Well, that's very nice of you." The nurse's eyes skimmed across to Logan. "You're one of the guys who are on the internet, right?"

His jaw tightened and he saw Grace visibly tense. "Yes."

"You poor thing." The nurse shook her head, returning her eyes to her work. "I've seen the media crawling through town. I think they should just leave you alone."

Logan relaxed, and he noticed Grace do the same.

The nurse stepped back from the bed. "Okay, all done, darling. The stitches are dissolvable so no need to return for removal, but I'll get the doctor back in here to have a final look before you go. She'll also go through concussion care with you."

Grace gave the woman a small nod. "Thank you."

When the nurse left, Grace lay back against the pillows, eyes closing. For a moment, she almost looked peaceful. The strain lines around her eyes softened. The muscles in her body visibly relaxed.

Logan could almost convince himself she didn't have secrets weighing her down.

Her eyes slid open and looked his way. "Are you okay?"

Logan almost laughed. Was *he* okay? "Grace, I don't mean to state the obvious, but you're the one in the hospital bed with stitches and a concussion."

"A mild concussion." She tilted her head to the side. "And I'm fine. You, on the other hand, look far from okay."

Obviously, he was doing just as shitty a job at hiding his self-loathing as he was at distracting himself from it. He sighed. "I shouldn't have yelled across to you." What he should have done was make his presence known in a much gentler fashion. Stupid idiot. "I'm sorry."

She was shaking her head before he finished, but stopped at a slight wince. "You do not need to say sorry. Like I said, this isn't your fault. I climbed up there. This is on me."

"Was the call really so important that you needed to?"

Something crossed her face. Worry? Anxiety? "It was my dad. There wasn't enough signal on the ground, so I was trying to get higher." She shot a resigned look to her phone, which had yet to turn on since falling on the rocks. Logan was pretty certain it was past saving.

"Is everything okay?"

She flattened the sheet on top of her legs. "He's okay."

He was coming to realize that she was very good at doing that. Answering his question but also not. Rewording his sentence to suit her answer.

"I'm sorry I was late," he said quietly. "I got held up at Blue Halo."

Her gaze flashed up, narrowing. "You need to stop apologizing. Like I said, none of this is your fault. You aren't responsible for me."

"I disagree."

She looked like she wanted to say more, but at that moment, the door opened and a new doctor walked into the room. Where the last doctor had been a middle-aged woman, this one was a young male.

"Hello, everyone. My name is Dr. Cassidy. Dr. Jenkins got rushed to an emergency, so I'll be checking over Miss Castle before she leaves today."

Grace's smile didn't quite reach her eyes. "Hi."

Logan gave the doctor a nod before the guy glanced down at her file.

"So, a mild concussion and ten stitches at the back of your skull."

"Feels about right." Grace chuckled softly. Logan didn't even crack a smile.

Placing the file down, the doctor grabbed a penlight from his pocket, leaned over and shone it in her eyes.

Logan saw the change in her immediately. It wasn't obvious, and the doctor probably didn't even notice. Her muscles tensed and her spine straightened. She leaned back a fraction, like her instinct was to get away from him and she had to force herself to remain where she was.

Whereas the female doctor had explained what she was doing before any procedure, this guy didn't. He simply leaned into her space. Had he not studied bedside manner?

Still, though, her response wasn't what it should be. And it wasn't the first time. He'd felt her tension and fear each time he'd touched her, and assumed it was a response to *him*. Maybe due to what he was capable of. Maybe because of what she'd done to him and his team. But now he wasn't so sure. Her fear went beyond them.

Was it all touch she was afraid of?

The thought left an uncomfortable feeling in his gut. Because there had to be a reason behind it.

Out of instinct, Logan rose to his feet and moved to her other side. She hadn't seemed to mind when he'd carried her to the car. In fact, she'd curled into him. Did that mean she was starting to feel safe around him?

Dr. Cassidy nodded as he straightened. "Definitely a mild concussion. I'm going to check your heart rate now."

Even though the doctor warned her this time, the second he lifted her wrist, her heartbeat picked up. The female doctor had done the same thing, but Grace's heart rate had remained steady. In fact, she hadn't reacted at all when the female nurse had touched her. Leaned over her body.

It was specifically a man's touch.

Her reaction wouldn't be noticeable to anyone looking at her, anyone who couldn't hear her heart pounding in her chest. It was as if she'd trained herself to remain calm, even though calm was the last thing she felt.

Dr. Cassidy frowned before releasing her wrist. "A bit high, but you might just be nervous. I'll check your stitches, if that's okay."

She gave a small nod before lowering her chin to her chest.

The doctor took a minute to look over the injury before dropping his hands and stepping back. "Stitches look good. Your job will be to keep them dry for the next forty-eight hours. You only need to come back in if you have increased pain. For the concussion, it's best to have someone with you the first night. Just so they can wake and check on you every few hours."

"I can do that," Logan said, before thinking better of it.

Grace's gaze flew toward him, but the doctor was already talking again.

"Great. Well, it was lovely meeting you both. Please don't hesitate to pop back in if you need us."

The second the doctor was gone, Grace argued. "You don't need to stay with me tonight, Logan."

"You're right. I think it would be best for you to stay with me."

She was already shaking her head as she climbed out of bed. In the process, her hospital dress rode up—and Logan's gaze zeroed in on a scar on her inner thigh.

A knife wound. It sat high, long enough to disappear under her sweatshirt.

What the hell?

"I'm really grateful for you bringing me here and staying with me, but you don't need to invite me into your home out of some misplaced guilt. Not to mention wake me every couple of hours overnight."

Pushing the scar to the back of his mind until later, Logan stepped in front of her. "You need someone. I'm happy to be that someone."

She looked more confused than anything else. "I don't..." She sighed, before looking down and shaking her head.

Like his hand had a mind of its own, Logan reached forward, placing his fingers under her chin and tilting her head up. He tuned into her heart rate, grateful that it remained steady. "You don't what?"

"I don't understand why you're being nice to me after...after what I did. I know that you feel responsible for my fall but—"

"It's not just that. It's the right thing to do."

When Grace remained silent, Logan's hand itched to run down her cheek. See if the rest of her was as soft as what he'd already touched.

He only just stopped himself.

"I have a spare bedroom. And I would feel a lot better if you stayed with me. I'll worry all night otherwise. You'd be doing me a favor."

He got a small smile from her. "Really? *I* would be doing *you* a favor?"

"Yes." He didn't smile back, instead telling her what he thought she needed to hear. "And you can trust me." He had a feeling she took a while to trust. But he hoped she at least knew that he wouldn't hurt her.

The smile slipped from her lips. And for a moment, her silence was loud. Loud with internal conflict. Uncertainty. She wanted to trust him, but she also didn't.

What had this woman been through?

She wet her lips. "Okay. Thank you."

Giving her a small nod, he turned, leaving the room and giving her a moment to get changed. When she walked out, he again had the urge to touch her. To put his hand on the small of her back. He didn't know why, but he didn't question it either.

Once they were in his truck, Logan headed to her motel. "I'll drive to the motel first and you can grab your stuff."

"Thank you." She fiddled with the phone on her lap. "I'm

guessing this thing isn't salvageable. I'll need to replace it tomorrow."

"To call your dad?"

There was a pregnant pause. "Yeah, to call my dad."

"What about your mom?"

Another pause. God, this woman seemed to have more secrets than a secret service agent. And that was saying something. "I'm not so worried about her."

Truth. But she didn't volunteer why she'd be worried about her father and not her mother.

He didn't press.

"What about you?" she asked. "Family?"

"Yep. I have my mom and dad, and my older brother. They don't live in Idaho." He hesitated for a moment, just stopping himself from telling her where they lived. He didn't necessarily think she would tell reporters, but his mom, dad and brother had been hurt enough. Logan wasn't taking any chances.

Like she knew exactly what was running through his mind, her head quickly turned toward the window. To hide the hurt?

"He's married with kids. I don't see them often enough," he finished.

A short pause. "You should visit them. I don't get to see my dad nearly enough."

Again, just her dad. "You must miss him."

She nodded absently. "Yeah."

Whether she realized she was doing it or not, her fingers were grazing her thigh, right over the scar he'd seen. And yet again, he was left wondering what exactly this woman was hiding.

CHAPTER 7

*G*race turned her car into Logan's long driveway. Flax lilies bordered the pavement while water glistened off the leaves from the earlier rain.

God, his home was beautiful. When he'd pulled in the previous day, her jaw had almost hit her lap. Not only were the grounds huge and gorgeous, with a perfectly manicured lawn, but the house itself was amazing. Two stories, with green vines growing along the facade on the outside, making it look all kinds of Mediterranean. And, of course, the interior matched the exterior.

Logan had mentioned something about needing to get security gates installed around the property. She'd been looking at him when he'd said it. Seen the slight tightening of his hands around the steering wheel.

Safety was important to him.

She didn't know the exact story of how he'd been taken, but she did know her own. It was soul-destroying. It broke down all of your preconceived notions of safety.

Shaking her head, she parked in front of the house on the side of the driveway.

She'd been planning to go back to the motel tonight. Logan had told her his team was due to get back tomorrow and offered to let her stay another night. She'd said no, of course she had, but then she'd called the motel and was told they were all out of rooms. Something about a rainbow run?

So here she was, back at Logan's. She tried not to let her nerves eat at her at the thought of having to confront the remaining four guys. She'd apologized to everyone else, she could do it again.

Grace climbed out of the car, moving inside with the groceries she'd just picked up, as well as the new phone that was still in its packaging. It hadn't taken her long to realize that Logan's house was almost completely devoid of food. So, grabbing some ingredients for dinner while buying a replacement phone was logical. Not to mention, she owed him for last night.

The second she stepped foot inside the house, she was surrounded by silence.

"Logan?" A few seconds passed before she moved to the kitchen.

It wasn't surprising that it was almost dinnertime and he wasn't home. He'd warned her that he had a full day at the office and would likely be home late. Still, she couldn't quell the stab of disappointment.

Memories of the previous night hedged her vision. Of Logan waking her with such care. Of him tapping her shoulder and remaining to her side rather than hovering. He was obviously good at reading people and what they needed. Or maybe just with her. Maybe she wore her emotions on her face like an open book.

It was strange to almost feel like she was attracted to Logan. For so long, she'd convinced herself she would never feel that kind of attraction again.

Healing wasn't linear. Not only did she help other women understand that, but her own healing had been anything but. It was normal to take one step forward and two steps back, especially at the start. She'd definitely done that. And even now, so many years after the event, when she finally felt normal again, she still wasn't fully healed.

Dropping the bags on the island, Grace took out the salmon and vegetables. She pulled out an oven tray, memories of how she'd been those first few weeks after she'd escaped replaying in her mind.

Broken. Utterly and completely broken.

Therapy had been the only thing to help her. It had *saved* her, there was no question about it. Learning about the power of therapy had been what inspired her to study the field herself. It was why she did what she did. So she could help women who had been as broken as her to function again.

Preheating the oven, Grace got to work on preparing the food.

Of course, now she wasn't even sure she'd ever work as a therapist again. After what she'd done, how could she? Sadness swept through her at the thought. Counseling women at their lowest point was hard, but it gave her purpose.

Scanning the room, Grace's eyes stopped on the radio. After a couple minutes of fiddling, she found a station with old school music. George Michael's "Careless Whisper" played softly through the room.

Immediately, some of the tension loosened from her shoulders.

Going back to the island, she continued to prep dinner. She allowed herself to be caught up in the music. Her hips swayed and quiet lyrics sung from her lips. This was her happy place.

By the time the salmon was in the oven and the salad done, Grace noticed it was almost seven and dark outside. Surely Logan wouldn't be too much longer.

She was just grabbing some plates from the cupboard when the lights in the room flickered.

She paused, studying the light fixture directly above her.

That's when it flicked off completely. And not just the lights, the oven beside her switched off as well. Even the music no longer played.

What the heck?

She could barely see a thing and didn't even have a phone to use for a light. What did people do when the power went out? Check the switch box? She didn't know where the thing was, and even if she did, she'd have no idea what she was looking for.

Grace was just about to head down the hall when scratching noises sounded from the back door. They were faint, but there.

Her heart jumped.

Maybe it was nothing. Or maybe it was a neighbor's cat looking for food. But then, why had goose bumps risen over her skin? Why was there a sick feeling churning away in her gut?

With slow steps, Grace moved toward the door. On the way, she caught a glimmer of moonlight reflecting off the knife she'd used to chop vegetables for the salad. Instinctively, she grabbed it, holding it in front of her.

She was probably being ridiculous. But if she'd learned anything in life, it was that it was better to be safe than sorry.

Stopping at the sliding door, she studied the yard through the glass. Although it was dark, she would have been able to see if someone was out there. There was no one. Not on the lawn, anyway. No movement. And no other noises sounded.

Dropping the arm with the knife to her side, she shook her head.

Christ, she was losing it. The power goes out and suddenly she's convinced herself there's someone there?

Turning away from the door, she made her way back into the kitchen. She'd just stepped toward the island when a hand touched her shoulder from behind.

A scream tore from her chest, so loud her ears rang. She swung the knife as she turned.

Immediately, a large hand wrapped around her wrist, halting the knife mid-flight, and stopping it from piercing his skin. Logan's big chest was in front of her.

She froze. Her world stopped.

Holy crap! She'd almost hurt Logan. *Would* have hurt him...if he wasn't who he was.

"I'm so sorry!"

She wanted to say more. She opened her mouth to do just that, but no words came. She could just make out his features in the dim light of the room. He didn't look angry. More confused. Shocked.

He looked above her head, studied the room, the windows, before his gaze returned to her. "Are you okay?"

Physically, yes. Mentally, she was turning into quite the paranoic. "Yes. The power went out, and I heard scratching at the back door."

It sounded ridiculous coming out of her mouth. Scratching could mean a whole lot of things. Birds. Cats. Heck, it even could have been a branch that had flown into the door. It did not warrant her grabbing a big-ass knife and swinging it around.

"Scratching?"

She shook her head. "I'm sure it was nothing."

"But it scared you?"

"Yes. But a lot of things scare me." Only half-joking, she cracked a smile.

He didn't. He waited.

Was he waiting for her to tell him why a lot of things scared her? Because if he was, he'd be waiting a long time. What could she say? That she lived her life in constant fear of being found? Identified by a man who had almost destroyed her?

No. She wouldn't be exposing that secret.

Logan placed his hand on top of hers, sliding the knife from her fingers and popping it on the island. Then he took hold of her hand, heading toward the door.

Immediately, his touch brought her comfort. The opposite of what she felt with other men. It was…nice.

He led the way outside, stopping at the fuse box on the side of the house. He flicked a couple of switches. The lights inside immediately came back on.

"Does that happen often?" she asked quietly.

He turned, studying the yard around him. "No. But I've been living here less than a month. I'll call an electrician tomorrow to investigate."

She didn't miss the way he continued to scan the yard as they re-entered the house.

They set the table together before sitting down to eat. Throughout dinner, Logan remained fairly quiet, his eyes scanning outside the window every so often. God, her paranoia was clearly rubbing off on him.

It wasn't until their plates were clean that Grace noticed the strain around his eyes. "You look tired."

He sighed. "I am. It was a long day."

It really was. The guy had left at about seven this morning and hadn't returned until twelve hours later. "I'm happy to be an ear to listen if you'd like to talk about it."

He ran a hand through his hair. "You know that half my team has been away. They've been working a job in Mexico. They finished in the early hours of this morning, but there was a hiccup."

A hiccup…that was particularly bad in his line of work, wasn't it?

"The guys are flying back to Cradle Mountain tonight. And when they return, it won't be just them." He stopped, his gaze cutting to her. "There will also be women they've rescued. These women have been through the worst kind of hell imaginable. Cradle Mountain was supposed to be a quick stopping point before they returned to their families and hometowns, but because of this hiccup…"

"Now it's not." It wasn't a question.

"Now it's not. My team will be guarding their rooms at the hospital until safe houses can be organized. The problem is, we've been told that will take a couple of weeks."

Grace wasn't sure why that was a problem. It wasn't ideal, that was for sure. If these women had been through something traumatic, family was important. But safety clearly needed to come first, and Logan and his team were in the safety business.

"You have special training in working with women who have been through trauma, don't you?"

Her brows rose, suddenly unsure where this was going. "Yes. That's what I specialize in. I did my internship at a women's trauma facility."

"Cradle Mountain has one therapist. He's sixty years old, but it's the fact that he's a male that's the problem. The hospital has been trying to get a female therapist up here since they found out one was needed, but female therapists, with the qualifications we need, are hard to source anywhere nearby. Particularly on short notice."

She swallowed hard. "Are you asking me to stay and counsel these women?"

She knew he was, but she wasn't sure why. She'd assumed he would be the first to never want her working as a therapist again.

"These women need someone, Grace. It's a desperate situation."

Desperate. So desperate that they were willing to ask a woman they didn't trust for help.

Ducking her head, she nodded.

She wanted to say no. She *should* say no. But what if it had been her who'd needed the help? What if, eight years ago, she'd been flown to a small town and someone could have helped her, but chose to protect themselves instead?

She probably wouldn't be here right now.

"Okay." She spoke the word so quietly, it barely reached her own ears.

Logan closed his eyes, the relief palpable. "Thank you." He opened them again. "The women are in bad shape. They were rescued from a sex trafficking ring in Mexico. Some have been held for years, others for shorter periods."

Grace's hands went clammy at the mention of sex trafficking. Not because she'd ever been subjected to it. But she should have been. That was supposed to be the plan...before Kieran changed it.

She swallowed in an attempt to wet her suddenly dry mouth, the food in her stomach now turning acidic.

Logan's brows pulled together as he studied her. "Are you okay?"

Get it together, Grace.

She focused on the song that played softly through the room. Jewel's "Foolish Games". She let the melody fill her, calming the turmoil.

When she spoke, her voice was even. She forced a smile to her lips. "I'm okay. And I'm glad that I can help."

CHAPTER 8

*L*ogan stepped into the conference room at Blue Halo. Five of his teammates already sat around the long table, Jason and Aidan the only men missing.

The guys who had been away on the mission—Flynn, Callum, Tyler, and Liam—all looked tired. But that was expected. They'd probably barely slept. And they looked frustrated as hell.

Logan knew why. He hadn't even gone with them, yet he felt the weight of the failure.

He took a seat at the head of the table. "How was the flight?"

Callum sighed. "Long."

It would have been. Partly from the switch between going from a raid, where there was noise and violence, to a plane of silence and stillness. And partly due to the terrified women they'd transported. Women who had been through the unthinkable.

"Are the rescued women at the hospital?" Blake asked.

Tyler nodded. "Jason and Aidan are watching their rooms now."

"Good. You said there were six women at the compound?"

Callum's jaw clenched. "Yes. Six alive."

A wild anger coursed through Logan. He was still feeling it when the Skype call from Steve came through on the laptop. It was already connected to the smart projector, so when he answered the call, everyone looked toward the interactive screen.

Steve's men sat around him at what looked to be a conference table. Everyone with expressions so clear they were unreadable.

Steve nodded. "Good morning, everyone."

Steve worked for the FBI in Intelligence. He was the contact who assigned their missions and liaised with them on everything. Both Logan and the FBI had only received the short version of what had happened.

Steve leaned forward. "How was the mission?"

Liam scrubbed a hand over his face. "There were six women in the building. All US citizens. All early twenties. All on your list." The list of women Steve had culled from missing women in the US who fit the MO.

"Do they all have the signature red hair?" he asked.

Sex trafficking operations didn't usually discriminate, especially to the point of hair color. This one did. Or at least, it had been for the last few years. It's what made this case so unique. It's also what made it easy to link missing women to this specific organization.

"Actually, a couple didn't," Liam said. "I'm thinking it's because the red wasn't their natural color."

Interesting that Ice hadn't forced them to keep the red hair, if color was a reason for taking them to begin with.

"There was a dead body in one of the rooms. Asphyxiation," Tyler added. Logan swore under his breath. "Death looked to be a couple days before we got there."

Flynn's hands were fisted on the desk as he spoke. "There was a shit ton of marijuana, as well as a few other drugs. A lot of alcohol."

"But Ice wasn't there?" Steve asked, frowning. The guy already knew the answer to that. They all did. But he clearly needed it confirmed again.

The energy in the room was low as Liam confirmed, "He wasn't there. Neither was his second in charge, Beau."

And there it was. The reason Logan's mood had plummeted yesterday. The reason it wasn't safe for the women to return to their families just yet. If the leaders of the organization were still alive, then the trafficking ring could be rebuilt. And if Ice was a possessive man, he'd want his women back.

It was a big blow.

"Damn." Steve shook his head. "Hason told us he was always there on weekends."

Julie Hason was a girl who had escaped only a month ago. She was the reason Logan's team had enough information to pinpoint the approximate location of the trafficking ring.

"She's been so reliable," Steve added, almost under his breath.

"Maybe it was Hason going missing that encouraged Ice to change up his routine," Logan suggested. It would be the smart thing to do.

"Possibly." Steve's jaw visibly ticked. "At least five of the seven men were there."

Liam nodded. "As we've already reported, the men are dead. We didn't have a choice."

It was a poor lie, and he had no doubt Steve saw right through it. But being part of an off-the-books operation meant they had more freedom.

Regardless, Steve didn't bat an eye. But then, he'd already read the report.

Callum leaned back in his seat. "We managed to question some of them. They didn't know Ice's real name and they had no way of contacting him. Apparently, he contacts *them*, and always through burner phones. Hopefully the women will be able to describe him in enough detail to get a drawing done."

"This guy is like a ghost," Steve said, frustration lacing his words. "He almost doesn't exist. He's been running the organization for eight years and we don't even have a first fucking name. We just know he has a fetish for American redheaded women in their twenties."

Unlike Ice, they knew more about Beau thanks to his long list of misdemeanors. From petty theft to bodily harm. He'd also been accused of sexual harassment by numerous women, but there'd never been enough evidence to lock him away.

"Anyway…you did good, boys." Steve scanned Logan's team around the table. "That house was in the middle of nowhere and you found it. I have it on good authority that it was like Fort Knox. Impenetrable. And you got in. Well done."

"That's what you pay us for," Liam said quietly.

"And thanks for liaising with the Cradle Mountain hospital. Making sure everything was in place to support the women, including a therapist. I'll do what I can to make sure the safe houses are ready as soon as possible. It will take a bit longer because of the support requirements for the victims."

Logan didn't need to look up to know that five sets of eyes sat squarely on him. He'd only spoken to Steve about Grace's involvement. He cleared his throat. "No problem. Let us know when you have an update on Ice's whereabouts."

Hanging up, Logan glanced at his teammates.

Flynn was the first to break the silence, having always been the most direct of the bunch. "Who's the therapist?"

Logan raised a brow. With the way his friend said it, it sounded like he already knew. "Grace Castle."

No one looked surprised. Someone from the team had already told them she was in town. Maybe even that she was currently staying at his house.

"It was me," Blake said, confirming his thoughts. "I told them before you got here."

"She's living with you?" Callum shook his head. "After what she did?"

He didn't blame his friend for his anger. Had situations been reversed, he would have felt the same. "There were no other female therapists who could make it to Cradle Mountain on such short notice. Especially any trained in trauma. Grace is here, in town, and she's exactly what they need."

"The woman can't be trusted," Tyler said firmly.

There was a tense beat of silence before Flynn spoke. "He's right, she can't. But I'd like to hear her story anyway."

"She's visiting the women at the hospital today. You guys can stop by my house tonight. She's expecting you." He didn't think they'd get more out of her than he'd gotten. And there were huge parts of her story missing. But at least they'd be able to hear her sincerity. Because she *was* sincere.

"I still don't think it's wise that she counsels anyone after breaching patient-therapist confidentiality," Liam said.

"Like I said, there was no one else. I was told the male therapist wouldn't work, so it was her or no one. It will only be for a couple weeks while Steve organizes the safe houses."

Besides, the women she'd counseled in Marble Falls had said nothing but great things about Grace. Her only sin was talking to the reporter. And Logan was almost certain she'd had a good reason for that. One that she didn't feel safe enough to share. Yet.

GRACE STEPPED INSIDE THE GRIND. The place was busy. But then, who wouldn't want to have a midmorning coffee at the most colorful coffee shop in town.

Moving over to the counter, she noticed Courtney wearing a pink top perfectly matching the pink stripes in her hair. Her pants were a shade of green that were ridiculously bright.

When the other woman looked up, she smiled at Grace. "Hey, hon. Coffee?"

Grace nodded. "Yes, please. In a big hot mug."

Courtney chuckled. "You got it. Grab a seat."

All the stools at the counter were taken, so Grace headed toward a booth by the window. Today was the day she was supposed to be leaving Cradle Mountain. Moving somewhere far away and disappearing.

Instead, she'd spent her morning unpacking her clothes into Logan's spare room—again. She'd tried insisting that she go back to the motel, to which Logan kept repeating that there was no point, and no room at the motel anyway. And he was right.

If she was honest with herself, she was kind of relieved. Not only because she was feeling comfortable around him now, but also because he made her feel safe. His strength. His size. Not to mention his unbelievable home security system.

Grace glanced down at her phone. She needed to call her dad today. Tell him her short-term plans. He wouldn't be happy.

Her stomach dropped at the thought.

She was meeting her new patients today. She sucked in a quick breath, knowing it would be emotionally draining. Counseling patients who had been through such significant trauma always was, no matter how experienced you were in the field.

She was just looking around when her gaze caught a couple outside the window. The man looked familiar. He was from Blue Halo. Blake, maybe?

She looked sad and he looked...discouraged? Definitely not happy. When the woman turned to walk away, he grabbed her wrist, pulling her close. Her eyes shuttered. When they opened, there was resolve there. Her lips moved, and whatever she said had him letting her go.

When she walked away, he ran a hand through his hair, obviously frustrated.

A hot coffee slid in front of her, then Courtney dropped into the opposite side of the booth, a glass of what looked to be orange juice in her hands.

"Mind if I join you? My feet are killing me and boy could I use some girl time."

"Working too much?"

She nodded. "Girl, I live and breathe this shop. I may as well set up a cot in the back."

"Well, I love company." Grace shot a quick look around the packed coffee shop, gaze zeroing in on the male and female servers. "Do you have many employees?"

"Eh, a handful. It's never enough. Luckily, Joey is amazing. He can run the show when I'm not here." She gestured toward the counter.

Grace looked over again to see a young man moving so quickly, he was almost on fast-forward mode.

Wrapping her fingers around the mug, she was about to lift it to her lips when she stopped and read the side. *I'm currently holding it together with one bobby pin.*

Grace laughed. Fitting. Very fitting.

Courtney smiled. "You looked a bit stressed."

"Yeah, you could say that."

She tilted her head to the side. "Are you okay?"

Well, the day's list included talking to her dad, counseling the women who had been rescued, and apologizing to the remainder of Logan's team...it was a lot. Not more than she could handle, but still a lot.

"I am. I'm staying in town for a couple weeks to counsel some women, actually."

"Ah, you're a therapist. That's why your eyes are so wise."

Grace almost spat out her coffee at the snort that bubbled in her throat. "Wise eyes?"

"Oh yeah. I thought that the second I met you." Courtney tapped her fingers on the table in thought. "You know, if you're here a couple weeks, I know something that would be great fun. Add some *color* to your stay."

Grace didn't know whether she should be excited or scared. "How?"

"It's called The Cradle Mountain Rainbow Run."

"Rainbow Run?" The reason she couldn't get a room at the motel.

"Yeah. It's kind of like The Color Run in that it's a fundraiser and there's color, but a bit different. It's taking place this Saturday. I've signed up for the race, but so far, I'm a lone wolf and in desperate need of a running buddy."

A fundraiser didn't sound terrible. "What does it involve?"

"Color. And running."

Grace laughed again. "Of course. Why didn't I think of that? How long exactly is the run, and where does the color come into it?"

"Well, it's ten miles, which you could also walk if you prefer." Walking. Definitely preferable to running. "Every mile, you get doused in colored powder, which is literally just baking soda, cornstarch, and food dye. It's the only day of the year I wear white." She lifted a shoulder. "And the only day I jog-slash-walk ten miles."

It would be the only one for Grace, too. "Where does the charity part come into it?"

"You pay a donation to participate. It's very popular here, and we always raise a lot."

Hm. She still wasn't too hot about the running part...

"I can already tell you're not convinced, so let me tell you the best part." Courtney leaned forward, her voice lowering. "At the end of the ten miles, there's a Finish Festival. After the kids leave and the sun goes down, there's music, alcohol, food trucks, and more colored powder."

Grace chuckled. Truth be told, she could probably use a little color and fun in her life right now. "Okay."

Courtney's eyes lit up. "Yeah? You're in?" She clapped her hands. "Yay! It will be so much fun!"

"As long as you don't mind me doing more walking than running." Probably a lot more.

"Easy, done. And worse comes to worst, we find a strong man to hitch a ride with."

It might become more of a necessity than a choice.

She was just lifting her mug to her lips when a woman slipped into the booth beside Courtney. Before either woman could say a word, the lady switched on what looked to be a tape recorder and turned to look at the coffee shop owner.

"Hi, Courtney. Good to see you again. I was wondering if you were ready for that interview?"

The second the words were out of her mouth, Grace recognized the voice. It was the woman who had followed her to the motel the other day.

Courtney rolled her eyes. "Look, Nicole, like I've told you a million times, I don't know anything about the guys. They only moved into town a couple months ago. And even if I did, I wouldn't tell you squat."

"They come here quite a lot, though, don't they?" the reporter persevered, clearly not perturbed by Courtney's refusal. She probably got it a lot. "Do they share anything with you about their lives? Do they ever act out of sorts?"

Out of sorts? What exactly was this woman's angle?

"I think they've been through enough," Grace said, already feeling angry at the woman without even knowing her. "They don't need reporters poking into their lives and publishing more stories about them."

The reporter turned her attention to Grace. "You're the woman from the motel. I went back, but you weren't there anymore. Sorry, I didn't catch your name."

"My name is none of your business."

Nicole smiled, but it didn't come close to reaching her eyes. "Honey, in the world we live in today, everything is *everyone's* business." She looked between them. "Would you women say you feel safe around them?"

Courtney lifted her juice and took a sip. When she placed it back down, the nearly full glass hit the edge of the table, tumbling into the reporter's lap.

The woman screeched, immediately jumping to her feet. "What the hell?"

Grace's mouth dropped open. She almost felt bad...almost.

Courtney gasped, covering her mouth with her hand. It was a terrible attempt at feigning guilt. "Oh, I am so sorry! I can be so clumsy sometimes. You should really be more careful who you sit next to."

Nicole reached across the table, grabbing a handful of napkins and her recording device, before storming out of the shop.

CHAPTER 9

*G*race closed the door softly behind her before moving down the hall of the hospital. Her breaths were deep. It had been a long afternoon. A long afternoon of putting her therapist face on and trying not to let each woman's story cut new scars into her soul.

It wasn't until the door to the bathroom was firmly locked behind her that she finally shuttered her eyes, each breath filling her chest.

Six women. Six different stories. Each just as harrowing as the last.

Three of the women had been taken from their homes. Locks broken. Intruder slipping in under the cloak of darkness. Plunging them into a world of terror.

The other three had just trusted the wrong people. Believed that men were good who weren't.

She loved her job. Helping women was her life. But today's stories hit so close to home. They almost made it impossible to remain distant.

These women's ordeals were worse than hers. She'd been held for a week. Abused by one man, rather than many. They had been away from their families for a long time, some for years, most of them now drug-dependent.

She could have turned into them. And she had similar scars, both internal and external.

Grace's fingers skimmed over the old wound on her thigh. Then she touched the one between her breasts. Visual reminders of what she'd been through. Of what she'd survived. It had taken years of work, years of therapy, for her to be able to just look at the scars. Touch them.

She breathed out slowly. Her heart still felt heavy, but taking a few moments had helped. At least most of the men who had been holding the women were dead. The women themselves had told her. Not all the men, but most.

Good. Men like that didn't deserve the air they breathed, as far as Grace was concerned. Eliminating them made the world that bit safer.

Walking over to the sink, she threw some water on her face before studying her reflection in the mirror. Dark circles colored the skin under her eyes. God, she looked as drawn out as she felt.

Not good. Not when she was about to apologize to four big, burly guys who noticed everything.

You've got this, Grace.

Giving herself a mental pep talk, she stepped out of the bathroom, immediately colliding with a large body. Strong hands went to her upper arms, steadying her.

The second Logan met her gaze, his brows drew together. "Hey, are you okay?"

Did he see her exhaustion as clearly as she felt it? "Yes, I'm fine. Are you just finishing your shift?" She'd seen him working security in the hall outside the women's rooms. Jason had been stationed there when she left.

A pause followed, during which he watched her closely. Analyzed her. Then he lifted his hand, gently rubbing his thumb below her eye, noticing what she just had. She felt his touch right down to her toes. And it didn't freak her out at all.

"Yeah, I am. I was wondering if I could grab a ride home with you? I came with Jason and he's sticking around a bit longer."

"Of course. Are you ready to go?"

He gave a small nod before lowering his hand. But instead of giving her space, he moved it to the small of her back. And that's how they walked to her car. With him touching her—and her feeling it everywhere.

The ride to his place was a quiet one. She caught every look he threw her way. There were questions in his eyes.

When they arrived at his house, she saw four cars parked outside. She parked beside them. His team was here.

Her hand went to the door, but she stilled when he touched her other wrist.

"I can tell the guys to come back tomorrow."

Boy, she must really look exhausted if he was offering that. "No. You don't need to do that. They deserve an apology sooner rather than later." When his hand didn't move, she frowned. "Logan—"

"If counseling those women is too much, you need to tell me."

"It's not too much. Their stories are heavy, and empathy is a key component of therapy. It would be worrying if I wasn't affected by their stories on some level."

Of course, it was harder, given her history, but Logan didn't need to know that. What he *did* need to know was that she was fit to do her job. That she was not going to fail these women. She had the education to provide them with what they needed.

"I'm human, and I have emotions," she continued. "But this is what I'm trained to do. I'm committed to working with these women to help them recover from their trauma for as long as they're in my care. And I have the training to cope with these situations."

Every word she spoke was true. And she hoped that Logan would be able to recognize that.

"Are you sure?"

"I am." Was she tired? Yes. Was she emotionally drained? Absolutely. But she wasn't going to let anyone down. She couldn't. "Now, let's go inside so I can apologize to your team."

Logan still didn't seem convinced, but instead of pushing, he opened his door and led them inside.

Four large men stood in the living room. They looked fierce and dangerous, and they took up all the space. It almost had her pausing mid-step.

As if they could sense her unease, a couple of them offered half smiles. Another took a seat in the recliner. The fourth remained where he was, his features unchanged.

Logan touched the small of her back, and this time, she almost jumped. "Grace, this is Callum and Tyler." He pointed to the two guys leaning against a wall, smiling. Then he nodded toward the man in the recliner. "This is Flynn. And that's Liam." The last man, Liam, was the one who hadn't sat or smiled.

"Hi." She gave them each a small smile, sure it looked wonky as hell.

Logan led her toward the couch, sitting beside her. Taking a steadying breath, she made eye contact with each man. "I came to Cradle Mountain because I owe each of you an apology. I'm sorry. I'm sorry for talking to that journalist, Phillip Barret, and telling him about what Project Arma did to you. I'm sorry about the exposure and media attention it has brought. I'm just...I'm sorry."

"Why did you do it?" Liam asked, muscles flexing in his biceps.

She was sure Logan had already told them everything she'd told him. But she understood their need to hear her say the words herself. "Because Phillip threatened me, and I was scared and alone. I didn't think I had any other options but to do as he asked." None that would end well for her or her father, at least. "I was thinking about me," *and Dad,* "and not about you. I'm sorry."

"We understand fear," Flynn said. "It can make a person do things they wouldn't normally do."

Some of the tightness in her chest eased. Until Liam spoke again.

"What did he threaten you with?"

It was the same question the other guys had asked, and she would have to give the same half answer. "He threatened to endanger my life."

"Endanger how?" It wasn't so much *what* he asked, but how he asked it. His tone had the fine hairs standing on her arms.

Logan's voice hardened. "Liam."

"What? The woman's apologizing but what is she actually sharing? How are we supposed to understand if we don't know *why* she hurt us? Her apology is flimsy as hell."

Logan stood, stepping closer to his friend. "Nothing about it is 'flimsy'. Her apology is genuine."

Liam stepped forward as well, his face contorting with anger.

Grace rushed to her feet. God, she hadn't wanted them to turn on each other. "He uncovered a secret of mine. Something that I'm desperate to keep buried."

The words rushed out of her mouth. For a second, she couldn't believe she'd shared that. It was more than she'd shared with anyone before—ever. She felt Logan's eyes on her, but didn't look his way.

"If he'd published my story instead of yours," she continued, only looking at Liam, "it would have been only a matter of time before not only my life, but the life of someone I love, was put in danger. I was selfish."

He folded his arms across his big chest. "I don't suppose you plan to tell us that story?"

She shook her head slowly.

Silence. Silence so thick, it hung in the air.

Something changed in Liam's expression. The anger decreased, replaced with something else. Something a little less threatening.

"I understand protecting the people you love," he said. "Does it make what you did right? No. But maybe I would have done the same."

More of the suffocating weight lifted.

Callum, the man who looked to be the biggest of his friends, cracked a smile. "I don't mind the media attention. That journalist...what's her name? Nicole? She's cute, and I like how determined she is. Plus, all the extra attention I've been getting around town really isn't so bad," he added. "*Finally*, I'm being treated the way I should be."

A few of the guys scoffed. And just like that, the tension in the room thinned.

Tyler lifted a brow. "What? Like a—"

A pillow was thrown at Tyler's head before he could finish.

As the guys bickered and joked around her, she actually smiled. And this smile wasn't forced. She knew her explanation left more questions than answers, and there was a chance Logan may start asking those questions before she left town. But for now, she felt good that she'd righted some of her wrongs.

CHAPTER 10

*P*eople were everywhere. Huge crowds of them, all dressed in white, ready to do The Cradle Mountain Rainbow Run.

Grace searched the sea of faces in the park. How the heck was she supposed to find Courtney? The participants all morphed into one giant cloud. She studied the throngs with apprehension, knowing that if she had any chance of finding her new friend, she was probably going to have to wade through them.

The problem was, she hated crowds. In fact, she usually did everything she could to avoid them. Because crowds meant touching.

Maybe she'd wait a few minutes. Keep her eyes peeled.

Glancing down, she adjusted her white sweatshirt. It was thick and warm, which was definitely needed in this weather. She'd also bought some white leggings, which, surprisingly, hadn't been hard to find.

It was her new sneakers that were uncomfortable. In fact, they were already rubbing. Maybe she should have walked around the house in them a bit before today? Too late now.

She'd actually been looking forward to the race. During the

previous three days, counseling the rescued women had become just a little easier. A highlight of each day was her morning pit stops at The Grind.

Courtney sat with her every time she popped in, and the woman never failed to make her laugh. She was like a human form of music for the soul.

Grace was just about to grit her teeth and brave the crowd when suddenly, the fine hairs on her arms stood on end. Not only that, but her hands felt clammy, her stomach doing an uneasy flip.

She could almost feel someone watching her.

Turning slowly, she scanned the area.

"Hey!" Courtney's beaming smile appeared out of nowhere, right beside her.

The air whooshed out of Grace's lungs. "Hey, yourself. I was just about to look for you."

"Ha. You would've struggled to find me. I only found you because you stayed out of the crowd. Smart. Step in there and poof, you disappear."

She'd pretend that had been her plan all along. "Glad I could help. You look great. White suits you."

The usually colorful woman was wearing exactly what Grace and everyone else was wearing. A white sweatshirt and white bottoms. But on Courtney, the ensemble didn't look simple. Instead, it made the pink stripes in her hair stand out, the green and brown of her eyes look even more radiant and unique.

"A blank canvas, my friend. I plan to finish this race looking like a rainbow of color."

"Well, I'm excited." She scanned the starting line, noting half a dozen people stood there holding containers of what had to be the colored powder. When she turned back to Courtney, she noticed a necklace peeking out of her top. "I think you forgot to take your necklace off."

"Nope. Didn't forget. I never take it off. It's a family heirloom."

"You're not worried it will get ruined?"

She lifted a shoulder. "It didn't last year." She glanced around. "Now, we need to check in." She tugged Grace toward the registration desk, stopping at the end of the line. "I can't wait to get muddy."

Wait. Mud? "Ah…muddy?"

"Oh, I didn't mention the tunnels?"

"No." Coffee every day, and getting muddy had never come up.

"My bad. There are tunnels and mud. It's super fun. The brown goes nicely with the bright powder on your clothes."

All Grace could do was laugh. What had she signed up for?

As the line grew shorter, they both stepped forward. That's when Grace felt it again. A tingly, cold feeling creeping over her skin.

What the heck was that?

Scanning the area for a second time, she tried to focus on individual faces. Was she just being silly?

"We're up."

Courtney's hand wrapped around hers, pulling her to the counter and forcing her out of her head. They each got their names ticked off and were given tie-dye buffs.

Courtney immediately put hers on her head like a headband. "When they douse you, use it to cover your nose and eyes. Trust me, you don't want to forget."

She hadn't even thought about her face. "Thanks for the tip."

"Okay, should we push our way to the front?"

Grace tried not to blanch at the idea, especially when the crowd looked even denser than it had moments ago. Honestly, where had all these people come from? Did they all live in Cradle Mountain? Surely not.

At Courtney's continued stare, Grace scrambled to come up

with a way of saying "hell no" without actually saying those words. Before she could, two tall men stopped beside them. Make that tall, *familiar* men.

Logan's hip almost touched hers, his woodsy, masculine scent filling the air. When she looked up, he smiled.

Her cheeks heated. Every day, she felt him warming up to her a little more. Every day, his smiles got a bit wider.

And it wasn't just Logan changing. Her own heart beat a little faster each time she saw him. Just like it was doing now.

God, she hoped the crowd around them blocked him from hearing.

"Well, look who decided to join the race," Courtney said, smiling at both Logan and Aidan.

Aidan lifted a shoulder. "Gotta give the town a show, don't we?"

Courtney put her hands on her hips. "Not if I beat you, buddy. Then it'll be *me* giving the show. I can see the headline now—Quirky Coffee Shop Owner Faster Than the Fastest Men Alive."

Grace studied the woman's five-foot-seven frame. "I'm afraid I won't be running with you, then." Especially not with the way she planned to lag behind everyone.

Courtney leaned in and whispered into her ear. "I'm not really that fast, but these Usain Bolt wannabes need to be taken down a peg."

Jason scoffed as he approached. "These guys wish they were that fast. *Me*, on the other hand…"

When Courtney didn't offer a sassy retort, Grace glanced at her friend to see the woman looking…nervous? Or maybe shy? She wasn't sure.

Aidan hit Jason in the shoulder. "I'm faster than you on my slowest day."

As the guys began to bicker over who was faster, Logan nudged her shoulder. "You look nice."

She tried to calm her fluttering heart. "Thanks. You didn't tell me you were doing the run." Grace, herself, had mentioned her participation a couple times. Even telling him about having to go shopping because she had nothing white to wear.

Logan lifted a shoulder. "It was a last-minute decision."

"So you just happened to have white outfits laying around the place?" Not that she was complaining. White looked good on him. It made his already tanned skin look even darker.

"Gotta be prepared for The Cradle Mountain Rainbow Run if you live in Cradle Mountain."

Grace grinned. "Just in case you wake up feeling the need to win a race?" Because, let's be honest, no one else would hold a candle to these guys.

"Nah, wouldn't be very fair of me to go hard. We'll probably hang around the back of the crowd with Blake and his daughter." Logan nodded off to their side.

Looking over, Grace saw Blake standing with a young girl who looked to be around four or five. Her brown hair was in two perfect pigtails, a white bow on each side. She was looking up at her dad like she idolized him.

Cute.

At that moment, Blake glanced over and nodded toward the guys.

"Guess we'll go join him. We'll see you during the race."

He tapped her hip lightly with his own before walking across the lawn.

When she looked back at Courtney, it was to find the woman's gaze glued to the men as they moved away. But not to all of them. It seemed her line of sight was following Jason.

"Are you okay?"

The other woman jumped, head spinning back toward Grace. "Me? Yeah, I'm good. Great. Fantastic."

Grace only just held back a giggle. "Are you sure? Because you went quiet for a bit there."

"Argh! It's so noticeable, isn't it? I just...can't be myself around him. I turn into a nervous wreck." Shaking her head, Courtney pulled out her phone. "Anyway, let's not let my ridiculous reaction to a crazy-sexy man derail our fun. Pre-race pics are just as important as post-race ones."

Pulling Grace close, Courtney snapped about a dozen pictures. She'd just tucked her phone back into her pocket when a loud horn sounded.

"Ah no. The race is about to start and we're all the way at the back!"

When Courtney grabbed Grace's arm, she tensed, already anticipating being tugged through the masses. "Actually, is it okay if we hang here? I'd prefer to be away from the crowd. Or if you want to go ahead, I'm completely fine going it alone." She didn't want to hold her friend back.

Courtney raised her brows. "Oh. Of course! No problem. I only start at the front because I like to get in the race pics. They usually splash them all over the Cradle Mountain paper. But someone else can have the glory this year. And don't be silly, no one's racing by themselves."

Grace breathed a sigh of relief. Not only because Courtney had agreed so readily, but also because no questions had been asked.

When a second horn sounded, everyone started moving.

The second Grace and Courtney jogged over the starting line, they were completely doused in colored powder from all directions. Grace only just got her buff over her eyes and nose in time.

When she looked down, she grinned. Blue, orange, and green powder were splattered all over her formerly white clothes. And not just her clothes. Her arms, legs, neck...

Courtney laughed beside her. "Feeling better already."

Grace laughed along with her friend. She felt like a living canvas. It was awesome.

She jogged the race with minimal talking. Minimal for *her*, that was. Courtney never stopped. Even when they got down on their stomachs and crawled through short tunnels, getting soaked in mud, the woman continued to ramble.

Grace learned a lot about her during the run. About her life in Cradle Mountain. The chaos of running a coffee shop. She also spoke in depth about her regular customers.

Every so often, she caught the other woman glancing around. Like she was looking for someone. Grace had a feeling she knew exactly who that someone was.

For the first time, Grace glanced over her own shoulder to look for Logan. She spotted him immediately, walking not too far behind with his friends. Blake's daughter was now on his back.

When Logan's gaze caught hers, he winked, and she stumbled, almost falling on her face.

Classy, Grace.

Not only had she been distracted by Courtney's chatter throughout most of the race, she'd also been trying—and failing—to take her mind off the rubbing of her shoes on her heels. At first the pain had been mild, but with every passing minute, it became more intense.

She should have known to wear Band-Aids with new shoes. Rookie mistake.

It was at about the halfway point—and a fifth dousing in powder—that the pain got so unbearable, she was grimacing with each step. It actually felt like razor blades were slashing across the backs of her feet.

Holy hell. Who knew blisters could be so dang painful?

Grace finally tugged on Courtney's arm, pulling them both to a stop. Grace was panting, exhaustion and pain weighing on her. "I'm so sorry, but I think I might need to stop."

Courtney frowned, her breathing not rushed at all. "Are you okay?"

"Yeah, I just have these blisters." *That are sending blazing trails of fire into my feet.*

Courtney shot a glance down, her expression sympathetic. "Of course we can stop. Why didn't you say anything?"

"Oh, no. You don't need to stop. I want you to finish. I might just have a quick rest and see if I can take a shortcut to the finish without shoes on." *Or just pass out on the side and not move for a good couple of hours.*

A shadow fell over them. Logan and Jason. Courtney almost jumped out of her skin when she spotted the latter.

"Hey. You guys okay?" Logan asked.

"Grace has blisters. She wants me to leave her behind." Courtney shook her head, keeping her gaze on Grace's feet. "No way am I gonna do that."

Logan frowned, him and Jason studying her feet in much the same way as Courtney. "I'll stay with you, Grace."

She opened her mouth to object, not wanting anyone to cut their race short for her, but then Jason turned to Courtney. "And I'll take over as your running partner."

Courtney's eyes widened. "Uh...I mean, sure...okay." She looked at Grace. "Or I can stay with you. If you prefer."

After witnessing her friend's reactions to Jason? "No. You guys go ahead. I'm okay."

When they continued, Logan gently wrapped his fingers around her elbow before helping her to the side, his touch just as electric as it always was.

They dropped to the grass, and Grace was about to reach for one of her shoes when Logan beat her to it, untying her laces and slipping the shoe off. He was so careful, so gentle, that she swallowed hard to keep from sighing.

Logan growled softly as he studied her sock. It was stained red. "Why didn't you stop earlier?"

Because she hadn't wanted to be a party-pooper. "I didn't want to be a hassle."

Slowly, he peeled off her sock. There was immediate relief when nothing was rubbing against her skin. As he studied her foot, his frown deepened, but he remained quiet.

Switching to the other foot, he did the same.

Grace glanced at the field behind them. "I can just cut through and finish it barefoot." She had no idea if there was a way to "cut through", but if there was, she'd find it.

Logan shook his head. "There's no shortcut. There's still five more miles, and some parts of the race are gravel."

Hm. The gravel didn't sound fun. "I guess I'll just put my shoes back on." Even though the very thought had her cringing.

Logan met her gaze. "Or...you could jump on my back. We could finish the run together."

Her mouth dropped open. Finish the race on his back? All five miles? "Won't that be annoying for you? Not to mention tiring. And heavy."

He shook his head. "Won't be any of those things."

She nibbled her bottom lip, wanting to say yes but not sure how she'd react to being wrapped around the man like a pretzel. Could she do it without freaking out? She didn't seem to react in fear to his touch anymore.

As the seconds ticked by, Logan sat and waited patiently for her decision, never rushing her.

"Okay." Her response was quiet.

He gave a quick nod. "Great."

Tucking her socks into her shoes, he tied the laces together before throwing them over his shoulder. When they stood, he turned his back to her and crouched down.

She only hesitated for a second or two. Then, slowly, she climbed onto his ridiculously hard, muscled back. Her heart started to pound in her chest. And she knew he'd be able to feel it.

"All good, darling?"

And just like that, the nerves ceased. A calmness that she hadn't felt in years settled over her system. Maybe it wasn't just Courtney who was music to the soul.

CHAPTER 11

For the first couple miles, the feel of Grace's warm body wrapped around him was heaven. His blood had pumped faster, awareness shooting through his limbs like an electric volt.

But now, every minute that passed became more unbearable. The soft breaths against his neck had his skin heating intensely. And the feel of her breasts pressed to his back, rubbing against him with each step…it was nothing short of torture.

He quickened his pace, all the while being careful not to jostle her too much. That was more for his benefit than hers though. More movement made everything worse.

When he finally saw the finish line coming up, he almost groaned in relief.

"I can jog the last bit if you want?"

Had he actually groaned out loud? "I'm fine." Damn if his voice wasn't gruffer than he'd intended.

"No, really, I'll jog." When she started wriggling in an attempt to shuffle down his body, he almost swore under his breath before crouching and helping her to her feet.

The woman was going to be the death of him.

She grabbed her shoes from his shoulder, jogging with them in her hand. He jogged alongside her, matching his pace to hers. Without her shoes on, the height discrepancy between them was even greater. Christ, he just about towered over her.

"Sure your feet are okay?"

"Yep. Without the shoes on, I could almost forget I have blisters. Lucky we're running on grass now." She shot a quick look up at him. "It still astounds me how fit you are. You can run ten miles, five with me on your back, and you're not even short of breath."

He probably could have run another ten carrying double her weight. "I'm not used to it, either. I've always been fit, especially after training as a special operations soldier, but this…" He shook his head. "It's different."

He could feel her eyes on him. "I'm sorry about what happened to you."

"Thank you." He lifted a shoulder. "It could have been worse. We were held on a huge property bordered by electrical fencing, but the house was large and comfortable. We weren't caged and were fed well."

"But you were still prisoners."

Every damn day. "As long as we went along with what they wanted—the training, the drug schedule—we were treated well and our families were safe. We definitely learned the art of patience. Biding our time until we were strong enough to fight back. It took two years. We attacked the guards, and I made it out. Then I met the guys in Marble Falls and, in the end, my team was freed."

"You risked everything for a chance at freedom."

There was something in the way she said those words, an undertone of heaviness, that had him looking her way. Her head was down so he couldn't see her face, but damn, he wished he could.

Had she escaped a similar kind of hell? The woman had been

through *something*. Her fear of being touched by men pointed to a past trauma.

The idea had his hands clenching into fists and anger creasing his brow.

As they approached the finish line, both Logan and Grace pulled their bandannas over their faces. The cool colored powder hit his face before he tugged the bandanna down to sit around his neck.

Grace's light chuckle had him looking her way. Her eyes sparkled in the sun and there was the slightest hint of dimples in her cheeks. Man, she was beautiful. The urge to tug her body into his was strong. So strong it almost caused him physical pain *not* to.

He gave himself a mental shake. What the hell was wrong with him? He barely knew the woman.

"Can't say I've ever been this colorful before," she said, scanning her body.

They headed toward the party area. Huge swarms of people congregated throughout the park, but he spotted his team, along with Courtney, immediately.

"It looks good on you," he said, trying and failing not to let his gaze linger.

"Yeah, I'll pretend I believe you."

And he'd pretend the mere sight of her hadn't been making him hard all over for days.

They'd almost reached his friends when a soft touch on his arm stopped him. He looked at Grace to see the smile was wiped clean from her lips. "Thank you. I know you have this super-strength and endurance thing going on, but you could have kept going with your friends. Thank you for helping me finish."

Unable to stop himself, Logan stepped closer, hand going to her upper arm, grazing the soft skin. "Happy to help."

Her blush wasn't subtle, pink touching her cheeks, a similar color to the powder they'd just been doused with.

Logan was almost sad when he had to drop his hand and head toward their friends.

"You made it!" Courtney said, studying Grace's feet. "How are the blisters?"

She lifted a shoulder. "Without shoes on, completely fine. Logan was my knight in shining armor and carried me on his back the rest of the race."

"He *carried* you?" Courtney seemed to melt on the spot a little bit, her gaze shooting between them. "That's so sweet. Maybe next year I'll wear shoes that give *me* blisters." She nudged her shoulder against Aidan's, making everyone laugh.

Logan scanned the area. "I could use some water."

"Well, you're in luck." Courtney pointed toward the drink trucks. "They serve PG drinks for the next hour. Then the kids get kicked out and the adult drinks begin."

"Alcohol?" Jason asked. "After a ten-mile race?"

Aidan lifted a shoulder. "Alcohol can be hydrating."

Courtney nodded. "Especially vodka. Maybe I'll get a margarita."

Grace shook her head. "Margaritas are tequila, not vodka."

Courtney frowned. "Oh. Mojito then?"

"No, that's rum." She chuckled. "If you want vodka, you could get a cosmopolitan? Or a martini. Or a Moscow mule."

"Ooh, Moscow mule, that sounds fancy."

Logan tilted his head. "You know your drinks."

She flinched. It was so subtle, he barely caught it. "I, um, worked in a bar. It was a long time ago. Like a lifetime ago. But you never forget what goes into a drink."

Was it just him or had there been a slight hitch in her voice? And if there was…why?

Before he could say anything, Jason groaned loudly. "Six o'clock, journalist incoming."

A few of them turned their heads. Logan didn't bother. He knew who it was. Most of the reporters had left town now, chasing other stories after hitting brick walls with them. But there were still a few around—and one who seemed to be here for good. And she was annoying as hell.

Aidan straightened, a smile curving his lips. "I'll handle this. I get a kick out of her frustration when I talk her in circles."

"She's all yours." Jason took a step away. "I'll grab everyone some water."

"I'll join you," Logan said, moving away with his friend.

The next couple hours passed quickly and involved a lot of trying to drag his eyes off Grace. Trying and failing. The woman was living in his house, and he still couldn't get enough of her. After what she'd done to his team, he should've been able to keep his distance.

The sun was just setting when Aidan joined him at a table, giving him an odd smile that said he'd caught Logan staring at the women. She and Courtney had been dancing for a while. And he'd been watching for almost as long.

He'd noticed a couple of things during his observations. For starters, she was careful to stick to the edges of the crowd. Any time Courtney attempted to move them into the throng, Grace shook her head.

She'd also had a couple of drinks, which had loosened her up. Helped her move more freely. The rigidity that she often carried in her spine was gone.

"Uh-oh."

Logan frowned at Aidan. "What?"

"What's that look on your face?"

"I don't know what you're talking about." He did, but Aidan didn't need to know that.

"You like her."

Actually, it was starting to feel more like an obsession. "Yeah. But I think someone hurt her. A man. And I think maybe they're still out there somewhere." Why else would she be so skittish?

The smile left Aidan's lips. His teammates were the same as

him. Protectors first, everything else second. And the idea of a man hurting a woman was as abhorrent to them as it was to Logan.

"Have you asked her about it?"

"No." He'd been tempted. A few times. "I think it's connected to whatever the reporter threatened her with." In fact, he was almost certain.

"If you want to get closer to the woman, I think you need to know her past."

Did he? Want to get closer to her? "She's leaving town soon."

"And the fact that she spoke to the reporter in Texas is stopping you."

Logan frowned at his friend. How was the guy so damn perceptive? "It would be easier if I knew exactly what had transpired between them."

Aidan nodded. "I agree. Unless you plan to force the words out of her, though, I guess it's up to her whether she's willing to share."

It was. The ball was in her court.

When Logan turned his attention back to Grace, he saw she'd stopped dancing in favor of scanning the crowd around her. She'd done that a couple of times already.

Had she seen something? Someone?

He studied the crowd, not noticing anyone looking her way. When he glanced back, she gave a small shake of her head before dancing again.

That's when the guy behind her caught Logan's attention. He seemed to be inching closer as he danced. He also wasn't so steady on his feet. Drunk.

When he suddenly stumbled sideways, falling right into Grace, the two of them went down. The guy didn't even attempt to stop himself from crushing her into the grass.

Logan was already moving. Fear flashed across Grace's face as the guy pushed up onto his elbows.

Grabbing the guy from behind, Logan lifted him off, throwing him to the side. Crouching beside Grace, he spoke softly. "Hey, you okay?"

She sat up quickly, her breaths moving in and out of her chest in quick succession. Her heart, which he could vaguely hear beneath the music, beat much too quickly in her chest.

The drunk guy returned, reaching to touch her shoulder. "Christ, lady, I'm sorry!"

Standing, Logan shoved him hard. "Don't touch her."

The guy squinted. "Hey, are you—"

"Someone you don't want to piss off? Yes. Now *go. Away.*"

The drunk guy lifted his hands, walking backward and stumbling as he went.

Turning back to Grace, he knelt, trying to catch her attention. Her gaze darted around the lawn, never focusing on one thing for too long. He touched her cheek, feeling her jolt immediately. Then she met his gaze.

"There you are. You're safe, honey."

She nodded too quickly.

"What do you need?" If it was for Logan to turn around and punch the asshole in the face, he would happily do it. Hell, if it was for him to clear the whole damn lawn, he'd get his team right on it.

Her arms wrapped around her waist. "Can you take me home?"

"Absolutely."

Gently taking her elbows, he helped her up before wrapping an arm around her waist and leading her toward his truck.

On the drive home, Logan cranked the heater, turning the radio on low. It wasn't until they were almost to his house that color finally started to come back to her face.

"I'm sorry," she said, breaking the silence.

"You don't need to apologize. That guy was all over you." *Asshole.* It was still making Logan rage.

She lifted a shoulder. "For the average person, how I responded would be considered an overreaction."

He paused. Interesting phrasing. "Are you not an average person?"

"I'm a constant work in progress."

Not really an answer, honey. "Aren't we all?"

She gave a small smile. "Yeah. But some of us have more work to do than others. More trauma to muddle our way through."

He was careful not to react to the use of the word "trauma". He'd suspected as much, but at the same time, his insides rebelled. They rebelled at the idea of any harm coming to *any* woman…but especially Grace. "I'm a great listener if you ever want to talk about it."

"Thank you."

God, but he wished the woman would trust him. "I want to help you."

He felt her eyes on him as he turned the corner onto his street. "You are."

When they reached his house, he pulled into the garage. He didn't get out of the car straight away. Neither did she. The dim lights of the instrument panel were all they had in the darkness.

She looked down at her hands. "You probably think I'm the biggest phony. Not only do I sell out my patients, I'm also a therapist who can't get over her own past."

"Then you know the challenges your patients go through. That healing takes time."

She nodded. "That's very true." When she looked up, her eyes were wide and vulnerable. "I meant what I said though. You *are* helping me. I don't know what it is about you, but you take away some of the fear that I've never been able to shake." When her eyes traveled down to his lips, awareness wandered through parts of his body that it shouldn't. "I wonder…"

When she stopped, eyes still on his mouth, a shot of need hardened him. "What do you wonder, Grace?"

"What it would feel like if I kissed you."

Fire, hot and heavy, burned through his veins.

He didn't make a move, somehow knowing that it was important for her to call the shots. "I wouldn't object."

Her eyes widened. Just slightly. For a moment, she remained still. Then, so slowly it almost killed him, she climbed over the middle console right onto his lap. Her legs straddled him, her heat pressing into his hardness.

Fuck, but he was already dying a slow death.

Then, her head lowered, and her lips touched his.

The first touch was akin to agony. Everything in him screamed for Logan to grab her head and make love to those soft lips. He didn't. He went as slow as her. Returning the gentle touch. Allowing every move to be determined by Grace. When she tentatively swiped her lips across his once more, his hands lightly touched her hips, unable to remain by his sides.

It was when her tongue slipped through his lips, though, that a soft growl tore from his chest. His hand went to the back of her head and he leaned in, tasting her sweetness.

A slow burn began in his chest, moving through his limbs.

He didn't know how long they sat there like that, exploring each other. He was sure the seconds had turned into several minutes. Still, when the kiss ended, it felt too soon. But then, hours would probably feel too soon.

Her lips were red and eyes half-closed as she eased back. "Thank you."

CHAPTER 12

*G*race lifted her coffee and took a sip. Memories of last night's kiss skittered through her mind on replay, lips still tingling from the feel of Logan's mouth against hers.

A smile tugged at her lips, and not just because the kiss was so good. Because there'd been no panic. No hesitation. The tendrils of fear hadn't even begun to seep into her soul. All she'd been able to think about was him. About how good he'd felt beneath her.

"Okay, what are you smiling about?" Courtney slid into the booth opposite her. "Wait." She held up her hand. "I know that smile. It's the 'I did something dirty' one. Oh my God." She leaned forward, lowering her voice. "Did you have sex with Logan?"

Grace almost spat her coffee right out. "Um, no." No way, no how. Just…no. "We kissed."

Courtney's smile widened. "Yeah, girl. Where?"

"Ah, in the car, after he pulled into his garage."

Which didn't actually sound that romantic, but, heck, it was probably the most romantic moment of her life.

"You must have some mighty strength, woman. If one of those

boys kissed me, and his bed was just a few steps away, I don't know how I'd stop myself."

"It's not strength, trust me," Grace muttered, almost to herself.

The grin on Courtney's lips dimmed. "What do you mean?"

Grace wrapped both her hands around the mug, enjoying the heat that filtered down her arms. Was it crazy that she actually wanted to tell Courtney a little of her past? Of what made her the person she was today? Having someone she could talk to would be nice. About what she'd experienced. About her wants, which mixed so intimately with her fears.

"Something happened to me," she said quietly. "It was a few years ago, but it was…bad. A man hurt me and I've been learning how to live again ever since. I still, ah, struggle with a man's touch."

Although Logan seemed to be the exception for some reason.

Immediately, Courtney reached across the table, her touch soft. "I'm so sorry, Grace."

She dipped her head. "Thank you. Last night was huge for me. A part of me almost believed I would never get past this trigger. That I would never be able to touch a man, kiss him, without panicking."

Logan was helping her realize that maybe she could.

Empathy, and a tinge of sadness, darkened Courtney's eyes. "I've only known Logan for a couple of months. But I can see the goodness in him. He has a pure heart. If there was anyone I thought you'd be safe with, it's him."

Grace felt that too. And not just safe in a physical sense. "You're right. I almost wish…" She paused, shaking her head.

"That you were here longer?" Courtney finished for her.

The woman was a mind reader. "Yes. To see where the attraction might lead." To see if she was capable of doing more than kissing a man.

"Do you have to leave?"

Did she? The media hadn't recognized her as being the whistle-blower. In fact, they'd paid her little to no attention. It would still be smarter to leave, but... "I'll check in and see if my patients might need me longer." There was always the chance the safe houses would be delayed further. And there was no way she could leave the women if that were the case.

Courtney leaned forward. "Just remember, the greatest rewards in life usually come from the greatest risks."

Fitting. Seeing as staying would be a risk. So, too, would attempting any kind of relationship with Logan. "Maybe I'm getting ahead of myself. It was one kiss. It's not like he professed his undying love and wants to marry me."

Or even that he's forgiven me.

Courtney scoffed. "A man doesn't carry a woman five miles on his back unless he at least likes her."

Grace wanted that to be true.

"Well, I for one hope you stay. This town is in low supply of women willing to listen to me ramble about nothing important over coffee every day."

"You didn't move here with any family or friends?" A partner maybe?

"Nope. I knew no one." She paused, seeming to consider her next words. "My cousin, also my best friend, died a couple of years ago. Less than a week later, I quit my job, packed up my life and moved here." She swung her gaze around the shop. "We dreamed about opening a shop like this."

It was Grace's turn to reach across the table, wrapping her fingers around Courtney's. "I'm sorry you lost her."

Pain flashed across her face. "Thank you." She lifted a shoulder. "Running this shop keeps her in my thoughts. But no, I don't see many young women around."

"What about Blake's daughter's mother?" Grace asked. She was pretty sure that was the woman she'd seen outside with Blake the other day.

Courtney nodded. "Yes, her name's Willow. She pops in every

so often, usually to drop Mila off when Blake's here. She never stays long. I think she's really busy with work and her studies."

That, on top of mothering, definitely sounded busy.

Lowering her gaze, Grace studied the mug Courtney was holding.

I'm holding this cup of coffee, so yeah, I'm pretty busy.

A laugh burst from her chest. "Willow's not the only busy person if your mug's to be believed."

"Hey! You don't need to be busy, just smart. And I was smart by hiring such a brilliant second-in-charge in the form of Joey."

Grace turned to look at the man behind the counter, who always seemed to be on the move.

Courtney lowered her voice. "So, do you see another kiss in the cards with the sexy soldier?"

Electricity tingled through Grace's stomach at the thought. "Well, I wouldn't say no."

～

LOGAN LOWERED HIS STANCE, watching his opponent closely, waiting for him to strike.

The guy matched him in size. They were both equally strong and fast. Even though Logan had special forces training, which was superior to that of his opponent's five years in the Army, they'd both been taken. Both been exposed to the enhancement drugs and trained at the compound.

Jason's fist came at him hard and fast. Logan dodged.

He countered the punch with his own. Jason mirrored Logan's move, ducking his head and narrowly missing the hit.

Kicking his leg out, Logan swiped Jason's legs from under him, sending him to the floor. Jason recovered quickly, kicking out his own leg and sending Logan down to join him. Then they were grappling, each man only getting the upper hand for a second before the power switched.

On a different day, Logan would have gone easier on his friend. He would have fought fair. After all, this was training.

But today, anger flowed through his veins. And the anger was red-hot.

Not at Jason. Not at anyone he knew personally.

Logan flipped their bodies so he was on top. His fist flew forward, nailing the guy right in the face. He was about to throw a second—he came pretty damn close—when crimson blood started flowing from Jason's nose.

Logan stopped, jumping to his feet. "Fuck. I'm sorry."

Jason stood slowly, not showing the slightest inkling of pain, as he grabbed a towel and wiped the blood from his face. "What's going on with you?"

Logan ran both his hands up his face and through his hair. It was that damn obvious.

Jason tilted his head. "It's Steve's phone call from this afternoon, isn't it?"

"Yes, dammit. I thought that asshole Ice would stay underground for at least a little while after we dismantled his organization. And *Ketchum*? Really?"

Not only had the scumbag taken another woman so soon after they'd shut down his operation in Mexico, but he'd taken the redhead from Ketchum—one town over from Cradle Mountain.

"I know. It's not good."

Logan could think of stronger adjectives to describe the situation. "Why was she taken from Ketchum? Because he found out it was us? Is this some kind of a sick warning?"

They weren't questions his friend could answer. But he *needed* answers.

"I don't know. But if he's close, he's just saving us the trouble of tramping across the country to find him."

Logan breathed out a hot, frustrated breath. "I don't like him being so close to Grace. I know she doesn't fit the description of the women he's taking. Wrong age. Wrong hair color. But I still don't like it."

Jason stepped closer. "This guy has been running his business on a very specific look for years. He's not going to detour and take someone different now."

Unless he knew about Logan's involvement and, further, somehow found out about him and Grace. Not that there really was a him and Grace. Not at the moment. But the woman was living in his house.

And he was just so fucking mad that there was another victim. There shouldn't have been—because Ice should be dead.

Logan's jaw ticked. "What the hell is the point of us being trained killers if we can't destroy the assholes we need to?"

"The point?" Jason raised his brows. "You think there's a point to what happened to us? There isn't. But we're using it to our advantage and doing what we can. Ice's days *are* numbered. So are this Beau guy's."

He knew that. He just wished he had a more definitive number of days. "You're right. I'm gonna head home."

Hopefully on the way, he'd calm the hell down.

Before he stepped out of the room, Jason took hold of his arm. "You sure you're okay?"

No. "I'm fine. I'll see you tomorrow." Grabbing his bag, Logan threw it over his shoulder before stepping outside and heading to his car.

He'd only been driving for a couple of minutes when he saw the tail. The driver was clearly trying to remain hidden but doing an amateur job of it.

When Logan turned the next corner, he stopped his car so that he was blocking the street.

Climbing out, he waited, watching as the person who had been following rounded the corner before slamming on the brake. That's when he saw who it was.

Nicole.

His eyes narrowed at the sight of her behind the wheel. Why was it that the other reporters could take a hint and get the hell out of town, but she couldn't?

The surprise on her face only lasted for a second before it was replaced by that cool, calm, professional smile.

God, even that infuriated him.

Logan walked forward, stopping in front of her door as she climbed out.

He forced himself to dampen the fire he wanted to throw her way. "What the hell are you doing?"

"Hello to you too, Logan. I was just coming to talk to you."

"By trailing me home?" At her silence, Logan had to work hard to control his voice. "There's nothing for us to talk about."

She took a voice recorder out of her pocket, the one she always seemed to have at the ready, and switched it on. "Two years is a long time to be held in captivity. Is there residual anger?"

Logan remained silent for a moment, praying to every God he knew to give him strength. Strength to not lash out at this annoying, godforsaken woman.

Then she pushed the goddamn recorder closer to his face so that it sat an inch from his mouth.

And he lost the last remnants of his cool.

Grabbing it from her fingers, he crushed it in his hand. Her mouth dropped open. The thing was in a million tiny pieces, so dismantled it was beyond repair as it fell through his fingers onto the road.

He kept his voice low and even. "You come near me with one of those things again, and it will be dust, too."

The smile returned to her lips. "A reporter doesn't always need words for a story. Actions work just fine. Anything else you want to do while I'm here? Beat your chest before throwing my car over your shoulder? Throw *me* over your shoulder?"

She was baiting him. And it was working.

Leaning down, he stopped when his face was inches from hers. He saw the flare of fear before she masked it. "Stay away from me, Miss Fleece. I'm not someone you want to piss off."

"What a lovely quote for my story."

Straightening, Logan forced himself to walk away before he did something he'd really regret. He'd never hit a woman before, and never would. But her car? Yeah, that was definitely at risk.

Lowering into his seat, he took off, pressing his foot to the pedal and driving away too quickly for her to follow.

CHAPTER 13

*T*he second Grace heard the door opening, a smile she couldn't stop stretched across her lips. She didn't look up from the stove straight away, but goose bumps pebbled over her skin.

Talking to Courtney about Logan that morning had been just what she'd needed. It had reminded her that she was strong. That even though she'd suffered something terrible and recovery was slow, Logan was someone she could trust. And maybe he was worth her taking some risks.

When footsteps sounded behind her, she turned.

Her smile faltered.

Logan looked...angry. She hadn't seen that look on his face since the night they'd first met.

The keys clattered on the side table as he dropped them.

"Hey. Are you okay?"

The man barely looked up, instead walking straight past her and opening the cupboard door to grab a glass from the cabinet. "Yeah. It's just been one of those days."

He filled the glass with water and took a sip, all the while looking out the window. She didn't miss the way his other hand clenched the counter edge firmly, his knuckles whitening. Or the rigidity in his shoulders.

"Do you want to talk about it?"

The glass went to the counter. He didn't place it down with force, but he didn't do so softly either. "A woman was taken last night while she was walking home from work."

Grace sucked in a sharp breath. "Oh no."

"She was taken from Ketchum."

The fine hairs rose on her arms. "That's only one town over. Are you sure she was taken by the same—"

"Yes."

Grace forced herself not to stiffen at the way he interrupted her. At his harsh tone. Anger rolled off the guy in waves, thickening the air around them.

"I'm sorry, Logan."

He rinsed the glass before stacking it in the dishwasher. "Why are you sorry? You didn't take her."

"I'm sorry that your team worked so hard to dismantle this organization and yet women are still being taken." Unbelievably sorry. Her heart bled for this new victim. Ripped away from her life and thrown into hell.

Taking a small step forward, Grace touched his back. "I can tell you're angry and frustrated. But remember, you've saved several women. Because of your team, they're free."

She almost thought she heard him scoff. "Thanks."

She frowned. His anger almost felt too...pointed to just be about the missing woman.

"Are you angry at me?" The words left her mouth before she could stop them. A question that, had she been smart, probably should have remained in her head.

When he turned around, Grace took an involuntary step back. On his face, there wasn't just anger. There was agony and...hostility?

"I'm angry at everything, Grace. I'm angry that I have these enhanced abilities yet can't use them to stop a sick bastard who enjoys taking and abusing women. I'm angry that my family found out about the hell that I lived through via an article plastered all over the internet. I'm angry that the last couple months were supposed to be spent settling into my new life in Cradle Mountain, a life of *normalcy*, but instead, I've been fending off reporters and pretending like I don't notice every goddamn set of eyes staring at me like I'm a roadshow."

For a moment, Grace was silent, words not coming to her like they normally would.

The man wasn't just angry. He was *enraged*. At her.

"I'm sorry." She'd said it before, but anything else felt inadequate. Disingenuous. She couldn't change what she'd done—and if she'd thought she'd been forgiven, she was wrong.

Logan scrubbed a hand over his face, suddenly looking more tired than anything else. "Last week there was an online article speculating that half our team was away on a government assignment. Completing missions that normal men can't."

How did that relate to—

"I can't help but wonder if that's how Ice got the idea that it may have been us who broke into his 'impenetrable' compound." He shook his head, glancing up. There was nothing gentle about the way he looked at her. "You shone a light on us for the world to see, Grace. Is it any wonder he's taken a woman so close by? Taunting us?"

Her chest constricted. Her fault. "You're saying that this particular woman was taken because of me."

Saying that out loud felt like razor blades sawing at her insides. She knew the hell that awaited this woman. She couldn't carry that weight.

"I'm saying that decisions have consequences."

When he started to walk away, Grace's words halted him. "You don't think I know that? Logan, the last eight years of my life have been one big consequence of my decisions. Of not recognizing danger before it was too late. You think you're the only one who's been hurt? Who's had time stolen from them? Freedom taken away?"

Christ, she wouldn't wish what she'd lived through on her worst enemy. And even though she'd gotten out, she hadn't been free. She'd been hiding, all the while a prisoner of her own mind. For *years*, the darkness had remained close, ready to consume her.

She shook her head before he could answer. "You're not. I know what I did wasn't fair to you guys. It's why I risked my safety by coming here. It's part of the reason I'm *still* here. But saying this woman was taken because of me isn't fair."

This time, it was Grace who turned to walk away. But before she'd taken more than a step, Logan grabbed her arm.

Every part of her rebelled against being touched at that moment. She yanked her arm so hard he was forced to release her.

"Explain it to me. Make me understand why you did what you did."

Understand? No. No one could ever understand unless they'd been through the absolute darkness and terror that had plagued her for longer than she could remember.

Her lips remained sealed.

A full twenty seconds passed before Logan sighed, turning away yet again. He was halfway across the kitchen before Grace spoke.

"If you knew there was a chance you could be taken again, what would you do?"

His feet stopped. Turning his head, he looked her square in the eye. "I would use whatever means necessary to eliminate any chance of that happening."

Exactly. "So I didn't act any differently than you."

~

LOGAN LIFTED the beer to his lips, downing a third of the bottle. Every minute that passed left him feeling like more of an asshole.

Drowning his sorrows in beer was a dumb idea, which was fitting, seeing as tonight seemed to be the night for them.

What the hell was wrong with him? Letting his frustration about Ice and the kidnapping and Nicole build up, then stepping into the house and exploding on Grace. He hadn't even meant what he'd said. Once he'd started, though, it was like he didn't have an off switch. Christ, he could kick his own ass. He should be better than that. He *was* better than that.

Blowing out a long breath, Logan took another drink. From his peripheral vision, he saw Jason step into the bar and head his way.

Great. Just what he needed.

Jason slid into the booth opposite, his brow rising. "Need some company?"

"The GPS trackers on our phones are for emergencies, asshole." Or maybe this *was* an emergency. Maybe he needed some emergency ass-kicking.

"When my calls and texts go unanswered, I start to get worried."

He didn't deserve friends like Jason. Or Grace. It was a wonder anyone put up with his jerk ass.

Jason lowered his gaze to the beer in Logan's hand before lifting it again. "What did you do?"

He probably wore his guilt like a mask for all to see. "I was an asshole." Which was putting it lightly. "I insinuated that it was her fault the woman was taken from Ketchum."

Yep. It sounded even worse out loud.

Jason didn't react. His friend may as well be a statue for how closely he kept his emotions to himself. But Logan could just imagine what the guy was thinking. It was likely no different to all the thoughts floating around his own mind.

"You *were* an asshole. So, what are you gonna do about it?"

"Well, currently, I'm searching for redemption at the bottom of this bottle." Not that he planned to drink any more. He already felt like an idiot for coming here rather than doing what he should have done at home—apologize.

"How's that going for you?"

"It's not." Logan leaned back in his seat, watching the small crowd of people drink and dance like they didn't have a care in the world. "Do you ever think back to the moment you were taken? Wish you'd done something differently?"

Jason frowned. "For a while I thought if I hadn't trusted the wrong people, told them about my suspicions, that maybe I wouldn't have been taken at all."

Jason had been employed in a lab when he'd started to suspect the drugs he was working on were being used for more than what he was being told. The day after he raised his suspicions, he was taken.

"But I'm starting to come to the conclusion that our cards were drawn long before they were played," he continued. "And even if they weren't, life's too short to stop and wonder about what might have been. Because while we're stagnant, the world will keep moving around us."

Fuck, but the man was wise.

Logan had been taken in the dead of night. That's why he woke at the tiniest noise now. Why his house had the best security system money could buy.

"It wasn't all bad," Logan said softly. "It led me to you guys. And I don't plan to stop using what they gave me to end men like Ice."

Jason nodded. "We just need to accept that we can't kill them all."

"But we can damn well try."

"Damn straight. Now what is your dumb ass still doing sitting here?"

Pushing his beer forward, Logan rose to his feet. "Being an

idiot again. But now I'm gonna do what I should have done an hour ago and apologize to the woman."

He just hoped she'd forgive him.

Moving outside, he pulled out his phone and called her number.

CHAPTER 14

A tear slid down Grace's cheek, but she quickly scrubbed it away. She didn't want to cry. She knew it was important to let her emotions out, to feel what she needed to feel, but right now, all she wanted to do was switch it off and be numb.

Lifting another T-shirt from the drawer, she folded it carefully before placing it in her suitcase on top of the rest.

Just when she'd thought she was moving forward, maybe even starting a friendship with a man who made her feel things—*beautiful, new* things—it all came crashing down.

Shaking her head, she went to the bathroom and grabbed a handful of her toiletries.

The worst part was, Logan was probably right about the girl being taken because of them—because of *her*. Anything else was just too convenient.

Grace dropped her toiletry bag into her suitcase.

She just had to hope that they'd find this girl in time. She'd heard the harrowing stories of the other women. She couldn't be responsible for it happening to this latest victim.

Sucking in a calming breath, Grace zipped up her bag, throwing it over her shoulder. Her footsteps were loud in the otherwise quiet house as she made her way downstairs. Logan had left almost straight after their fight. The resounding click of the door as it closed behind him had felt like he was dropping a brick right onto her heart.

Pausing at the front door, Grace cast a quick glance around before heading into the kitchen.

She should leave a note. Tonight, the man had hurt her, but before tonight...

Thank you for allowing me into your home. You are a wonderful man, and you have helped me more than you know.

Grace xox

Things might not have ended the way she'd hoped, but the man had taken her in when all he should have felt was distrust. He'd made her feel safe. Reminded her that a man's touch could feel good.

Her eyes misted again at the thought, but she shoved the emotions down. She could feel it all later. For now, she wanted to leave. Get out of this house and into a motel before he returned. The last thing she wanted tonight was to face more of his anger-fueled accusations.

Tugging the door open, Grace clicked the lock before pulling it closed behind her. She climbed behind the wheel and took a steadying breath before driving down Logan's long driveway.

Using the car's Bluetooth, she called her dad, wanting to hear his familiar, calming voice. Talk to someone who loved her.

The phone rang. And then it rang some more. A solid five rings later and Grace knew he wasn't going to answer.

Logan's words repeated in her head.

"You shone a light on us for the world to see, Grace. Is it any wonder he's taken a woman so close by?"

And she'd shone that light on them to take the light off *herself.*

Pain shot through her, so sharp she had to press a hand to her chest. Selfish. So damn selfish. To save herself and her father, she'd hurt others. She hadn't known that there would be such massive repercussions. But it didn't change the fact that every-thing was her fault.

What made it worse was that, even if she could go back, she wasn't sure she'd do anything differently. She wasn't sure she *could* do anything differently.

Was she capable of allowing her father's actions to be found out?

No.

When tears pressed against her eyes yet again, blurring her vision, she pulled to the side of the road. Turning off the engine, she leaned her head back, closing her eyes.

There had been a flicker of hope today. A small possibility of starting a relationship. But she couldn't have any of that. Not at the moment, anyway. And that was just something she needed to accept.

"You'll be okay, Grace."

What she needed was a good night's sleep.

She'd just switched the engine back on when a car in her rearview mirror drew closer before pulling over to stop behind her. Even though it was probably just a concerned local checking on whoever was on the side of the road, she flicked her locks, safety always at the forefront of her mind.

She waited a moment for them to get out and check on her. A few seconds passed. Then another few.

When the car remained idle behind her without any doors opening, a sliver of unease trickled down her spine. Who was in that car? And why had they pulled up behind her, on an empty road, under the dark night sky, just to sit and do nothing?

Easing the car out onto the road, she said a silent prayer that the person wouldn't follow. The hope was short-lived. A second later, they were on the road behind her.

When their high beams flicked on, Grace's heart began to pound against her ribs. They followed so closely that she had to angle her rearview mirror away so the light didn't shine into her eyes. Blind her.

Pressing her foot down harder, Grace upped her speed. In the side mirrors, she could see the person behind copying her action, the distance between them remaining constant.

Who the hell was this person and what did they want?

Turning a corner, the car did the same.

Were they closer now? Their engine definitely sounded louder. She sped up again, knowing she was surpassing the speed limit.

At the sudden sound of her phone ringing, Grace jolted in her seat. She answered the call without checking who it was. "Hello?"

"Grace. It's Logan." There was a small pause. "I can hear that you're in the car. I don't blame you for leaving. I was wondering if we could talk?"

Her eyes flew to the side mirror again. Oh, God, he was so close she could barely see his headlights now. "Logan, I—" She gasped when a pedestrian almost stepped onto the road in front of her. Swerving, nearly losing control of the car, she only just regained it. The man jumped back just in time.

"Are you okay?"

"I don't know." She raised her voice over the deafening sound of the engine. "There's someone behind me. He's close. *Really* close. And his lights are so bright I can barely see. I'm scared whoever it is is going to hit me. And I'm driving way too fast."

She was now driving more than fifteen miles over the speed limit. Fear rushed through her limbs, making her fingers tremble.

"Where are you?" Logan's voice had hardened. There was an edge of worry lacing his words.

That was a good question, where was she? She had no idea. She'd stopped paying attention to street names the second she noticed the car.

Scanning the street, her eyes landed on a roadside diner.

"I'm just about to pass a diner. Albert's Diner, maybe? Or

Allen's." Her words were running into each other. Her eyes flicked from the road to the mirror and back again.

"Take the next left. I'm at Tucker's Bar. It's not far down that road."

"I don't know if I can slow down without them hitting me." And the idea of trying terrified her.

"That road's going to end in about two miles anyway." *Oh, sweet Jesus.* "You can do it, Grace. Release your foot slowly off the accelerator and gently press on the brake. If he hasn't tried to hit you so far, maybe that's not his goal."

The calmness in Logan's voice eased some of her own panic.

Slowly, Grace eased her foot onto the brake. She was careful to keep her eyes off the car behind, knowing if she saw him inch closer, she'd lose her nerve and speed up again.

When the turn suddenly came up, she knew she was still going way faster than she should be. But she was out of time.

Holding her breath, she spun the wheel. The sound of rubber squealing against asphalt was loud, the smell almost as overwhelming. The car slid sideways, and it took a lot of maneuvering to maintain control and get back into her lane.

The car behind made the turn in exactly the same manner, high beams yet again threatening to blind her.

What was this guy's plan? How long did he intend to tail her?

"Are you okay?"

She brought herself back to the sound of Logan's deep voice. "I made the turn but he's still following me."

"The bar isn't far down the street."

"Okay."

She just had to pray that the guy behind didn't do anything rash.

At the sight of the bar ahead, Grace's limbs began to tingle with an odd mix of dread and relief. There were people standing out front. Half a dozen maybe. She spotted Logan immediately, his huge outline noticeable as he stood close to the road.

Pressing her foot on the brake slowly, she almost sighed in relief when the car behind did the same. In fact, the distance between the two cars began to increase.

Was he finally leaving her alone?

She'd almost made it to where Logan waited when suddenly the car behind her sped up again, ramming into her.

Grace screeched as he hit her back right corner, sending her careening toward Logan and the other people outside the bar.

Logan jumped out of the way just in time, sweeping others aside with him.

Grace was still trying to gain control by madly turning the wheel. But it was too late. She saw the utility pole a second before the car collided with it.

The seat belt cut across her chest at the impact, air bags exploding.

Then, there was stillness.

A second later, her door was pulled open.

Without a word, Logan reached across her body, unclasping her seat belt and lifting her out.

LOGAN STOOD TO THE SIDE, watching as the tow truck drove away with Grace's rental car on the back. She'd argued that the thing was still drivable, but Logan wasn't taking the chance.

His muscles were just as tense as they'd been an hour ago when he'd watched her crash into the pole.

"You're okay to go home."

Grace smiled at the paramedic as she stood. Logan slid an arm around her waist, hating the way her body tensed at his touch. "I'll take you home."

She didn't say a word but at least she allowed him to lead her across the parking lot.

The police had only just left. Grace hadn't been able to see the car, only the headlights, but Logan had gotten a glimpse. The vehicle was a dark green Honda. That was all he knew. It wasn't a lot to go on. And certainly not enough to get an identity of the driver.

Had it been a reporter? Or was it someone else? The idea of the latter left a sick feeling in his gut and had him tightening his grip around her waist.

Stopping at his truck, he helped her into the passenger seat, not missing how stiff her body felt. On his way around, he threw her bag in the back before sliding behind the wheel.

She'd been leaving him, probably heading back to the motel. And he didn't blame her at all. Not after how he'd spoken to her. The things he'd said. But he couldn't let her stay on her own. Someone had just been trailing her. Hit her car with their own and sent her into a damn pole.

Pulling out of the parking lot, he headed toward his house. It took about four minutes for her to notice.

"Logan, I'd like you to take me to the motel. I've called ahead and they have a room for me."

His hands tightened on the wheel. "I can't do that."

He expected an argument. Strangely, he didn't get it.

He shot a glance her way, hating how tired she looked. Hating the sight of the small bandage on her forehead from where the airbags had forced her into the window. More stitches.

When they arrived back at his place, her door was open before he had a chance to get around. He tried to put his arm around her again for support, but she pulled away so quickly she almost fell down.

Jaw tensing, Logan grabbed her bag and trailed behind. It wasn't until she moved into the guest bedroom that he finally said what he needed to say. "I'm sorry."

She paused, partway to the bed. Her back was to him, so he couldn't see her face, but God, he wished he could.

"You don't need to apologize for expressing how you feel."

Her words were frustratingly formal and detached. It was only the slight shake in her fingers that gave away her nerves.

He took a small step forward. "I was angry at the situation and projected that anger onto you. That's not how I feel."

Sure, he'd been frustrated that she wouldn't explain her actual reason for talking to the reporter, but he didn't blame her for the woman in Ketchum being taken.

Grace turned, dark shadows under her eyes and exhaustion visibly weighing her down. "There was truth to what you said, Logan. I felt the honesty in the emotions you expressed. And that's okay. You're entitled to be angry with me. If I were in your position, I'm sure I'd be angry, too."

"Grace." Another small step forward. Almost close enough to touch her. "I screwed up. I shouldn't have lost my temper. I promise you, it won't happen again. Ever. The only person responsible for the woman going missing is the man who took her."

That's where the blame started and ended.

"We're going to find her." Another step. When she didn't retreat, he raised his hand, grazing her cheek. "And we're also going to find out who caused you to crash your car today."

For a second, there was silence, her brown eyes flickering between his. "I don't want to be a burden for you."

The last thing she represented in his life was a burden. "You're not. You're my guest. And I want you to stay. I want you close. And not just to keep you safe."

The smallest flicker of emotion in her eyes. Then, finally, a small nod. "Okay."

Some of the dread that had been twisting away at his stomach, clawing at his insides, eased. She wasn't leaving him. Not tonight.

CHAPTER 15

*L*ogan hung up the phone. Leaning back in his seat, he replayed Steve's words in his head, allowing a tendril of hope to unfurl.

There'd been a sighting of Beau Prater. The asshole had been caught on video surveillance at a gas station on the outskirts of Jerome.

So he wasn't in Ketchum, but he *was* in Idaho. Still close.

Logan blew out a long breath. He needed to call Tyler and Liam. Send them out to search the small town. Prater probably knew that airlines were being watched, so he'd likely be driving wherever he needed to go.

They would catch him. There was no way Logan was letting those lowlife scumbags continue to run their sex trafficking ring. And if they were close to Cradle Mountain because they wanted the women that Logan's team had rescued back under their control, there was no way in hell that was happening either.

Darting his gaze to the time on his laptop, Logan sighed, closing it. Five-thirty. Time to go.

He'd been trying to leave the office a little earlier lately. The earlier he left, the more time he had with Grace. There was just something about her that pulled him in. It might be her quiet resilience. Or the way her eyes lit up just before she smiled. Or maybe it was that when he talked, she really listened, genuine empathy in her gaze.

Hell, it was probably all of it.

When he was with her, it was a battle to keep himself from touching her. A battle he often lost. The need to kiss her again damn near tortured him.

A few days had passed since the accident. They still hadn't found out who'd been driving the green Honda. It had to be one of those damn reporters. When he found the asshole responsible, he'd be making sure the guy not only left Cradle Mountain, but that he knew he wasn't welcome to return.

Logan pushed to his feet. When footsteps sounded from beyond the Blue Halo offices, he paused. A woman's steps. Her heels clicked against the wooden staircase in light succession. The door to Blue Halo creaked as it was pushed open. Logan remained where he was, listening. Would she stop at the reception desk? Or would she continue further into the building?

When the clicking of her heels continued down the hall, Logan's brows pulled together. Who the hell was this woman and where did she get the balls to just come straight in?

He didn't have to wonder for long. A second later, Nicole Fleece stepped into view from outside his office, only stopping once she stood on the other side of his desk.

"Good evening, Logan. I almost thought I'd missed everyone."

"And yet you still waltzed right in."

One of her perfectly manicured brows rose. "An unlocked business door usually means the public is welcome."

"You are neither public, nor welcome." And the woman knew it. "You're media. Now leave."

Rather than turning, she lowered into the seat opposite his desk, bag dropping to the floor with a resounding thud. "I'm here to negotiate with you."

"Why the hell would I negotiate with a reporter, especially one I've been telling to leave town since she got here?"

"Because you want to hear what I have to say."

Doubtful. He was just eyeing the door again when she indicated to his seat with a nod of her head. "Please, sit, Logan. I'll hurt my neck having to look up to meet your gaze."

If she thought he cared about that, she clearly had an inflated view of his concern for her. But the woman obviously wasn't going anywhere, so unless he planned to physically carry her out of the office, he was stuck.

He lowered slowly. "You have five minutes. No more."

"Wouldn't want to keep Grace waiting, would we? I'm actually surprised you forgave her after outing you the way she did."

Outwardly, Logan didn't react at all, every muscle remained perfectly still. Internally, he rebelled against Grace being brought up. He wanted her kept firmly out of anything to do with this woman.

"I'm not discussing Grace. So, if that's why you're here, you should walk right back out."

Nicole gave him a smile that was as fake as her tan. "I've been watching her. She seems like a good person. I mean, you've forgiven her, so her ethics can't be too skewed. Which raises the question, why would she have spoken to Phillip?"

Where was the woman going with this? "Because the guy's an asshole and he threatened her."

"I'm not sure if you're aware of this, but I met Phillip. A few times, actually. He was a good reporter. Great with research. That was his sword. Digging stuff up and using it against a subject. He would never stoop so low as to threaten someone with physical assault. He was smarter than that." She tapped the side of her head. "No. He found something on her. Something so bad that she gave up information on *you*, to keep herself out of the public eye."

Logan leaned forward, needing this woman to get to the goddamn point. "What do you want?"

"I want an inside story on your experience with Project Arma. I want to know everything, the good, the bad, and the ugly."

He knew what she was going to say, but he asked anyway. "And if I say no?"

"I switch my focus. From you to Grace. I dig until I find out exactly what her secret is. Exactly what Phillip found. And I expose her."

Logan breathed through his rage. It bounced off him like tiny sparks of electricity. The woman didn't have a shred of compassion or boundaries. The idea of her anywhere near Grace's business had his blood boiling.

"I want a signed contract that I see and approve the article before it's published," Logan said through gritted teeth. "And if there's anything, even a single word, that I don't like, it's out."

He'd do the stupid article if it meant saving Grace from this woman. But he'd give Nicole the information *he* chose to give.

She tilted her head to the side. "You don't trust me, Mr. Snyder?"

"Not even a little."

Her lips lifted at the corners. Yeah, she knew she'd won. "You're not really in a position to choose here."

"This is me being nice. The alternative is you stay, and I make your life a living hell." Every damn day.

She didn't look scared. Not one bit. "Lucky for you, I'm in a negotiating mood. Done. Do you need to run this by your team?"

"Yes. I'll talk to them in the next few days and you can get the contract sorted." Given the two choices, he was almost certain he knew what his team would choose. They were protectors, just like him. And besides, he only planned to give an inside look into *his* life in Project Arma. Not those of his brothers. That was the deal.

"Fine. I'll call in a few days." She stood. "I knew we could be adults about this."

She turned and was almost at the door when Logan spoke. "Do me a favor and tell the others to leave."

She looked back at him over her shoulder. "Others? You mean other reporters? Logan, I'm all that's left. No one else has my grit or tenacity."

Logan tried not to tense as Nicole made her way down the hall. That couldn't be right. It *had* to be a reporter who had run Grace off the road.

Logan reached for his phone and sent a message to Wyatt. He hadn't asked the man for help on this yet. Mostly because he'd thought the local police would find the dirtbag who'd run Grace into the pole. Days had passed, and they hadn't. Logan was taking matters into his own hands.

Even though Wyatt lived in Marble Falls, he could still access street surveillance here in Cradle Mountain. Hopefully, the guy would be able to get a license plate on the green car.

Logan also sent a message to his team, asking for a meeting the next morning.

Rising from his chair, he headed out of the building and toward his car, wanting to get to Grace quickly, hating any time he was away from her after the crash. His house had great security, but still, him being there with her was the ultimate protection.

The second he pulled into his garage, he heard the music. And just under it, he heard the soft hum of her voice.

Some of the tension eased from his shoulders.

Grace loved music. He'd come to that realization after living with her for a single day. The soft lyrics sounded from the kitchen while she prepared food. From her bedroom while she got ready in the morning. It even played in the bathroom while she showered.

She didn't seem to discriminate either. Every song was different. Different eras. Different genres.

Tonight was Michael Jackson's "Man in the Mirror".

Opening the door, he paused at the kitchen entrance, getting a perfect view of her swaying hips from behind. She was stirring whatever was in the pot on the stove while singing the words to the song in flawless harmony.

Fucking perfection.

He wanted to move across the room slowly. Surprise her by sliding his arms around her middle and nuzzling her neck. But he knew that sneaking up on the woman wasn't a good idea. Instead, he cleared his throat.

Grace still jumped, but probably less so than if he'd suddenly been surrounding her.

She placed her hand to her chest. "Logan. I didn't hear you come in."

"That's because I'm a ninja." She chuckled as he began walking toward her slowly, closing the distance.

"You are. And it doesn't help that I lose myself in the music sometimes."

He wasn't complaining. When he took the next step, he heard the slight increase in her heart rate. "I love that you love music so much."

"I do." Those two words came out quieter than her last.

"I missed you."

Her eyes widened a fraction. "You did?"

He placed his hands lightly on her hips. "You sound surprised."

"You saw me at lunch."

He had. He'd brought over food from the diner in between her seeing patients. Jeez, he was becoming addicted to the woman. "I know. It's been forever." He studied her eyes. Then her lips. When her gaze shot to his lips too, a lightning bolt of awareness rushed through his system. "I really want to kiss you right now."

A small tremble rocked her body. When her tongue poked out of her mouth and wet her lips, he almost groaned out loud.

"You should."

Fuck, but those two words made him hard all over.

Sliding a hand into her hair, he tugged her head up, kissing her slowly. Swiping his lips across hers and pulling her hips into him.

He'd intended to stop there. One taste, then let her go. But she leaned into him. Pressed her chest against his, moaning deep in her throat.

Logan growled, swinging them around and lifting her onto the island. He paused for a moment, waiting to see if there was hesitation. Resistance of any kind.

There was none. Instead, she wrapped her legs around his waist, bringing him closer.

The fingers on her waist slid beneath the material of her shirt, stroking her soft skin.

Grace hummed.

Slowly, so slowly that she could stop him at any time, Logan slid his hand up, until his fingers closed around her breast.

There was the slightest pause.

He readied himself to move away—until she pressed her chest into his hand, her lips moving once more against his.

He massaged the soft mound, loving the soft groans of encouragement he received. As he shifted his hand to her other breast, he grazed across something...

Scarring. Etched into her otherwise smooth skin between her breasts.

Grace's body stiffened before she took her lips from his and pushed him away.

"The sauce is bubbling," she said quietly under her breath.

It wasn't. But he let her go.

Another scar. He hadn't forgotten the one he'd seen on her thigh. How had she gotten them? *Who* had inflicted them?

He wanted to know exactly what had happened to the beautiful, tortured woman in front of him. But with one look at her rigid spine, he knew he wasn't going to. Not now, anyway.

CHAPTER 16

*H*e'd felt it. The scar on her chest. The one etched so deeply into her skin that the very sight of it had once repulsed her.

He hadn't said anything. He hadn't asked a single question. But she was sure the questions had been there, ticking away in his mind.

Taking her eyes off the dishes she was washing, Grace shot a glance at Logan from below her lashes. Before he'd felt the scar, before she'd felt him pause, every little part of her had wanted to go further. Further than she'd gone with any man in a very long time. And he'd wanted that too. She'd felt it.

Cleaning the last dish, she turned to watch Logan as he wiped down the counter.

The room was almost silent. At some point during dinner, the music had stopped, and she'd barely noticed. Too distracted by the questions in her head.

But now, the silence was deafening. She almost wanted to bang her hand on the counter or stomp her foot, anything to bring some sound into the room.

"I'm not ready to talk about it," she blurted, before snapping her mouth shut.

Logan paused. When he lifted his head, his face was so unreadable she didn't have a clue what he was thinking. "It?"

"The scar on my chest. There's also one on my thigh. I don't want to talk about either of them."

His nod was slow. "Okay."

Some of the tension eased from her chest.

He straightened. "Should we watch another episode tonight?"

Her brows rose, surprised at the easy change in topic. Surprised, but definitely not unhappy about it. "Sure."

Logan's small smile made her heart give a little kick. He moved across to her, his heat pressing into her shoulder as he rinsed the cloth. A small shiver ran down her spine, traveling all the way to her toes. "I need to find out who the killer is," he said quietly.

"You and me both."

They'd been watching a murder mystery on Netflix. To be honest, it was always a struggle to pay attention to the show when Logan was right beside her, often touching her in some way, thigh against thigh. Shoulder against shoulder.

Logan tossed the cloth away. "My money's on the mother."

All signs pointed to it being the mother. But... "That would be too easy. I think it's the gas station attendant. He has shifty eyes."

"Shifty eyes?"

Grace chuckled. "Yeah. They flicker too much, like he's nervous. Either that, or keeping his eyes peeled for anyone who might accuse him. If he focused a bit more, I might trust him."

This time, Logan threw back his head and laughed. The smile slipped from Grace's lips. The only way she could think to describe him in that moment was beautiful.

"Okay, detective." He slipped his fingers through hers and the fine hairs on her arms rose. "Guess we'll find out who's right soon enough."

He led her to the couch and Grace immediately tucked her legs under her, skin prickling when Logan sat close, pulling a blanket over both their laps. His wonderful heat radiating up her side.

When the show started, Grace did what she always did, watched, pretended to focus, when really thoughts of Logan took precedence. His hand was now on her thigh, and Lord All Mighty, it was doing strange things to her insides.

Placing her hand on top of his, she traced her finger along his veins, never taking her gaze off the screen in front of her. So much of her adult life had been spent avoiding a man's touch, but with Logan, she craved it. It was like an addiction she couldn't get enough of.

What was it about this man that put her at ease, when every other man spiked her fear? Was it because when he looked at her, he really *saw* her? Like he could see the tangled web of her soul. Or was it the strength that vibrated off him? Not just the physical strength, but the mental. Emotional.

Like her body had a mind of its own, she angled herself more toward him. With her opposite hand, she trailed up his forearm, grazing across his bicep.

Everything about him was huge. But the more she thought about it, the more she was sure it wasn't his size or looks that attracted her. No. It was *him*. The man inside the sparkly case. The man who was kind and gentle and protective.

Turning her head toward him, she studied his features. Saw the way his lips tugged up at the corners.

"Grace." His voice almost sounded like a warning.

"Yes?"

When his eyes met hers, there was desire there. The brown of his eyes almost black. "You're killing me with those strokes."

She stilled, barely realizing her fingers had been moving.

"I really like you, Logan." Her words were almost a whisper.

Voice so small, it probably sounded like she was talking to herself.

"I like you, too."

His words worked their way into her chest, breaking down some of the barricades she'd carefully constructed around her heart.

For almost a decade, she'd been so careful. Never pushing her limits. Always working to heal herself without jeopardizing her progress.

This man made her want to take risks. To explore these newfound confidences. These new feelings.

Slowly, Grace climbed onto his lap, straddling him with her thighs in much the same way she had in his truck that day. His eyes flared, his grip taking hold of her hips.

She trailed her hands up his chest, grazing his skin lightly, before curving her fingers around his neck. Even that felt well-muscled.

Logan was so still, she almost wondered if he was breathing.

Lowering her head, Grace touched her lips to his. His hands tightened on her hips. When he tugged her closer, and her core pressed against his hardness, a gasp escaped her lips. Logan took advantage of the moment, slipping inside her mouth.

Her nipples pebbled against his hard chest, desire pooling in her core.

She pressed herself closer to him, never quite feeling close enough. She wanted to lose herself in the man. Feel things she'd never felt before.

They continued to kiss for endless minutes until, at some point, the control shifted from her to him. And God, did the man know how to make love to her mouth. He sipped and swiped, his hands caressing her hips in rhythmic motions.

A yearning claimed her. Demanded she give more. Take more.

The barrier of clothing between them suddenly irritated her.

As if he read her thoughts, Logan's hand slipped beneath her top. And just like he had earlier that evening, he trailed up her stomach, pushing up her top and closing his hand around the mound of her breast.

Grace's whimper was swallowed by his lips. The blood roaring in her ears, blocking out the background noise of the show that had long been forgotten.

Logan cupped and massaged her. When his thumb found her hard peak, he grazed back and forth, causing the need to heat and rupture inside her.

Grace rubbed her core against his lap, trying and failing to get some much-needed relief. Logan switched to her other breast, and the agony deepened. The searing need was like no other. The *man* was like no other.

Gently, Logan lay her back against the couch, hovering over her. His hand went back to her breast, his mouth meeting hers again.

More of his weight pressed against her.

That's when things shifted. First it was the beads of sweat on her forehead. Then it was the body chills when moments before she'd been so deeply heated.

Her skin began to crawl at his touch, her heart thudding violently against her ribs.

His body weighed her down. A single hand restraining both of hers above her head.

Unbreakable.

His other hand grazed across her naked skin, making her flesh crawl and her stomach rebel. Her throat was dry and raw from screaming so loud, but she didn't stop. The desperation to get away like a living, breathing parasite inside her.

She struggled, but his strength was overwhelming.

"Grace?"

Her breaths were coming out in short gasps. Her body shaking violently. But she couldn't stop it. Any of it.

The weight lifted off her. He touched her arm and she spiraled again. Thrown back into hell.

"Don't touch me! Get away!" It took every ounce of strength to get the words out. To make her terror-filled voice work. "God, please, leave me alone!"

Memories she never wanted to relive again cascaded through her mind like an avalanche. Making her want to peel her skin from her body. Rid every part of her that had been touched by *him*.

~

IT WAS like a switch had flicked. Logan recognized it the second it happened. One moment she was with him, craving his touch as much as he craved hers, the next she was somewhere else completely.

Immediately, he rose. At first attempting to touch her arm, soothe her. But at her sharp cry, he pulled back. Shifting away and giving her some space.

Grace pushed herself into the corner of the couch, wrapping her arms around her legs and curling herself into a ball. A part of Logan's heart cracked at the sight of her trying to make herself so small. He'd never seen this level of fear. Of sheer desolation. And he had no idea how to handle it.

Her body continued to tremble violently. Her soft sobs filling the air.

His hand twitched to reach out and touch her again, wanting to comfort the woman. But he didn't. Touch didn't represent safety to her right now. Particularly not a man's touch. He had to get through to her a different way.

Logan kept his voice low and gentle. "Sweetheart, can you hear me? It's Logan."

Nothing. She was now rocking back and forth, her head

tucked so firmly into her knees that he couldn't see a single part of her face.

"You're safe," he said quietly. "No one is going to hurt you. No one is going to touch you."

"Stay away from me." Her words were so low and pained, they shattered Logan. "Please! Please don't touch me."

Later, he knew he would feel the full of weight of anger that someone had instilled this pain and fear inside her. But for now, he needed to focus on helping her find her way back to him.

He tried a couple more questions, but didn't get anywhere with them. Her fingers were now digging into her arms, penetrating her skin.

Fuck. He needed to do something, and he needed to do it *now*.

Scanning the room, his eyes stopped on the speakers.

Music. She always had a song blasting. It was when she seemed her most relaxed.

Grabbing his phone, he connected it to the Bluetooth speakers and chose one of the songs he'd heard her singing on numerous occasions—Rising Appalachia's "Resilient".

The music began to filter through the room, its soothing melody wiping out the sounds of her loud, ragged breaths.

At first, there was no change in Grace. The pain and fear all but bled out of her. It wasn't until about two minutes into the song that the rocking slowed. Then it stopped, her body going still. It was another thirty seconds before her heart rate began to slow.

When that song ended, another began. Logan waited. Watching as she regained her grasp on reality.

Finally, Grace lifted her head. Pain. It was front and center on her tear-stained face. God, he hated it. But at least the fear was gone.

Her mouth opened and closed a few times. Like she wanted to say something but didn't know what.

Logan kept his distance, waiting for her, for whenever she was ready.

"I'm sorry," she said quietly.

Sorry? That wasn't what he wanted or needed to hear. "Are you okay?"

Her gaze went to her knees. She was still hugging her legs like she was trying to hold herself together. "I thought I would be okay tonight. Every other touch from you has been wonderful."

"Do you want to talk about it?"

He hoped she said yes. He was so ready to listen. And not to some watered-down version. He wanted to know everything. Every little fractured part of her.

He knew he wouldn't like it. Hell, he'd probably feel a rage so deep in his soul he'd never fully recover. But he didn't care.

"I suppose I owe you an explanation—"

"You don't owe me anything, Grace. I would like you to tell me, but only if you're ready."

She rubbed her thumb over the scratches she'd just created on her arms. "Eight years ago, I worked in a bar called Sunnie's. I mostly worked nights, particularly on weekends. But it was a Wednesday night when I first noticed him. He sat in a corner booth and he just...watched me. My entire shift. I remember feeling his gaze on me wherever I went and hating it. He didn't even try to hide it."

Logan clenched his jaw. His muscles tightened in anticipation of what was coming next.

"He came in again the next night. And the one after that. This continued for weeks. On the days he wasn't there, I somehow still felt his eyes on me. I knew he was somewhere. Watching." She paused to breathe deeply. "I called my dad. We've always been close. He was worried too, and he hired a guy to watch me during my shifts. A professional bodyguard."

Logan didn't miss the small tremble that rocked her body.

"A few nights passed where I didn't see or feel him. I

remember feeling relieved. Thinking I wouldn't see him again. That Mitch's presence had scared him off." She shook her head. "One night, I finished my shift but Mitch wasn't there. He usually trailed me home. I thought maybe an emergency had popped up. I got home to find…"

She stopped, her features anguished.

"What did you find, honey?"

"The guy killed Mitch. His body was…it was bad. I barely opened my mouth to scream before someone hit me. The next thing I remember, I opened my eyes in a basement."

Logan's heart hammered so violently against his ribs it was almost painful. "What happened next?" He was almost certain he knew, but he needed her to confirm it.

Her words were quiet, but it didn't soften the weight of what she said. "He held me in his basement for a week. I was…raped. Drugged."

Fire, hot and intense, burned through Logan's body, scalding him from the inside out. Every part of him rebelled against her words, wishing them to be untrue but knowing they weren't.

He'd hoped he'd been wrong. Prayed for it. But now, having it confirmed…it almost destroyed him. Made him want to find the asshole and tear him limb from limb.

When her breaths started coming out shaky, Logan shifted closer. "Grace." When her eyes didn't meet his, he lifted his hands slowly, placing them on her arms. Finally, she looked. "I'm sorry. So unbelievably sorry that happened to you. If I could turn back time and protect you from it, I would. You're safe with me. Always."

For a moment, she just watched him, pain still etched onto her face. Then, slowly, she crawled onto his lap, tucked her head into his chest and cried. Silent tears that soaked his shirt.

Logan held her close. His hands moved in slow, rhythmic circles on her back. Wanting to be whatever she needed.

He had questions. Lots of them. How had she gotten away? Where was this guy now—behind bars or dead?

He was hoping for the latter.

All that could wait. For now, he just needed to hold her and try to stop the overwhelming rage and desolation from consuming them both.

CHAPTER 17

"*I* couldn't see him, but I could feel him."

Grace remained quiet as she listened to her patient talk. Her patient was describing the night she'd been taken from her home. She spoke with such strength that Grace's hairs almost stood on end.

"I stepped inside and locked my doors. Then went around the entire house, turning on every light."

"Why did you turn on the lights, Antonia?"

She lifted a shoulder. "I felt safer in the light. I felt safer being able to see." Then she shook her head, regret flickering across her face. "But I didn't see him coming."

"What happened next?" Grace asked quietly.

"When I turned on the light in my bedroom, this cold, sick feeling came over me." Grace's skin chilled. She knew that feeling. She'd experienced the same moments before her own abduction. "It was like my body knew that my world was about to change, before my mind did."

Grace gave a gentle nod from her position on the chair beside the bed where Antonia sat. The other woman's hands rhythmically smoothed the sheet over her thighs.

"He came out of nowhere. I still don't know where he was hiding. I could probably ask, I bet it's in my file, but does it matter?" She shook her head. "He placed something over my mouth, and that was it. Everything went black, and when I woke up, I was in this basement. I didn't stay there for long though. A couple hours. Then I was thrown into a trunk and taken to the compound."

Grace was careful to keep her face neutral, even though her skin crawled.

She'd woken in a basement. Although, where Antonia had only been held a few hours, Grace had been held a week. A week of hell.

Antonia looked up, her pale blue eyes clashing with Grace's. "Can I tell you something?"

"You can tell me anything."

"The first morning I woke up here, I stood in the bathroom and I looked at myself. I literally just stood there for…God, it had to be close to half an hour. I was looking for something familiar in my reflection. I couldn't find it. It was like I was looking at a stranger. I felt disconnected from my body. Hollow."

"That's very normal after what you went through."

She sighed. "That day you walked in here, I didn't want to listen or talk to you. I didn't want to talk to anyone. I went into my head and imagined…" She chuckled. "I imagined this bubble around myself. It was my bubble of safety."

"The bubble was a coping mechanism." Grace's coping mechanism had been a dark fog. A fog that she'd let block out everything and everyone else.

"You said something that penetrated the bubble, though. You said, 'There's nothing shameful about asking for help'."

They were the same words that had been said to her. Words that she'd desperately needed to hear. "It's true. There isn't."

"It suddenly hit me, I *did* feel shameful. Shameful for a crime I didn't commit. I felt *at fault* for something I held no responsibility for. For so long, I thought maybe I'd done something to put myself in that position."

Grace leaned forward. "You didn't."

"I know that now. You also said, 'if you can't speak your truth, the pain is released somewhere else, and that place is not always good'."

Grace's chest warmed at the knowledge that her words had a positive effect on this woman who'd been through so much. "It's my job to give you a safe space to release your pain."

Safety was key for trauma survivors. It was something that had usually been taken away. Stolen.

"And you do." Antonia looked up, meeting Grace's gaze. When she released a long breath, it was like the woman was breathing out some of the pain she'd been holding. "I feel confident in my recovery, Grace. I feel determined. I want to be better. I want to stop being a victim and start being a survivor."

God, the woman's strength was unbelievable. "I'm so happy to hear that, Antonia."

"I know our sessions will be changing to Skype sessions, so I want to thank you in person before I go. Thank you for allowing me to speak without interruption or judgment. For letting me feel heard and listened to. When you look at me, you really look. Which is...big. For so long, people have looked through me. Seen me as an object."

"I am so proud of you."

The woman beamed from the bed. Even the fact that she could smile so soon after being rescued was...gosh, it was amazing.

"I was actually thinking that maybe I could work toward helping other women like myself. Like at a shelter or something."

"I think that's a fantastic goal. And I love that you're looking toward and planning for your future."

Antonia continued to smile as she nodded.

Grace stood, their session coming to an end. When she said

her goodbyes and walked out of the room, she was still smiling. Smiling at the tremendous progress her patient was making. At her strength. Her grit. It was nothing short of amazing.

Her patients were due to leave Cradle Mountain soon. Some would struggle more than others. Some would have faster progress. Antonia was by far the furthest along in her recovery.

Grace gave Flynn and Liam a smile as she said goodbye. They were guarding the rooms that day. Then she made her way down the hall. In the women's changing room, she stopped at the mirror, studying her reflection. The bags under her eyes were still as dark as they'd been that morning. Sleep had not been her friend last night. Not after her panic attack. Her first in many years.

She would have thought she'd be wiped out after the attack and talking to Logan. That it would make her so exhausted she slept like a log. Not the case at all. She'd tossed and turned for hours.

But although she was exhausted, her talk with Antonia had made her feel just that bit lighter. The woman was so strong. And so determined to be better. It fueled Grace's fire to get better herself.

For so long, she'd ignored her fear of intimacy with a man. No more. She needed to tackle this head on.

Giving her reflection a quick nod, Grace turned, grabbing her bag and heading to the front desk. She began filling out the last of her patient forms. Glancing at her watch, she noticed it was five minutes past five. Logan must be running late.

Taking her phone out of her pocket, she sent him a quick message.

Just walking out now.

She hadn't gotten her phone back into her pocket before his response came through.

Wait for me inside, honey.

She paused, glancing up at the doors. She'd wanted to get

some fresh air after being inside all day, but knew Logan was just trying to keep her safe. They still hadn't figured out who'd been driving that green car. It must've been a journalist getting desperate and trying to create a story. Who, exactly, was the question.

I will. See you soon. x

His next message was faster than his first.

xx

She'd only taken a couple of steps away from the reception area when the lady behind the desk called for her.

"Grace Castle?"

She turned her head. "Yes?" Grace had spoken to the woman a couple of times but couldn't remember her first name. Jen, maybe?

The lady held out an envelope. "A man dropped these on the floor as he was leaving…"

Grace frowned as she noticed what looked like pieces of paper tucked into the open envelope. "And they're for me?"

"They're *of* you."

Of her? She took the envelope from the woman's fingers and stepped away from the reception area. Her stomach did a little flip when she took out the contents. They weren't just pieces of paper. They were pictures of her. One of her and Courtney sitting in a booth at The Grind. One of Logan carrying her during the Rainbow Run. Another of her dancing at the Rainbow Run.

A chill swept through her.

What the hell? Who had taken these? Was it one of the reporters? She knew she'd felt eyes on her during the Rainbow Run. Surely it must be the same guy who ran her car off the road.

Anger boiled in her gut and threatened to overflow. How dare this person? Following her around town? Taking photos of her without her knowledge or consent? It was stalking.

She was close to blowing up when her phone rang.

Yanking it out of her pocket, she just about growled at the person. "Hello."

"Gracie, it's me, Dad."

"Dad! I've been trying to call you."

"I'm sorry, darling. I've taken some leave from work and have been trying to keep a low profile. I've turned off my normal phone and gotten a new burner. Are you out of Cradle Mountain?"

She nibbled her lip. "Uh, not exactly. I took on some patients but will be leaving soon."

There was a brief pause. "Are the reporters still there?"

Lie. She had to. Otherwise, the worry would kill him. "They're gone." Most of them *were* gone, so it was a small lie, right? Her father didn't need anything else to worry about. "How are you, Dad?"

"I'm good. I've been keeping a close eye on the case in Phoenix. They didn't find Kieran after he left his prints at the woman's house, and there have been no more attempted kidnappings."

Of course not. It didn't surprise her at all. The guy was a master at remaining hidden. "But you're safe?"

"I'm safe. You don't need to worry about me, honey."

"I love you." She loved and missed him so much, her heart hurt.

"I love you, baby girl."

CHAPTER 18

*L*ogan dropped his phone into the middle console of the truck, starting his engine. Grace said she'd wait inside. Good.

It had been another long day of security consultations and paperwork. At least he'd gotten a morning training session in with Blake. A short session was better than nothing.

Flynn and Liam had spent the day at the hospital guarding the women. Logan had met with the rest of the team after his workout to discuss his upcoming meeting with Nicole. They were all in agreement that he would do the interview. Even though he hadn't shared anything about Grace's history, they knew it was heavy. Knew it was something that couldn't, or shouldn't, get out.

He hadn't told Grace about Nicole and the interview. He'd been planning on it, but then they'd kissed, and the kiss had been followed by making out on the couch after dinner...then her panic attack.

A muscle ticked in his jaw at the memory of what she'd told him last night.

He'd just turned a corner when his phone rang, Wyatt's name popping up on the screen.

"Hey, Wyatt. You found anything for me on that green car?"

"I found it on some traffic surveillance. It was a rental, under the name of a Scott Pilgrig. He's a reporter for the Idaho News 6 team. Mid-thirties. Caucasian."

Logan frowned. Why would a reputable reporter trail Grace around town, running her into a pole? Was he so desperate for a story that he was willing to risk losing everything? Was he trying to make *her* the story? It didn't make sense.

Unless it wasn't Scott driving the car…

"Nicole Fleece told me she was the only reporter left in town." Of course, she could have been lying. Logan didn't trust the woman. "Do you know which hotel or motel he's staying at?"

"Unfortunately, no. His colleague readily admitted he was due to return to the office today, but he never showed."

Big fucking red flag.

"I know. Not looking good," Wyatt said, reading his silence. "I'll keep looking into it from my end."

Logan turned onto the street with the hospital. "And I'll keep an eye on Grace from mine." He pulled into the hospital parking lot. "Did you find anything on her?" he asked quietly.

He almost cringed, hating that he'd gone behind Grace's back to find information. But after her revelation, and when she didn't reveal the guy's name or whether he was alive or dead, there was no way Logan *wasn't* taking matters into his own hands.

That's why he'd sent Wyatt security footage of Grace from Blue Halo and asked the man to run a facial recognition search. It was also why he hadn't pushed her for more information last night. There were other means of finding out what he needed to know.

Grace wouldn't be happy. But now that he knew her past, it was a matter of safety. He cared about the woman and he needed her to be okay.

"Yes, I did. You sure you want to know?"

He knew what his friend was really asking. Was he sure he wanted *Wyatt* to tell him before Grace did. Because once he knew, there was no going back.

"Tell me."

"Her real name is Grace McKenna. When she was twenty-one, she was kidnapped from her home. A week later, she was picked up by a man driving on Route 128 in Massachusetts. The medical reports read severe dehydration, malnourishment, deep lacerations to her chest and thigh, as well as sexual assault."

Logan scrunched his eyes shut. Hearing the details was damn painful, but it needed to be done.

"Who was the guy?" he asked through gritted teeth.

"Kieran Hayes. He got mixed up in drugs in his teenage years. There's not much information on the guy in the system. Not even a picture. He was raised by a single mom who lived in a trailer park in Stockton, California. His mother OD'd and died when he was eighteen. Nothing in the system for him bar Grace's report, and he disappeared after Grace got away."

So the asshole was alive. *Goddammit.* "Shouldn't she have been placed into a safe house?"

"According to the police report, she was assigned one, but never made it there. She disappeared shortly after being released from the hospital."

"Disappeared?"

"Yep. And on her seventh year of being missing, she was officially declared dead."

Jesus Christ. He leaned his head back against the headrest, his brain moving quickly, sifting through all the information.

"Who would have helped her create her new identity?" Logan asked, more to himself than to Wyatt. "Because a bartender definitely wouldn't have the skills or resources on her own."

"Her father was, and still is, a US marshal. He would have had the means to create a new identity and make sure it was bulletproof."

And there it was.

The reason she'd talked to Barret. The reason she didn't ask for help. The reason she was still hesitant to tell Logan everything. The final piece of the Grace McKenna puzzle fit into place. "He would be in a lot of trouble if that ever got out."

"To protect his daughter," Wyatt said, "I'm sure he saw it as a risk worth taking."

Of course. Most parents would move heaven and earth to protect their kids.

Logan sighed. "And her mother?"

"Passed away when she was little. Heart attack. Looks like her father raised her."

"Another reason she wants to protect him." He undid his seat belt. "Wyatt—I need you to find this Kieran guy."

"Already on it."

If Logan found him, he was a dead man. "Appreciate it. And Wyatt, are we able to keep this information between us?"

He trusted Wyatt's team, but they weren't family to him. Not like his guys. And if this information got out to the wrong people, neither Grace nor her father would be safe.

"Was planning on it. Talk again soon, Logan."

Hanging up, Logan climbed out of the truck.

He spent the entire walk to the doors debating whether to come clean to Grace about what he'd learned. How would she take it? Not well, he was guessing. Not when she worried for the safety of herself and her father.

He needed to tell her, though. Especially if he wanted a relationship with the woman. He just had to hope she'd forgive him for the methods he'd used. Trust him to not put her or her father at risk.

Logan spotted her the second he stepped through the door.

She held a phone to her ear in one hand, and small pieces of paper in the other.

"I love you."

Logan heard her father's voice through the line before she hung up. When she turned her head, her eyes widened slightly at the sight of him.

He smiled in an attempt to put her at ease. "Hey, honey. Ready to go?"

Pushing the phone into her pocket, she returned the smile and nodded. He didn't miss the strain lines around her eyes.

His gaze darted to her hand. "What's that?"

Her smile slipped, eyes narrowing. "Someone took photos of me. They dropped them on the floor as they left."

"Photos?"

Taking them from her outstretched hand, he flicked through the images, just biting back a curse. "What the hell?"

She lifted a shoulder. "I'm assuming it was one of the reporters."

His hand went to her cheek. "Who gave you this?"

Her gaze shifted to the front desk. "The receptionist."

Slipping his fingers through hers, he tugged her behind him, stopping at the desk. The woman looked up. Her eyes widened slightly, a reaction he was used to ever since the community found out about his team.

"Hi." The woman sounded slightly out of breath.

He smiled. "Hi. We need more information on who dropped these pictures. Is there security footage we could check?"

"Um, there are cameras, but it's live footage watched by our security team. It's not recorded."

Dammit to hell. "Could you describe the man for me?"

"I can try. He was wearing a gray sweatshirt. He was bald. Shorter than you, maybe six feet. Slim build…that's all I really remember. Sorry."

Hopefully it would be enough to either match or dismiss

Scott Pilgrig. He'd ask Wyatt to send through pictures of the reporter later tonight.

"Thank you."

Turning around, hand still holding Grace's, he led them out of the hospital. The second they stood on the sidewalk, he scanned the street.

He made his way to the car, one hand firmly on the small of Grace's back.

"The green car was a rental," he said as he helped her into his truck. "A reporter by the name of Scott Pilgrig leased it."

He walked around, climbing behind the wheel.

Grace nodded. "Makes sense. He probably sees me as an easy source of information. Although, why he didn't just come and talk to me, I have no idea."

Yeah, Logan wasn't sure what the hell was going on. But he planned to find out.

He shot a glance across to her as he drove out of the parking lot. "Grace, I need to know—how did you get away?"

He hadn't intended to ask that question right now, but suddenly, he needed every detail he could get.

Grace took a deep breath before turning her head toward him. He might not have been expecting to ask it, but maybe she'd been expecting to hear it. "He kept me in his basement for a week. He was supposed to deliver me to his boss. He... He worked for a trafficking organization."

Logan tensed.

Grace hurried to continue. "The last couple days, he'd started talking about how he couldn't give me up. How he wanted to keep me as *his*." He saw the shiver that rocked her spine. His hand immediately went to her leg. "That night, when he came into the basement, I could tell he was on something. Some sort of drug. His eyes were bloodshot, and he was acting really paranoid. He just kept saying he couldn't lose me. He couldn't let anyone else have me."

She found a string on the side of her pants and began to fiddle, focusing on it. "He pulled out a knife. Said that he needed to mark me as his." When the fingers playing with the string began to tremble, Logan's hand shifted so that it sat over hers.

"What happened next?" His voice was tight and low.

"He attacked me. I remember his weight on top of me as he cut. He wasn't trying to kill me. Just scar me. He went for my thigh first. Then my chest. The pain of the knife slicing over my skin...it was something I'll never forget."

Fire laced his blood. "Then what, honey?"

"When he went for my face, he shifted his body just enough for me to knee him between the legs. His movements were more sluggish than usual because of whatever he was on. He dropped the knife, and I just lunged for it, grabbing it and stabbing him in the stomach. Then I ran. I had no idea where I was or where I was heading. I just knew I needed to get as far away from the house as possible."

So damn strong.

"I ran until I reached a road. I ran in front of a car, forcing the driver to stop. The rest, I barely remember. It was a blur of white hospital walls, nurses trying to talk to me... By the time the house was located, he was gone," she finished.

He opened his mouth, readying himself to tell her about Wyatt. About what he'd learned. Then Grace sighed. Leaned her head back and closed her eyes.

God, he hated how tired she looked.

"Let's do something tonight."

The words just slipped out. He would, of course, make sure she was guarded by him and his team. But she needed at least the illusion of freedom.

"Anything that doesn't involve danger or threats or men who do unspeakable things sounds good to me."

Lifting her hand, he kissed the back of it. "Done."

CHAPTER 19

Cool air moved through the open windows. The smell of popcorn and nature filled the air. Grace had never been to a drive-in cinema before. In fact, she'd barely gone to indoor cinemas. Not since she was a teenager, anyway.

Her hand twitched to reach across to Logan. The movie was half over, and they hadn't touched. Not once. What was worse, he'd had a frown on his face the entire evening.

Thoughts of her conversation with Antonia were still floating through her head. Of Antonia's strength. Determination. Her courage.

Grace had spent years carrying her trauma around with her like a big weighted bag. She'd worked so hard to heal others, without ensuring that she herself was fully healed. And it was only now, when she wanted to progress in her relationship with Logan, that the cracks were beginning to show.

Every single day, she taught women that recovery and survival only happen because a person *chooses* for them to happen.

Antonia was choosing to survive. To *live*. And God, but that was inspiring.

Grace wanted to choose the same. To take back control of her sexuality. To take back the power that was stolen from her and break the spell that Kieran had been holding over her for so long.

She smiled as she reached across the console and put her hand on top of Logan's. He immediately wrapped his fingers through hers.

The man was everything.

Leaning her head back against the seat, she watched as a girl on the screen left a building, a backpack on her shoulder. Grace could have laughed. She had no idea what the building was, or even the girl's name. Yeah, she had no hope of catching up now.

Turning her head, she looked out the passenger window—just as a face appeared in front of hers. Grace screeched, seconds before recognition hit.

Placing her free hand on her chest, she took a deep breath. "Courtney, what the heck? You scared the crap out of me!"

Courtney smiled, looking way too amused by Grace's fright. "Logan would have heard me. You should be angry at *him* for not warning you."

She glanced beside her at Logan, and he had a hint of a smile on his face. "I was too distracted by your hand in mine."

Hm. She'd accept that answer, she supposed. "From now on, you need to focus," she joked, turning back to Courtney. "I didn't know you were here."

She lifted a shoulder. "Joey and I decided to catch a movie. I saw Logan's truck and thought I'd come over. Wanna get a soda with me?"

Well, she wasn't watching much of the movie. She turned to Logan. "Do you mind?"

"Go ahead. I'll join you in a sec."

Giving him a small smile, Grace climbed out of the car and followed her friend.

"How come you're here with Joey? Wait, it's not a—"

"Oh my God, don't say the word date." She shook her head,

like the very thought was absurd. "No, no, no. We're friends, nothing more. The guy's like a younger brother."

Yeah, he looked younger. Twenty, twenty-one maybe? "Oh. Does he feel the same?"

"Of course. And he's seen my pathetic bouts of nerves around Jason, so he knows I'm hopelessly obsessed with the man. Not that I'll ever do anything about it."

Grace frowned. "Why don't you just ask him out?"

"Ah, because to date a person, you'd actually need to be able to talk to him. Whenever I *do* talk to him, I ramble so much that I can't stop." Courtney kicked a stone. "It's crazy, isn't it? I try to live each day without fear, which is a conscious decision, by the way. I moved to Cradle Mountain even though I knew no one. I used all my savings to open my coffee shop. But with Jason, I just feel so dang nervous, like someone has cut my tongue right out of my mouth. Argh, it's pathetic!"

Reaching for Courtney's hand, Grace gave it a gentle squeeze. "Not pathetic. It sounds like you like him a lot, so the possibility of him not liking you in return scares you." She lifted a shoulder. "It's normal. Matters of the heart are hard and complicated."

Courtney sighed. "You're so wise. I need more of that in my life. And you're right. I need to grow some balls and ask the guy out."

That wasn't what she—

"Thanks, Grace. Maybe I'll write him a letter. Or an email."

They both laughed as they came to a stop at the end of the food and drinks line. "Or a text."

"Yes! Text. Why didn't I think of that? Hey, what about you? How's the date?"

"We haven't done a lot of 'date' stuff. We've just been watching the movie." At least she assumed *he* was watching the movie. She'd done more staring off into space and thinking about anything and everything.

"So kiss him."

Grace almost laughed. "Kiss him?"

"Yeah. There's still a whole lot of movie left. Certainly, enough to bring some passion into the night."

Hm. The passion part didn't sound terrible. "Maybe."

"I love that you two are together. You're a great fit. And such a good-looking couple. You could model on the front page of a magazine together."

"Er, I'm not sure about that, but thank you. What I feel when I'm with him is so different to what I feel with anyone else." Understatement of the century. "I honestly didn't think I would ever want this kind of relationship again. But with him...I want everything."

The kisses. The hand holding. The sneaky, under-the-table touches that no one could see. The love.

Courtney's eyes softened. "So beautiful. You're like two pieces of a puzzle, finally united."

"He's such a wonderful man. I don't know how I got so lucky." She barely felt deserving of his affection. Especially after what she'd done to him and his team.

Suddenly, Courtney pulled Grace into her arms and hugged her. It was a big, you're-going-to-be-okay kind of hug that almost had Grace feeling emotional.

"He's lucky too," Courtney whispered. "You are beautiful and intelligent and strong."

Grace hugged her friend back. It was the strong part that stayed with her. Because she didn't always feel strong. Sometimes she felt a stone's throw away from breaking.

"Thank you, Courtney."

When they reached the counter, Grace got her soda first then stood over to the side to wait. She was idly looking at the vacant field to her right when she saw it.

A car entering the gates, stopping not too far away.

Out of nowhere, a camera popped out of the window, pointed

directly at her. Through the darkness, she couldn't see the color of the car—but assumed it had to be green.

Unease swirled in her gut. Was it the reporter? Or was it someone else?

She needed to know. As if her feet had a mind of their own, they took a step toward the car. Then another.

She hadn't made it far when strong fingers wrapped around her arm and tugged her to a stop.

Turning, she saw Logan's less-than-impressed face looking down at her. "Where are you going?" Even though he didn't sound happy, his thumb was rubbing small circles on her skin, making her arm tingle.

She opened her mouth to answer, but before she could, a bright light shone on them. Immediately, she scrunched her eyes closed.

Logan's fingers tightened around her arm. "What the hell?"

Opening her eyes, she squinted, trying to see. Suddenly, the car's engine got loud.

She barely had a chance to register what was happening before she was pulled off her feet and thrown to the side. For a second, she was airborne. Then she landed on a big, hard chest, which immediately rolled her below him.

She didn't have time to feel fear over being caged because Logan was already tugging them both up, hands going to either side of her face. "Are you okay?"

Her heart was racing a million miles a minute, but she wasn't hurt. "I'm okay."

Logan's neck twisted as he looked behind him. She peeked around his shoulder to see the car was gone.

Suddenly, Courtney was beside her, eyes so wide they almost bugged out of her head. "Oh my God, that guy almost hit you guys! Are you both okay?"

She nodded, trying to work up a reassuring smile for her friend, but knowing it didn't quite come off.

Logan took his phone from his pocket. "Wyatt. The green car just tried to run Grace over. I want you to use every resource you have to find the driver." There was a beat of silence before Logan nodded. "Appreciate it."

Logan took Grace's face in his hands again, fury rolling off him. Even though she'd almost just been turned into roadkill, she couldn't deny the affect the man's touch had on her. "Are you sure you're okay?"

"I'm okay, Logan." Shaky, but alive and uninjured. Thanks to Logan.

He studied her face for another beat before dropping his hands. Immediately, one of them curved around her waist. "Let's get out of here."

She gave Courtney a quick hug before heading to the truck. She didn't miss the way Logan scanned the area the entire way back, like he was expecting the guy to come out of nowhere. Maybe jump out of the bushes.

When they got to the truck, he helped her inside before sliding behind the wheel and driving home.

The trip was done in silence, the air so tense she felt it in her bones.

When they pulled into the garage, he got straight out, going to the passenger side and helping her down. Then she had to jog to catch up with him as he stalked inside. It took two massive strides to match every one of his.

When they reached the living room, she touched his arm, relieved when he finally stopped. "Hey, are you okay?"

His face was clear. Too clear. The man was intentionally trying to shield her from whatever he was feeling. "Yes."

Not true. Not in the slightest. She didn't need to be a human lie detector to recognize that.

Stepping closer, she placed her hands on either side of his face. "Talk to me. I can tell you're not."

She wasn't sure if it was wishful thinking, but she could have sworn his muscles eased a little. Hands going to her hips, he leaned down, touching his forehead to hers. "I hate you being in danger, Grace. I hate that we can't even go out without something happening. What if I hadn't been there? What if that asshole had hit you?"

She tried not to react to his words. Instead, focusing on the touch of his head against hers. "You were there, Logan. You were exactly where I needed you to be."

"Every day I spend with you, my feelings grow. The thought of losing you is...terrifying."

Her heart jolted in her chest, leaving her breathless. "I feel the same way."

She didn't want to lose him. But staying in Cradle Mountain had never been her plan. Not long term.

When he lifted his head, his eyes were pained. "I need you to be okay."

Another jolt to the heart. Another moment of breathlessness.

Other than her father, no other person had needed her to be safe. "I will be."

Suddenly, he was kissing her. His lips capturing hers with an intensity she'd never felt before. Grace kissed him back. Giving him everything she had. Taking all that he offered.

"Is this okay?" he asked between moments of ravaging her lips.

"Yes." *So much yes.*

When his hands lowered, lifting her into his arms, she wrapped her legs around his waist. She ran her fingers through his hair, trying to get closer, trying to give the man more, take more.

She didn't know how long they remained like that. Maybe seconds, maybe minutes, connected so deeply that time became insignificant. But still, it wasn't enough. She needed to be closer. The fire inside her demanded it. Demanded *him*.

She tore her mouth away, whispering the words she thought she'd never speak again. "I want you, Logan."

When she kissed him again, he only returned it for a second before holding her cheeks, searching her eyes. "Are you sure?"

She knew that she couldn't live in fear forever. And that right now, she needed this man more than she'd ever needed anything else. She was ready to take back the control she'd barely fought for the last eight years.

"Yes."

CHAPTER 20

*D*esire burned through Grace, causing her heart to pound violently against her ribs. Her breasts ached as they rubbed against his chest.

Logan stopped beside the bed. Her entire body grazed against his as he lowered her to her feet, so much so that she felt every hard ridge. The moment his hands dropped, Grace felt the loss. The loss of his touch. His warmth. It almost brought a chill to her limbs.

Slowly, Logan slid off his shoes. His hands then went to the base of his shirt, lifting it over his head.

Almost involuntarily, her gaze slid over his bronzed, muscled chest. Power. Strength. He was both those things. And for tonight, he was hers.

When his hands went to her cheeks, her gaze pulled back up to his deep brown eyes. So clear and open that she swore she could see inside the man.

"How far do you want us to take this, Grace?"

She took a small step closer, feeling his heat, his energy, radiating off him in waves. "I want all of you."

She wanted everything.

His features didn't change, but an array of emotions flickered in his eyes. Desire. Heat. Apprehension, maybe? Hesitation?

"I don't want you to do something you're not ready for," he said quietly.

This man, this beautiful man, always trying to protect her.

Hands going to his chest, she caressed his skin. Silky smooth. His heartbeat pounded against her palm, its rhythmic cadence almost becoming a part of her. "I trust you. And I trust myself." To stay in the moment. To not let the ugliness of her past seep into her current reality.

She pressed a kiss to his chest before stepping back. Holding his gaze, she toed off her own shoes. Then, clutching the bottom hem of her dress, Grace tugged it over her head.

A tickle of fear tried to feed its way into her bones. But this time, it was fear of his reaction. Fear of what he would think about the scars that disfigured her body.

Logan's gaze didn't shift from hers, intensity swirling inside their depths.

His hands went to his jeans, removing them first, then his briefs. She watched, imprisoned by her mounting desire.

Stepping closer, Logan put his hands on her shoulders, turning her gently so that she faced the bed, his front pressed to her back.

His hands lightly ran down her arms, leaving a trail of fire wherever they touched. Her hair was swept off her neck, replaced by Logan's lips. A soft kiss placed right below her ear. The next on her neck. Then her shoulder.

She was vaguely aware of his hands shifting to the clasp of her bra. Of the lace falling to the floor with a soft whisper. One of his arms sliding around her waist. The other enclosing a breast.

A soft whimper escaped her lips, her pulse quickening. He took advantage of her exposed neck, feasting on her skin while he cherished and massaged her soft mound.

His kisses were too intoxicating. Like tiny bouts of electricity traveling from his lips right down to her core. Every so often he would pause, sweet endearments leaving his lips. About her beauty. Her sweetness. How their hearts were beating in sync.

When he shifted to the other side of her neck, she eagerly turned her head, sucking in a sharp breath when he also switched to her other breast at the same time.

It was an assault on her senses. A delicious torture. Her body throbbed for him.

She could feel his hardness behind her, but he made no move toward the bed.

"Logan." She whispered his name so quietly it barely floated through the room.

"What do you need, honey?"

Every little part of him.

Turning in his arms, she held his gaze for a moment before reaching up and pressing her lips to his. This man was starting to feel like home, his lips so familiar she'd just about memorized them.

She felt his hands at her hips as they tugged down the last piece of material that separated them. He took a step forward, gently pushing her until the back of her knees touched the soft mattress.

Logan's arm wrapped around her, lifting her, showcasing his immense strength, before laying her in the center of the bed.

She expected him to cover her body with his own. Press her to the mattress. Instead, he remained to the side, kissing her shoulder again. Then the top of her chest. He paused at her breasts, just for a second, then he was taking one of her pebbled nipples between his lips, feasting on her.

A strangled cry escaped her lips. She writhed beneath him, squirmed and arched as his tongue swirled her peak. With his fingers, he played with her other peak, flicking and tugging and grazing with his thumb.

The desire inside her mounted. A physical ache cocooning itself in her core, driving her to the edge.

After torturous minutes, Logan lowered himself down her body, shifting so that his head was above the apex of her thighs.

Her breath caught as his head lowered. Then, his tongue was swiping her clit.

A jolt of fire, so hot she felt like she was burning from the inside out, blasted through her body. The unbidden cry that released from her lips was so loud it echoed through the room, splintering the silence.

He swiped his tongue over her again, his hands encircling her thighs, his shoulders widening and exposing her. It was heaven and it was hell at the same time. He played with her body like she was an instrument he was intimately familiar with. Like he knew exactly what she needed to go higher.

He was relentless.

With every passing second, she became more feverish. More *desperate*. Soon Grace was rocking her hips. Whether she was trying to get away or closer, she wasn't sure, she just knew that she needed more of him.

"Logan..." She was close to the breaking point when finally his head lifted. His soft kisses trailed up her body until he hovered over her, their lips fusing together. He held most of his weight off her as he lifted his head. Grace almost wanted to cry at the separation.

"One more time, Grace—tell me you're sure."

She wrapped her legs around his hips, tugging him closer. The contact was shattering, in the best possible way.

Her hands went to either side of his head, stroking his cheeks with her thumbs. "I've never been more sure of anything. I want you, Logan."

He leaned across the bed, grabbing a foil wrapper from the nightstand and tearing it open. He sheathed himself quickly before returning to her. A bit more of his weight pressed against her this time. His hardness was right there at her entrance.

For the first time, a small trickle of doubt hit her. Her breath stuttered in her throat.

What if she couldn't do this?

She felt Logan tense, his intelligent brown eyes seeing everything as they studied her face. "Grace..."

At her silence, he quickly rolled onto his back, taking her with him so that she straddled him. "You're in control, Grace."

Wetting her lips, Grace lifted herself up, wrapping her fingers around his length and positioning him at her entrance again. Slowly, she lowered, feeling the delicious stretch of her walls around him until he was seated inside her depths.

Logan's hands went to her hips, the muscles in his arms visibly bunching. The man almost looked like he was in physical pain.

She lifted her hips slowly before sliding back down his length. Pleasure cascaded through her limbs. Logan's fingers tightened on her hips, digging into her softness, while her own fingers dug into the hardness of his chest. A perfect symphony of yearning and fire simmered inside her as she began to move up and down, igniting the most exquisite need.

Soon, it didn't feel like enough. She needed more. She wanted to feel his weight against her chest. She wanted to hand the control over to him.

Slowing her pace, she touched his shoulder, pulling him as she eased to her side.

A frown marred his brows, but slowly he went with her, rolling until she was on her back once again. She could see the doubt raging inside him. "Are you sure?"

Her hand moved to his neck, stroking the skin. "I trust you."

His features softened. "You tell me to stop, and I stop. No questions asked." He grazed her cheek with his finger.

He lowered his body, and she felt him right there. They didn't break eye contact as he slid back inside her.

There was no doubt. His weight now felt like a safe haven.

When he was seated inside her, he stilled, one hand cradling her cheek. "Everything okay?" His voice sounded strained. Like it was using all of his strength to remain as he was.

"So much better than okay."

His eyes shuttered. When they opened, they were the most beautiful shade of chocolate brown. "Stay with me, baby."

He started to move, lifting his hips and lowering in slow, even thrusts. Closing her eyes, she breathed him in. Her hands gliding over his muscled arms, his hard chest.

Every movement was measured. Controlled. Healing. She could see the toll it was taking to keep his thrusts slow. Her fingers dug into his arms, urging him to move faster. He did, but only slightly. She still felt the tension in his body.

The man surrounded her. Claiming her. It was beautiful and intense and emotional.

Logan lowered his hand, touching her core. A soft cry released from her throat as she bowed off the bed. His finger moved in rhythmic circles while his thrusts remained deep and even.

It was when his head lowered, his mouth capturing hers, tongue slipping between her lips, that she finally broke.

She cried out as the orgasm took her, her body convulsing and throbbing. Logan kept moving, his arms straining to hold his weight, before suddenly he buried his head in her neck as he growled and tensed.

Then there was stillness. Their deep breaths the only sound penetrating the quiet.

Tears hit the back of her eyes. She'd just done something she thought she'd never be able to do again—and it felt amazing. "Thank you." She breathed the words, not sure how she would ever be able to let this man go. He'd changed everything.

CHAPTER 21

*T*he sheet bundled around Grace's waist as the first rays of sun poked through the window. Logan took a moment to study the scar on her chest. The cut had been deep, running from between her breasts, down her ribs.

Blood boiled in his veins at the sight.

Where was the asshole who'd done this? If he had the means to remain hidden for over eight years, then the guy had significant resources.

Reaching out, Logan lightly touched the old wound.

Grace's breathing shifted from long, deep breaths to shorter ones. Her eyes scrunched once, twice, before slowly sliding open.

God, he could just get lost in her eyes.

When she looked at him, a flurry of emotions crossed her features. Surprise. Desire. Hesitation. And finally, when she looked down at her chest, at his finger on her scar, uncertainty.

She didn't pull away though.

"For a long time, I couldn't bear to look at it," she said quietly.

He switched from forefinger to thumb, grazing over the mark. "It's a reminder of your strength. A reminder that you're a survivor." She was so strong. So much stronger than she even knew.

She nodded slowly. "That's what I've spent years retraining my brain to believe."

His hand shifted to her waist, caressing her silky-smooth skin. "I need to tell you something, Grace."

The change in her was subtle. The slightest tightening of her muscles. The little hitch of her breath. "Okay."

"When you first got to town, I asked Wyatt to do a background check on you."

No reaction. She'd probably expected it, but she also knew how airtight her carefully constructed identity was.

What she *didn't* know was the extent to which he'd gone to learn her story.

"Then yesterday, I sent him video surveillance footage of you from Blue Halo to run through facial-recognition software."

Grace shot up into a sitting position, dragging the sheet with her. "You what?"

Logan sat up slowly. "I know your real last name is McKenna. That your father is a US marshal, and probably the person who set up your new identity."

Her eyes widened. Real fear washed out every other emotion. Because she didn't trust him with that information?

"Who else knows?"

"No one. I asked Wyatt to keep it to himself and I haven't told my team." *Yet.*

She was shaking now. "If it became public knowledge, my father would go to jail."

He would. There was no doubt about it.

Reaching out, he touched her cheek, relieved when she didn't pull away. "I need to tell my team. They can help find Kieran—"

She was on her feet in seconds, sheet pulled from the bed, covering her body. "No."

"Grace—"

"I need him to be safe!"

"He will be."

Her brows dipped. "I don't know your team. I don't trust them enough."

"Then trust *me*."

He held her gaze, watching as she bit her bottom lip, indecision flickering over her face. *Trust me, honey.*

He almost repeated those words, but she needed a moment to think. She needed to come to this decision alone.

She wet her lips. Gaze dipping to the floor then shooting back up again. "Barret knew."

Logan nodded, not surprised. He'd started to suspect as much. "How?"

"He'd been working as a reporter in my hometown eight years ago, when it happened. He'd even researched and written an article about my abduction. So, when he saw me in Marble Falls, he recognized my face. He also knew I'd been declared dead. Knowing who my father was, he pieced it together immediately."

The asshole.

She shook her head, a mix of anger and sorrow on her face. "He said if I didn't tell him everything I knew about Project Arma, about what Evie and Samantha had divulged, that he'd expose me." Tears began to fill her eyes. "It went against everything in me to do what I did, Logan. If it was just me, I would have chosen to remain silent and run."

His muscles tensed at her admission.

"But my dad is involved. I couldn't let him pay the price for protecting me." A tear spilled over her cheek. "I'm so sorry."

Rising to his feet, Logan tugged her into his arms. Her body still trembled. "Barret was scum for putting you in that position." If he was alive, Logan would have beaten the shit out of him. "You protected your dad because you love him. You were put into a terrible position."

"When they couldn't find Kieran, I knew my days were

numbered. Kieran has money. And my dad didn't trust the system any more than I did...so he made sure no one would find me."

Sitting on the edge of the bed, Logan tugged her down onto his lap. Her hand went to his chest.

"He made sure my new identity was bulletproof. I dyed my hair and ran."

Logan studied her long hair, reaching up to stroke a soft tendril. "What's your natural hair color, honey?"

"Red."

His hand stopped mid-stroke, unease settling like a rock in his gut, slithering up his stomach to his throat.

The sex trafficking ring, the red hair...

The man who took her *couldn't* be connected to the trafficking ring they were trying to destroy...could he? Surely, the world wasn't that small.

Grace's phone began to ring, cutting through Logan's thoughts.

She leaned to the side to grab her cell, answering the call. "Hello, Grace speaking."

"Grace, this is Nurse Kelly. One of your patients, Lizzie Bodes, is having a panic attack. We need you to come in as quickly as you can."

Grace was on her feet immediately. "I'll be there in a couple of minutes."

CHAPTER 22

*L*izzie was having a panic attack? Why? What had triggered it? Those questions rushed through Grace's mind as Logan drove them to the hospital. Lizzie had been doing so well. Making so much progress. But Grace was intimately familiar with the fact that regressions were common.

Still…something had to have caused it.

Logan pulled into a parking spot, and Grace was out of the car before it came to a stop. She heard the curse from Logan seconds before he was by her side, hand on the small of her back. She looked up to see him scanning the parking lot like he was watching for—maybe even expecting—danger.

Pushing through the entrance doors, she jogged into the corridor, seeing Tyler down the hall. She'd almost reached Lizzie's room when she heard it—loud cries. They sounded tortured, filled with raw fear. The sound had Grace's spine tingling with dread.

Pushing inside the room, she stopped at the sight of Lizzie pressed into the corner of the room, knees pulled up to her chest and head in her knees. Exactly as Grace had been the other night at Logan's.

The other therapist, Ted, was crouched in front of her, trying to talk, while a doctor stood at the back of the room, syringe in hand.

Walking forward, Grace placed a hand on the therapist's shoulder. "Thanks, Ted. I've got it from here."

He rose, nodding to the doctor before they both left the room. Grace turned to see that Logan remained, standing just inside the door. She moved over to him quickly. "Logan—"

"I'm not leaving."

She frowned. "She's not a danger to me. She fears men. And you can hear everything from the hall."

His features remained hard. "I'll stand in the corner."

She wanted to argue, unsure why he was pushing the issue, but by the look of his set jaw, she knew it was a battle she wouldn't win. "Fine, but this is the one and only time. And you need to sit down and try not to look so...big."

Which was an impossible request, but she still said it.

Taking a calming breath, Grace turned back to Lizzie. The woman's knuckles were white. Cries still wrenched from her chest, so fear-driven they made Grace's heart hurt.

Moving closer, she crouched down. "Lizzie, it's Grace."

Nothing. No reaction whatsoever.

"I want to help you, Lizzie. Will you let me help?"

Again, nothing.

Grace tried a few other strategies, telling the woman she was safe. Reminding her of where she was. Even talking about the woman's pet dogs back home.

Nothing seemed to work. So she changed tactics.

Pulling her phone from her pocket, Grace sat down, crossing her legs. Flicking through the tracks on her phone, she paused when she found the one she was looking for. It was one her therapist had played for her, and one she continued to listen to in her darkest moments.

There were no lyrics to the song, just calming, melodic piano music. She played it softly, every so often speaking words of safety. Reminding Lizzie that she was in Cradle Mountain with Grace. That no one would hurt her.

It took about eight minutes for Lizzie to go quiet. And another five for the violent shakes in her limbs to subside.

Eventually, Lizzie lifted her head. Her eyes were still slightly glazed. Her bottom lip trembling.

Grace kept her voice gentle. "Hi, Lizzie. It's Grace. You're at the Cradle Mountain Hospital, and you're safe."

She repeated the words she'd been saying for the last thirteen minutes. Panic attacks had a way of deafening people. Blocking out the world and only showing the ugly that existed in the mind.

"I'm not safe." Her words were barely a whisper.

"You *are* safe, Lizzie. Security is guarding your room. I'm here. No one is letting anything happen to you." She didn't mention Logan. On the chance Lizzie hadn't seen him, she didn't want his presence sending her back into a panic.

Lizzie shook her head slowly. "No. He was here. I saw him."

From her peripheral vision, she saw Logan leaning forward. She willed him to remain where he was, not wanting to lose any progress she'd made.

Lizzie said the next words so quietly, Grace almost missed them. "Ice was here."

Ice? Here at the hospital? That wasn't possible. "Sometimes after trauma, the mind can convince us of things that aren't real."

Lizzie was shaking her head before Grace had finished speaking. "No. He *was* here!"

Grace nodded slowly. The women had each provided descriptions of Ice, but they'd all been slightly different. Which was normal. Trauma could skew what a person remembered. "Okay, what did he look like?"

"My door was open, and he walked past. He looked different. His head was shaved, and he was wearing a huge sweatshirt that made him look bigger. It was when he looked up that I *knew* it was him. Not only did I see his eyes, but he was wearing the ring that he always wore. A ring with three skulls on it."

Grace's very bones chilled, a low buzz whistling in her ears. For some reason, that was a detail none of the women had mentioned before.

Kieran had worn a ring like that. On his middle finger.

She remembered the pain of the ring cutting through the skin of her cheek when he hit her. The way he habitually touched the ring with his thumb when he stood in front of her.

"He lifted his hand to touch his face. He did it on purpose. He wanted me to see. He always wore it on his—"

"Middle finger," Grace whispered, finishing the woman's sentence.

Grace worked hard to keep her breathing under control. She refocused on the music that still floated through the room, willing herself to remain in the moment.

She desperately tried for a small smile. "Even if the man you saw was from the compound, he can't get to you. You have security stationed outside your door at all times. You're protected."

"For now."

It was like Lizzie had plucked the words right out of her mind from eight years ago. Right before her father had stepped in.

Suddenly, every fear and insecurity that she'd worked so hard to control bubbled to the surface. It took every ounce of her strength to press it down. Suffocate it.

Lizzie didn't need her fear, she needed reassurance that she was safe. That Ice hadn't been in the hallway.

Grace locked her knees, forcing herself not to rise. Not to run or let her fear suffocate her. She remained on the hospital floor for a long time. Nodding. Smiling. Saying all the right things. All the things she knew Lizzie needed to hear. When inside, she was falling apart.

When she eventually left the room, she almost collapsed right there and then. *Would* have collapsed if Logan's strong arm hadn't wrapped around her waist and held her firm.

She leaned into him, sucking the breaths in hard and fast. "It's him."

Every second she'd been in that room, she'd felt more certain. Like, once the seed had been planted, it just continued to grow.

"How do you know?"

She tightened her grip on his arms, knowing her fingers were digging into his flesh. "He had the same skull ring." It was one of the many things that haunted her nightmares. Grace breathed through her panic.

Without letting go of her, Logan reached for the phone in his pocket, placing it at his ear. "Steve, did you arrange for the hospital surveillance footage to be recorded?" Logan nodded as he listened. "I need access. Ice might be here in Cradle Mountain."

Ice. Kieran. All this time, her enemy...the very man Logan was hunting.

"Thanks." Glancing down at her, he put his phone away, then placed his hand on her cheek. It immediately calmed some of the storm raging inside her. "Do you want to watch the footage?"

No. But she needed to. She couldn't leave here wondering. "Yes."

His jaw ticked. He'd heard the lie. But she wasn't changing her answer.

He turned his head to glance at Flynn. "Notify the team of what's going on and keep your eyes peeled."

Flynn nodded, having heard everything. He pulled out his phone.

Breathing out a heavy breath, Logan curved an arm around her waist and led her down the hall. They turned a corner and, at the end of that hall, another.

Logan stopped in front of a door and pushed it open. Inside

sat two security guards with about a dozen screens in front of them.

One of the guards was just hanging up the phone. "Logan, I take it?"

He pulled her farther into the room. "We need to see the hallway footage outside room eight from about an hour ago."

The guy nodded to the other guard, who immediately started pressing buttons. He pointed to a screen at the top. "This is the camera we're looking at."

It rewound for a few minutes before the footage played on a slow, fast forward. People came and went, none of them significant.

Then she saw him. A bald man, with a big, baggy sweatshirt.

Logan stepped forward. "Stop. Rewind about thirty seconds and play at normal speed."

The guy did as asked. When the recording started, Grace took two large steps toward the screen. At first, it was impossible to see his face.

"Stop," Logan said.

The recording stopped. The bald man was now looking up, right at the camera. Like he wanted them to see him.

"Can you enlarge that?" Logan asked.

The man enlarged it. Then enlarged it some more.

Suddenly, Grace's entire body flooded with adrenaline that made her limbs weak. "It's him."

His dark eyes. The haunting face.

She was staring right at the man she'd never wanted to see again. The man who had tried to take everything from her.

Logan wrapped his strong arm around her again. His touch was her only anchor to reality. He spoke to the guards, but Grace barely heard.

Shortly after, he led her out of the room, basically carrying her because her legs were trembling so badly they almost didn't work. Bit by bit, she was shutting down.

She was sure that if she tried to speak, no words would come out of her mouth. All she could think was one thing...

Get out. Out of Cradle Mountain. Leave. Disappear.

If Kieran was here, she couldn't be.

Would she be able to disappear a second time? She couldn't ask her father to risk his career and freedom again to create *another* identity for her. So what could she do?

When they got in the truck, she felt Logan's eyes on her. But she didn't say anything. She couldn't.

He'd only been driving for a couple of minutes when his phone rang.

Using the car's Bluetooth, he answered the call. "Wyatt, now's not a good time."

"A body was discovered on the outskirts of Cradle Mountain today. It's been identified as Scott Pilgrig. He's been dead for over a week."

CHAPTER 23

*L*ogan clenched the steering wheel hard, rage pumping through his system. The asshole who had hurt Grace, and the man his team was chasing, were one and the same. And he was here, in Cradle Mountain.

He wanted to find the son of a bitch and tear him apart limb by limb before setting his body ablaze. What was his game? Why was he here? Why the hell had he taken the photos of Grace and left them for her to find? To taunt her? Terrify her before he made his attempt to grab her?

No way in hell was that happening—and it would be a deadly mistake for the guy to try.

He shot a glance at Grace. She was quiet, her spine unnaturally straight.

Reaching over, he wrapped his fingers around her knee. There was the tiniest jolt. Like she'd been caught up in her mind and he'd tugged her out with a touch. "It'll be okay, honey."

Without looking at him, she gave a small nod.

She didn't believe him. Her nod was merely reflex.

He trailed his hand up to hers, placing it on top. Ice cold.

Logan pressed his foot harder on the gas. He needed to get home, contact his team, and have an emergency meeting.

Now that they knew Ice—Kieran Hayes—was in Cradle Mountain, they could narrow down their search. In theory, it should be easy. But Logan knew better than anyone that nothing was easy in warfare, and this was most certainly a war.

"I'm going to call my team over and we're going to come up with a game plan. We'll find him."

More silence.

His jaw tensed. He wished she'd say something. He was almost certain that even though she was here in person, her mind was elsewhere. She'd gone inward to protect herself, and who knew when she'd come out again. Tightening his hand around hers, trying to warm her, Logan breathed through the churning in his gut.

Once he pulled into his garage, he'd barely stopped before Grace was climbing out. The woman looked like she was on a mission. To do what?

He trailed closely behind as she went straight to the guest bedroom and pulled out her suitcase.

Hell no. If the woman thought she was leaving, she had another thing coming. She was clearly so caught up in what she'd discovered that she wasn't thinking straight.

"Grace, you're not going anywhere."

She didn't stop. Didn't even pause. Her suitcase now lay open on the bed, clothes being thrown in madly as she moved faster. So desperate to get out, she wasn't even folding anything.

"If you leave town, he'll follow." More clothes thrown in. "Grace, stop."

When yet again she didn't react to his words, he walked up to her, taking her wrists in his hands and turning her to face him. He held her as gently as possible, while also making sure his hold was unbreakable.

"You're not leaving."

Terror and determination glazed her expression, confirming for him that her actions were straight-up inspired by fear.

"But I am, Logan."

GET OUT. Leave town. Disappear.

Those were the only thoughts she could manage right now. Her thin connection to the only safety she understood.

But Logan was stopping her. For the first time, his touch felt like shackles. Restraints designed to hold her in place, rather than keep her safe. Because she wasn't safe. Not while she was in the same town as the man she'd spent years hiding from. She couldn't be.

"Let me go."

Kieran was here, in Cradle Mountain. *Had* been since...God, maybe since she'd been in Cradle Mountain herself. Watching. Toying with her.

Kieran didn't fear Logan or his team. He didn't fear anyone. The man was so confident that he wanted her to know he was within reaching distance. He wanted her to *fear* him before he took her.

Just like last time.

"Grace, you're not thinking—"

"He did this last time. Stalked me while I worked. Wanted me to know that he was watching." She shook her head, the panic now bubbling up her throat, choking her. "I didn't get out. I didn't leave. I trusted someone else to protect me and they ended up dead! I can't make that mistake again!"

Nausea swelled in her stomach, but she pushed it down. She couldn't be sick now. She had to stay on her feet. Keep moving. Survive.

"I'm not just anyone," Logan said quietly.

"Do you know how I found my bodyguard? In pieces. First, I

spotted the thumb. Then a foot..." She was certain she would have found more of the guy if Kieran hadn't taken her so quickly. Grace's voice caught, but she forced herself to finish what she was saying, needing Logan to understand. "Kieran killed him and cut him up!"

An old fissure that she'd thought was healed cracked open in her chest. A sob tried to escape, but she swallowed it, not allowing it out into the light.

"I know you're fast and strong, but you're not bulletproof. I don't want you to die protecting me."

If something happened to Logan because of her...God, it would kill her.

She tried to wrench her arms free of his hold, but yet again, his grip was impenetrable.

Logan stepped closer, his proximity almost suffocating her. Her mind in a battle between wanting him close and pushing him away.

"No one will get past me or my team. No one will hurt me."

She wanted to believe that. But for eight years, fear had motivated her to stay hidden. Kieran knowing where she was and her remaining safe, didn't go together. It didn't make sense in her muddled brain.

She tried yanking her hands away yet again, but his hold didn't give. Not even a little. "Please, Logan!"

Every second she stood there, her breaths came out quicker. Her heart soared faster in her chest. Another second passed and the shaking in her limbs intensified. If he didn't let go, it would become more violent. Then she'd succumb to the panic.

As if he'd read her mind, he finally released her wrists.

She didn't think. Just turned back to her suitcase and continued packing. Where would she go? It had to be somewhere far. She'd drive as far as she could, for as long as she could, without taking a break. She'd tried small towns; now she'd go big.

She'd also need to call her dad.

Oh, God—her dad. He'd be so worried. What happened to her had almost destroyed him as well.

For a moment, she stopped. Closed her eyes and sucked in some deep breaths.

Focus, Grace. Panicking won't help.

All panic did was slow you down. She had to accept that she wasn't safe. Accept reality. Then survive.

Grace went to the bathroom to grab her toiletries. She felt Logan's eyes on her the entire time. Intense as they watched. Tracked her. She had no idea what his plan was. She couldn't think about that right now. She literally didn't have the energy.

Shoving the last couple of items into her bag, she lifted it before heading into the hall. Luckily, she'd finally gotten another rental car late yesterday. One small saving grace.

Crossing to the front door, Grace came to an abrupt stop when Logan appeared out of nowhere, barricading the exit.

"I'm sorry, Grace. I can't let you leave." He took up all the space. There was no way to get past him.

"Logan, you need to move."

He stepped toward her. Grace stepped back.

"I care about you. And I'm not letting you go God-knows-where unprotected."

"You don't have a choice."

Another step forward. Another step back.

He shook his head. "Fear is clouding your judgment. Stop and really think about what you're doing."

She was intimately familiar with fear. She'd lived with it for years. Fear of being found. Fear of ending up in that basement again. Fear of being touched, not just by Kieran but by anyone.

Her stomach twisted as she whispered her next words. "You can't keep me here."

He reached for her again, but she flinched away. "Grace—"

"No! You don't get to decide how I keep myself safe! You weren't there. He took me from my *home*! A home that was supposed to be my safe place. He held me in his basement for days. Hurt me, tortured me. I almost died because of him!"

The ever-present trembling in her limbs had now become so violent it was like the earth was moving beneath her feet. The small semblance of sanity that she'd been hanging on to by a thread finally snapped.

"He destroyed me, Logan! I shattered into a million pieces, and it's taken years for me to put myself back together, and I'm still not whole. I'll probably never be!"

She was shouting now. Each word wrenched from somewhere so deep, she had to dig to the depths of her soul to find them.

"I can't do that again. I can't be thrust back into that hell! I won't survive."

When the last word left her mouth, her legs buckled. Her sobs were tortured and carnal. The black cloud of fear that had muddied her mind since the hospital finally clearing, and pain—piercing and raw—took its place.

Strong arms came around her before she hit the floor, scooping her up and holding her close.

Air caressed her skin, then she felt Logan dropping onto the couch. She leaned into him. Wanting his heat to replace her cold. His strength to replace her weakness.

She cried long and hard. For the parts of her that had been stolen. For the years that had been lost. For the fear that had become her very existence.

Logan held her the entire time. His hand rubbing her back in soothing circular motions. His silent support was louder than any words could be.

Minutes passed, many of them, until finally she had no tears left to cry. Her limbs felt heavy, her chest aching. Her cries became soft hiccups, and the shirt beneath her cheek was soaked.

She felt his face pressing into her hair, stopping beside her ear. "I need you to be okay. I need you to be safe." There was a small pause. "I need *you*, Grace."

She nuzzled herself closer to his powerful chest. "I need you too. But I can't lose you—and I can't lose myself." Because she would. If Logan was hurt because of her, if she was taken again, she would lose it all. "It's hard for me to trust someone else with my safety."

"I know. I'm a risk. But so is leaving. I'm asking you to choose me."

Choose Logan. The beautiful man who had broken down her walls and pierced the hard casing of her heart.

Could she stay? For him? Trust him with her life, even though Kieran was so close? Seconds ticked by, but the time felt meaningless. It was the thoughts darting through her mind that took up all the space.

Finally, she whispered one word that both terrified and soothed her. "Okay."

Suddenly, the pressure on her chest lightened.

Someone was going to fight by her side to bring down the man who hunted her.

In one swift move, Logan stood, keeping her in his arms. He moved down the hall toward the bedroom. Not hers, not the one she'd just emptied of everything she owned, but his. The room where they'd spent the previous night together.

Tugging the sheet down, he lay her in bed, removing her shoes and then his own, before climbing in after her.

They were both fully clothed, and it was the middle of the day, but Grace didn't question it, not when she felt Logan curl around her, surround her. His strength...her everything.

CHAPTER 24

*L*ogan slid out of bed, careful not to wake Grace. It was early morning, the room was still dark, but he could see everything.

Moving around the bed, he pressed a gentle kiss to her forehead. A soft sigh fell from her lips as she snuggled her head deeper into the pillow.

Everything in Logan called for him to protect this woman. Keep her close. That's why there hadn't been a single hope in hell that he would have let her disappear into the world without him there to keep her safe.

Walking out of the room, he headed into the living area. Jason and Aidan were already waiting for him. Blake had his daughter last night, and the rest of the team was either at the hospital or working with Steve to hunt down Kieran Hayes and Beau Prater.

Logan dropped onto the couch. "Thanks for coming over so early." Fortunately, they all functioned well with minimal sleep.

"How is she?" Jason asked.

"She was set on leaving. The fear in her eyes…God, it tears me up just thinking about it."

Fear had completely consumed her. He'd work as hard as necessary to chase it away and replace it with safety.

"If she's here, the asshole will probably stay," Aidan said quietly. "It will make it easier for us to get him."

Fuck, that left a sick feeling in his gut. But he needed this guy caught. Not just because he needed to die for what he'd done to Grace and every other woman he'd hurt, but also because otherwise, she'd spend a lifetime looking over her shoulder.

Not going to happen.

"I spoke to Wyatt," Jason said quietly. "He's looking into local businesses here in Cradle Mountain, working out which ones have surveillance footage that he can hack. He's going to use the footage of Kieran from the hospital for photo recognition."

"He found the car, though," Aidan added. "It was left on the outskirts of Cradle Mountain, near the border to Ketchum."

"Figures." The asshole wasn't dumb enough to continue driving the thing. "Her patients are going into witness protection tomorrow. After that, I plan to keep her with me until he's caught."

"Wyatt's also searching for Prater using similar methods," Jason said. "But he's broadening his search to surrounding towns for the guy."

The sound of his phone ringing from the bedroom pulled his attention. Logan cursed under his breath, realizing he'd forgotten to grab it before coming out. And the thing wasn't on silent.

He was just standing when he heard the rustle of Grace climbing out of bed. A few seconds later, she entered the room, his phone in hand.

She stopped at the sight of Jason and Aidan, her eyes widening just slightly. She was still wearing her clothes from yesterday after they'd fallen asleep in them, her hair was rumpled...and damn, but she was cute.

"Hey." She nibbled her bottom lip. "Sorry, I didn't realize...I'll leave the phone and go."

She walked the phone over to Logan, but before she could step away, he took her hand, tugging her to his lap. "It's okay. This involves you, too."

He pressed a kiss to her head, enjoying the way she curled into him.

When his phone rang again, he noticed it was Steve. "Hey, what's going on?"

"We got Beau Prater."

Jason and Aidan straightened, while Logan's hand tightened on Grace's waist. The phone wasn't on speaker, but he knew everyone could hear, including Grace, since she was so close. "Your friend Wyatt helped us locate him, then your team ran him out of Ketchum. My guys found him on the border of Ketchum and Bellevue. The girl was with him."

He felt Grace stiffen. With relief or apprehension, he wasn't sure. He stroked her side as Steve continued.

"We'll keep her safe tonight before transferring her to one of the safe houses tomorrow. We'll also take Prater into custody and try to get information from him on Kieran's location."

"I want to question him," Logan said immediately.

Steve sighed. "Logan—"

"I know what you're going to say, that your boys can do it. That it's their job. But I can do it better."

Not only was he thoroughly trained in interrogation strategies from his time in special forces, he was also more motivated than anyone else to extract the information.

Steve sighed. "Fine. I'll make it happen. But you need to do it this morning. Within the next hour. We're detaining him in Bellevue for now. There's too much red tape for me to wade through after that."

"Done."

Hanging up, Logan looked at Grace.

She was frowning. "I hope she's okay."

He prayed for the same thing. Pressing a kiss to her head, he met her gaze. "I hate to ask you this, but are you okay—"

"Yes." She cut him off before he could finish. "It's important for you to be the one to question Prater, and I want to be where *you* are. So, yes, I'll go to Bellevue."

He nodded. "Thank you. I'll need you to remain in the hall with one of the guys while I go in, but you're safe with them."

~

NERVES RATTLED GRACE'S STOMACH. She was anxious about being in the same building as a man so similar to Kieran. So *close* to Kieran.

She took a deep breath as Logan parked the car in the police station parking lot. Reaching out his hand, he wrapped it around hers. And that's how easy it was for the man to make her feel safe. "Jason will sit with you in the foyer. I'll be just down the hall."

She nodded, even though the very thought had her heart beating wildly. Not because she was worried about herself, but for Logan. Theoretically, she knew how much stronger, faster, and just generally more lethal Logan was, but mentally and emotionally...she didn't want Logan anywhere near the guy.

Logan remained silent for a moment, studying her closely. Suddenly, he shook his head and started the engine again. "I'll have the guys question him. You and I can spend the day together doing something else."

"What? No!" Her seat belt was off and her door open before he could start reversing. "This is important to you, so you're doing it."

She jumped out of the car, hearing his curse seconds before the car switched off again and he was in front of her. She turned toward the station, but Logan shifted, blocking her path. Two warm, hard hands went to either side of her face.

"Are you sure you're okay with this?"

"Yes. Let's get this done, Logan." The sooner it was done, the sooner everything was over...hopefully.

Sighing, he leaned down and pressed a kiss to her lips. It was a kiss that tugged at her heart, that had her wanting to pull him close and never let go.

At the sound of footsteps, they parted slowly. Jason and Aidan walked up beside them. Together, the four of them walked into the police station. They'd only just stepped inside when a door opened down the hall and shouting sounded.

A man with sandy-blond hair and tattoos scattered across his body was being tugged out of a room by police officers. Aggression and violence thickened the air around them. When he looked up, he briefly scanned Logan, Aidan, and Jason.

Then his eyes landed on Grace.

His struggles momentarily paused, his feet rooting to the floor. "Holy shit—it's *you!*"

Grace almost took a step back at his words. At the way a hundred percent of his attention sat solely on her.

Logan moved in front of her, blocking the man's view. Jason and Aidan edged closer, warming either side of her.

Even though she couldn't see him, his voice carried to her ears. "Grace fucking McKenna! Your hair's different but I've seen your face enough times..."

Her blood ran cold at the sound of her name. Her real name.

"He's not going to stop, you know." He sounded farther away now. "Even after all these years, he's just as obsessed. He's going to find you! Your time is limited, sweetheart!"

A door opened and closed. The voice disappeared from the air but remained in her head. Haunting her.

Turning, Logan cradled her cheeks. "Hey. Look at me, honey."

She did. She watched Logan's deep brown eyes as they washed over her face.

"You're safe."

She nodded. She was. "I know. Safe with you."

His lips pulled up at the corners. "Safe with me."

She nodded toward the hall. "Go get some information from that asshole. I'll wait here."

He chuckled softly, his mouth touching her forehead, his lips lingering, before he straightened and walked down the hall with Aidan.

Jason nodded his head toward a bench, waiting for her to sit first before lowering beside her. Beau's words were still repeating in her head, but Logan's voice was louder. Washing out the doubt and fear that tried to creep in.

Turning to look at Jason, Grace noticed he had a frown on his face. It was a look of concentration. He was listening, or at least trying to.

Were they close enough to hear? Could he hear over the noises of the police foyer? The sound of footsteps and shuffling papers and other movement?

"Are you worried about Logan?" The question slipped out before she could stop it.

Jason turned to look at her, the frown gone. "About him in that room? Or him in general?"

"About the lengths Ice...Kieran...will go to in order to get rid of him and take me."

"No."

So sure. "You're that confident in his safety?"

"Yes."

Memories of her last bodyguard flashed through her mind. A shiver rocked her spine. "I know he's tougher than most guys, but he's not invincible."

Jason dipped his head. "True. But he's as close as they come. He's been through the best training in the world, both during his time in special forces and with his time at the Project Arma compound. Add in everything else he can do, and he's definitely the man you want watching your back."

It made sense. It did. But when feelings were involved, sense sometimes took a back seat. "I still worry."

"I know. I can see that. But trust me, the man stops at nothing to protect his own...and he's definitely claimed you as his own."

CHAPTER 25

*L*ogan and Aidan stood with Steve. The door to the interrogation room where Prater was being held remained closed just behind the special agent.

"You've got thirty minutes," he said quietly, before stepping away from the door.

More than enough time.

Pushing inside, Logan found Beau sitting at a small table, handcuffs around his wrists.

The guy had the balls to smirk. "I recognize you guys. You're the freaks who were in all those articles. Shot up with those enhancement drugs."

Logan moved farther into the room, but he didn't sit. "What do you know about Grace?" After what the guy had already said in the hall, Logan was only just hanging on to his temper.

Beau chuckled. "Hey, all I know is that the woman's been stuck in Ice's head for years. He has a fucking picture of her that he keeps in his wallet. It's sickening."

Logan's jaw ticked.

"Why wasn't Ice in Mexico when we raided the compound?" Aidan asked.

"Surprised? You shouldn't be. The second that bitch Julie escaped, he knew he needed to change things up. If you'd arrived a week later the whole setup would have been gone. Ice was in the process of acquiring a new location. I was just lucky I wasn't there, either."

"Yeah, well, your luck's run out."

Beau smirked again. "We'll see. Money has a way of helping situations turn around—and I've made plenty over the years."

Logan leaned across the table. "Where is he?"

"You think I know? He doesn't tell anyone shit. How do you think he's kept off the grid for so long?"

Logan shot around the table before the guy could blink, yanking him to his feet and shoving him hard against the wall. He pressed his forearm against the man's throat, applying enough pressure to cut off most of his air supply.

Panic flared through Beau's eyes. Then fear.

Good.

"Tell me what you *do* know then."

"Why?" Beau spluttered. "You're not gonna kill me."

Logan raised a brow. "You think death's the worst I can do? I have half an hour with you. No one's watching. No one's coming to save you. I know a million different ways to break you without killing. I can send you to the brink of death, pull you back, then do it all over again. You want that?"

When Beau remained silent, Logan pressed harder, knowing the exact moment he cut off the guy's air supply completely.

"Something you should know about me—I don't stop until I get what I want. And I have a lot of pent-up rage right now. So, you not talking works great for my current mood."

Beau's face went a deep red shade, then purple, before Logan finally eased his arm back a touch. The guy spluttered and coughed.

When he still didn't speak, Logan threw him into the side wall —hard.

Beau cried out, blood dripping from his face as he crumpled to the floor.

Logan was on him again in under a second. He tugged the guy to his feet, pushing his front against the wall while pulling his arm back and up.

"All it would take is a little bit of pressure to dislocate the limb," Logan said into his ear. He lifted the arm higher.

A deep groan vibrated through the guy's chest. "Fine, stop! I'll talk!" Logan paused but didn't lower the arm. "Ice watched you guys tear up the facility in Mexico through his hidden security cameras. He was in a goddamn rage! Called and said he was flying to Cradle Mountain to murder each of you one by one."

When Beau paused, Logan shoved him against the wall again. "What happened next?"

"The next time he called, he was…different."

"Different how?" Aidan asked.

"Excited. I've known the guy for nine years and *never* heard him sound like that. Now I know it must have been when he found *her*." Beau muttered that last part under his breath, before continuing. "He told me the plans had changed. Sent me to Ketchum to take a redhead. He wanted you guys to know he was close. That he was in control."

"Is that why you only take redheads? Because of Grace?"

"Yes." He said the word through gritted teeth as Logan stretched his arm higher still. "The second Ice took over the operation, he made it a rule that all the women had to be Caucasian redheads in their early twenties. As far as I know, I'm the only one he ever told why."

Aidan stepped forward. "How did Ice come to take over?"

"It happened after *her*. Grace McKenna was an assignment. An assignment that Ice was given because he took all the snatch-and-grab jobs. He was, and always has been, good at getting in and out of places without being seen."

Logan breathed heavily through his nose, only just holding on to his rage.

"He was supposed to snatch her up, bring her to the compound. When a couple weeks passed and Ice still hadn't completed the job, boss wasn't happy. Shortly after, Grace got away from him. And two days after *that*, our boss was shot in the head in his own home. Ice took over. We all suspected it was him who made the kill. After all, if he hadn't, our boss would have killed *him*." Beau bucked in Logan's hold. "Can you let go of my fucking arm now?"

Instead, Logan pulled his arm higher, pressed the guy harder against the wall. Beau cried out. One more tug and the thing would dislocate.

"Why is he so obsessed with her?" Aidan asked.

"Who the hell knows!" Beau was just about gasping the words, rising to his toes to alleviate the pressure on his shoulder. "It was like once he had her, she was just...his. The man hasn't stopped thinking about her since."

"She was never *his*," Logan growled. "And very soon, the bastard will pay for his crimes."

Beau scoffed. "You'll have to find him first. Why do you think you didn't get Ice's location or contact details from the guys in Mexico? Because he's careful. He doesn't let anyone know a single thing about him. Eight years of being their boss and they didn't have so much as a phone number. You don't find Ice unless he *wants* to be found."

"We'll find him," Logan said quietly.

"Will that be before or after he finds *her*? Because he has the means to disappear from the face of the planet. And once he has her again, he won't let go. Not a second time."

～

"So you didn't get much information?" Grace asked, pushing the pasta around her bowl with a fork. She wasn't that hungry, but Logan had gone to the effort of making food, so she was eating it.

Logan placed his fork on the table. Where her bowl was almost full, his was almost empty. "He didn't have anything on the guy's location and doesn't have a way of getting in contact with him."

So, a big fat diddly-squat. "But he knew my name." McKenna. No one had used that name in such long time. Not since before Logan had yesterday, anyway. Hearing it again today had been another shock to her system.

"He did. He knew exactly who you were. Ice had shown him a picture."

Kieran had kept a picture of her? God, the very idea made her skin crawl. After all these years, she'd really hoped he would forget about her. "I can't believe Kieran still wants me. I must be pretty memorable."

She was half-joking. Logan didn't crack even the beginnings of a smile.

Was there anything she could have done differently all those years ago? Worn different clothes? Smiled less? Smiled *more*?

"The guy's sick in the head, Grace."

She pushed a piece of pasta up the side of the bowl. "Mitch was the best of the best. We actually got along really well. We had lots of chats while he was guarding my home. While he walked me to and from my car. That night, I just assumed he was either called away or watching me from afar. I didn't know he was..." Dead. Butchered. "He was strong. Former military. Big. I remember thinking about how safe I was with him. How nothing would get past him."

She saw the way Logan's jaw clenched.

"It's another reason I didn't tell the guys back in Marble Falls. I didn't want them to have to protect me from Kieran. I didn't want *anyone* to have to put themself in that position for me ever again."

Logan's expression softened. "I understand why you did what you did."

"But do you forgive me?" She hadn't realized until this very moment just how much she needed to hear him say the words.

"There's nothing to forgive. Do I think you should have trusted Wyatt's team to protect you? Yes. But you did what you thought was best. The blame lies solely on Barret for putting you in that position."

Grace breathed out a long breath.

Logan opened his mouth, looking like he wanted to say something, but stopped.

She tilted her head to the side. "What is it?"

He scrubbed a hand over his face. Suddenly, she got a sinking feeling in her gut. "Steve, our FBI liaison, approached me after I got out of the room with Beau. He ran your name through the system after that asshole shouted it. Steve knows who you are, Grace. And what your dad did."

Grace shot to her feet so fast, her seat tipping backward. She scanned the room. Where was her phone? She needed to call her dad. Warn him the police were coming.

She'd taken three steps before Logan's large body appeared in front of her, hands going to her shoulders, holding her in place.

"Grace, stop."

"I need to call him!" She wrenched herself away, but Logan's arms just slipped to her waist, tugging her close.

"He's safe." His forehead went to hers. "Steve's a good guy. He's also a father, so he understands why your dad did what he did. He's going to take care of it."

She looked up, almost not wanting to believe what she was hearing in case she was wrong. "What does that mean, 'take care of it'?"

"He didn't share the details, but he said he was going to make sure both you and your father were okay."

Okay? So...not put in jail? Not punished for the crime he'd committed to save her? "And you trust him?"

"Yes."

Grace could have collapsed at the sudden weightless relief that flooded her body.

Logan's arms tightened before he lifted her off the floor. Her legs immediately wrapped around his waist. Then she was kissing him. Or maybe he was kissing her, she wasn't sure.

Everything was a blur, their lips meeting hungrily, his hands gliding through her hair, her fingers clutching at his shirt like he was a lifeline.

Shifting her lips away from his, she trailed kisses across his cheek, all the way to his ear. "Thank you. For everything." Every little thing he'd done to make her life better. Easier. Safer.

CHAPTER 26

*L*ogan's body turned molten at Grace's limbs wrapped around him. At her breath against his ear.

Tightening his hold, he moved to the bedroom, his lips never leaving hers. He stopped beside the bed, cupping the back of her neck, deepening the kiss. Her lips on his, in combination with her sweet little moans, had his blood soaring in his ears, deafening him.

Carefully, he lay her on the mattress. When he hovered over her, he studied her face, searching. Complete trust. It was all he saw.

It cracked his heart wide open.

Rising to his knees, he removed his shirt, then his jeans. Crawling down her body, he grasped the top of her jeans. The sound of a button popping open was loud in the otherwise silent room. So too was the sound of the zipper sliding down.

As he pulled her jeans off, he lowered his head, pressing a soft kiss to the scar on her thigh. She stiffened below him, but when she didn't pull away, he did it again. He kissed every inch of the scar.

Her body slowly relaxed, and Logan trailed the rest of the

kisses down her legs to her feet. Reaching up, he slid both hands beneath her shirt, pushing the material up her torso. This time, he trailed kisses up her stomach. When he reached her chest, he quickly removed her silk bra before pressing a kiss to the scar there. Then another.

This time, she didn't tense. But he heard the gentle acceleration of her heart rate. The quiet whoosh of air being sucked into her chest.

"You're beautiful, Grace. All of you."

A soft sigh escaped her lips.

"How did I get so lucky?" he asked quietly, more to himself than to her.

At first, her lips tilted up. Then the smile left her face as she said the four words that rocked his world. Shifted it and colored it a new shade.

"I love you, Logan."

For a moment, words were lost to him. Emotions pummeled him, so intense they tied his tongue and stole his voice. But when uncertainty tinged her expression, he forced the words out of his mouth, needing her to hear his truth.

"I love you, too, Grace. I've loved you for a while."

Her eyes misted, then shuttered. He caught a tear with his lips as he kissed her cheekbone. "Hearing those words is…it's everything."

"*You're* everything, sweetheart."

Their lips fused together again, and he felt and absorbed the electricity that buzzed between them. Lowering his head, he trailed kisses down to her chest, taking one hard nipple between his lips. Back arched, she pushed herself farther into his mouth.

He licked and sucked her sensitive peak, loving the soft whimpers and cries she didn't quieten or soften. Lowering a hand, he stroked her core. Her entire body trembled beneath his touch.

When he glanced up, his breath came out in a hiss at the sight of her. Her head was back, fire dancing in her eyes. The fire of need and lust and trust, all fused together.

He pressed a finger inside her. Watched as a carnal moan tore from her lips.

Fucking exquisite.

His thumb remained on her clit, his finger continuing to thrust as he moved up her body, his eyes never leaving hers. She began to writhe beneath him. Rocking uncontrollably.

He inserted a second finger, crooking it, pushing farther inside her. Her entire body jolted, her breath catching in her throat.

"Logan..." Her voice was almost a whisper that sizzled through the room.

Rolling to the side, he grabbed a foil wrapper, tearing it open and sheathing himself. He was back in seconds.

"Remember, if you want me to st—"

Her finger went to his lips, silencing him. "With you, that will never happen." She tugged his head down until her lips were at his ear, her breath brushing across his skin, almost burning him. "Nothing in this world compares to the comfort, love, and security you bring me."

Her confession caused a wild storm to rage inside him. God, he could live a hundred years with this woman and love her more each day.

Slowly, so slowly he was almost in physical pain, he slid inside her.

This was home. And it was also torture.

Grace wriggled her hips before leaning up. She latched onto his neck, nipping his skin with her teeth. Logan growled low in his chest before lifting up and thrusting back in.

His insides turned molten, lava pooling in his gut. He pulled out and thrust back in again. Every time he returned to her, he got the same overwhelming feeling that he was exactly where he was supposed to be.

He alternated between kissing her and watching her, loving the array of emotions that washed over her face. Pleasure. Need. Desperation.

For him, there was mostly one thought skittering inside his mind. *Mine.* The woman felt like she was made for him.

Grace tugged at his hair with one hand, her nails digging into his shoulder with the other. Her breasts bounced with every movement as he rocked faster, her long neck on display.

Rolling so that they both lay on their side, Logan continued to thrust, but he also reached between them, touching her clit, pressing his thumb against her and rubbing.

She whimpered and writhed, nails digging into him harder.

He moved his thumb in rapid circles, enjoying the sound of her breathing as it shifted, becoming more erratic.

Fuck, he was so close. But he needed her to get there first. He needed to feel her shatter around him.

Lowering his head, he latched onto her neck.

She let out a cry, so much louder than any he'd heard before, right as her entire body tensed and arched. She came apart, and it was the most beautiful and primal thing he'd ever seen.

Almost simultaneously, he broke, everything in him letting go.

His mouth found hers as his hips slowed, his body still throbbing inside her.

"God, I love you." His words sounded guttural. *She* did that to him.

He felt her lips stretch into a smile. "I love you, too. And I'm going to tell you every single day until the day we die."

And he'd live for those words. Every damn day.

CHAPTER 27

*T*wo days had passed. Two days of Grace sleeping in his bed. In his arms.

Logan almost groaned out loud at her small wriggle. Every little move she made caused her naked body to brush against his.

It was torture. Even the slow, sexy sighs she released in uneven intervals caused his body to harden to an unbearable degree. He nuzzled her hair with his face, breathing in the woman who had quickly become such an integral part of his life.

Since Beau's arrest, everything had been quiet. The women had been moved to safe houses, including the new victim who had been found with Beau. And Grace had continued counseling them online.

Logan hated the quiet. Quiet meant unpredictability. It meant time for the enemy to strategize. Plan.

Yeah, it wasn't ideal. He'd much prefer it if Kieran showed his face. Logan wanted to fight the guy head on, but right now, he was blind. He tightened the arm that curved around Grace's body. Everything in him told him to keep her close.

At Grace's deep inhale, Logan knew she was waking. Her ass

ground against him again. Another deep, sexy sigh hummed through the room.

Damn, but the woman was killing him. "Grace, if you keep that up, I can't be held responsible for my actions."

She went still. He could almost hear the smile that was no doubt stretching her lips. "Hm. You mean…this?"

She wriggled again, but this time, the movement was more purposeful. Grinding against him in an attempt to cause maximum discomfort.

Growling deep in his throat, he rolled her, pressing against her front. Bracketing her body with his arms and legs.

He studied her face, not finding a single thing beyond love and trust. "Don't say I didn't warn you."

Lowering his head, he feasted on her neck, rocking his hips against her. She rotated between bouts of laughter and moans, squirming beneath him.

When he lifted his head, he saw the smile on her lips. It was wide, and it was magnificent. Christ, but he wanted more of those.

She lifted a brow. "You think I'm the only one affected right now?"

The woman was onto him. Lowering his head, he pressed a softer kiss to her lips. She purred. "I have to get to the office," he said between feather-light kisses. "I have a workout, then I'm speaking to Nicole."

She tensed. He'd already told her about Nicole. About the ultimatum she'd given him. And she'd been just as annoyed as Logan.

"I'm sorry—"

"Not your fault." At all. He slid a piece of hair off her forehead, gliding his thumb over her skin as he went. "I'm going to do the story and get rid of the woman. Sounds like a good deal to me."

She nibbled on her bottom lip. "But if it wasn't for me—"

"Then I would be one very unhappy man," Logan finished, kissing her again.

She gave a small chuckle. "No, you wouldn't, because you wouldn't know what you were missing."

He knew it was meant as a joke, but he couldn't smile back. "And wouldn't that be a damn tragedy."

The smile slipped from her lips. "Just…be careful. I don't trust her."

Oh, Logan didn't trust the woman in the least. But then, he didn't trust many outside of his team. "She can ask whatever she wants. I'll choose what I answer and how I answer it."

"Good."

She began to push on his chest to get out of bed, but Logan shook his head. "Rest. Jason will be here soon to stay with you while I'm gone. You can laze in bed all day."

"Uh, even more reason to get up. I don't need your friends thinking I'm a stay-in-bed-all-day kind of girl."

"Hm, doesn't sound terrible to me."

She pushed again. This time he rolled to the side, watching as she headed to the bathroom completely naked.

Letting her go was hard. Leaving the house was even harder. Probably why, when he eventually got himself dressed and out of the house, he was running late.

He took the stairs up to Blue Halo two at a time, realizing he had less than half an hour before Nicole was due to arrive. Jeez, at this rate, his workout would consist of a couple of push-ups and that was it.

Entering the workout room, he saw Blake already there. The guy was pounding the bag like he was trying to destroy the thing. Clearly something was bothering him, but Logan remained silent. If Blake wanted to talk about it, he would.

Moving to the other side of the room, he started his workout. He was about twenty minutes in when his friend finally took a break. Even though Blake had gone damn hard on the bag, he was barely out of breath.

Logan shot him a glance. "You okay, buddy?"

Blake opened his water bottle, downing half before responding. "Nope."

"Is this about Willow?"

Willow was his ex. Though, anyone who'd seen them together knew that Blake was still in love with her. They'd been together before Blake had been taken by Project Arma, and for some reason had been unable to recapture that relationship when he finally escaped.

Now, their only connection was their four-year-old daughter, Mila.

"Of course it is. Willow just…"

When Blake didn't finish, Logan frowned. "What? She's not keeping Mila from you, is she?" He didn't think she'd do that. Heck, she'd moved across the country so Blake's daughter could be close to him. But—

"No, she would never do that. She does everything she can to make sure we have a good relationship."

"What is it then?"

He ran his hands through his hair. "I love her, man. But we just can't seem to find our way back to each other."

Blake sounded tortured. It damn near tore up Logan.

Walking over to his friend, he pressed a hand to his shoulder. "I'm sorry, buddy. Project Arma hurt a lot of relationships. It was probably a huge shock for both her and Mila to have you return two years after disappearing, and an even bigger shock to learn what was done to you." He tightened his hand on his friend's shoulder. "That would take anyone a long time to get over."

He frowned. "It's not just Project Arma. I made a lot of mistakes when we were together. I want to prove that I can do better. *Be* better. But she doesn't seem willing to let me."

Blake hadn't shared that detail before. In fact, he'd shared very little about his relationship while they'd been held in the Project Arma compound together. "We all make mistakes. It's part of being human."

"Yeah." Shaking his head, he glanced at his watch. "Don't you have the meeting with that reporter soon?"

Fuck, what was the time? Shooting a quick look at his own watch, he realized he had five minutes to spare.

Squeezing Blake's shoulder, Logan jogged to the bathroom and rushed through the quickest shower he'd ever taken before throwing on a T-shirt and shorts. Then he headed to the front. He passed his office, noticing it was empty. When he got to the foyer, he stopped. Also empty.

He was five minutes late. Had she already come and gone?

No. Not after the way she'd all but hunted him down and threatened him for this interview. She could just be running late, as well. But then again, she didn't strike him as the kind of woman to be late for anything.

Sitting behind the front desk, he quickly scanned through their surveillance footage.

She'd never arrived.

Pulling out his phone, Logan noticed he had no missed calls or messages. Searching through his recent calls, he found her number and dialed. It went straight through to voicemail.

Blake stepped into the foyer, one brow raised. "She's not here?"

"Nope. And no messages."

"Odd. She chased us down for an interview like a mad woman. Maybe she's just running late."

"Maybe." But maybe not. And for some reason, Logan's stomach felt tight with dread.

A KNOCK on the door had Grace momentarily leaving the sandwiches she'd been preparing. She took a couple steps but stopped when Jason stood.

"I've got it."

When he looked through the peephole, she could have sworn she saw his lips quirk up just a little before he tugged open the door.

Courtney stood on the other side, two cups of coffee in one hand and a paper bag and envelope in the other. When her eyes met Jason's, her mouth fell open.

He stepped back. "Hi, Courtney. Come in."

"I didn't know you'd be here." She didn't move. She barely looked like she was breathing. Grace almost laughed. "I mean, I don't mind that you *are*. It's Logan's house, he can invite whoever he wants. But I didn't bring you a coffee. Or a donut."

When Courtney started mumbling about going back to the shop and bringing more coffee and food, her words ran together. As her speech sped up, Grace moved across the room. If there was ever a time her friend needed saving, it was now.

Stopping beside Jason, she noticed he had a bemused smile on his face. "Hey, Courtney. It's so good to see you."

"It is," Jason confirmed quietly.

Courtney's cheeks tinged pink before she stepped inside. "You can have my coffee, Jason."

He shook his head as he closed the door. "I couldn't do that."

She pressed one into his chest, looking up to meet his gaze. "No, I insist. I'm ashamed to admit I've had two already."

"Okay, if you're sure." Jason took the coffee, sending a wink her way before heading back to the couch.

If possible, the red on Courtney's cheeks deepened. She headed to the kitchen, plonking onto one of the island stools. Grace heard Jason flipping channels on the TV as she went back to work on the sandwiches, not missing the way Courtney gave a quick look over her shoulder before flicking her gaze back to Grace.

"Want a sandwich?"

Courtney shook her head. "No thanks. I worked the morning crowd, so thought I'd pop in on my way home and share my exciting news."

Grace could always use some of that. "Yes, please, share away."

Courtney straightened, her eyes brimming with excitement. "Okay, so a couple months ago, I entered this competition. The *Living in Idaho Today* magazine was looking for Idaho's 'most unique coffee shop'. They've even partnered up with some radio stations and will endorse the winner. I thought, what the heck? I'm unique, The Grind is unique—let's enter."

"You most certainly are, in the best possible way."

"I'd actually completely forgotten I'd entered, but then this morning, a guy from the magazine called to tell me I'd been shortlisted." Courtney leaned forward, her eyes widening with excitement. "I'm one of the top ten contenders, Grace!"

That didn't surprise Grace in the least. "That's wonderful! And what you've created at The Grind is amazing. Your shop is as unique and quirky and fun as they get." Moving around the island, she pulled Courtney into a hug.

Her friend sighed. "Thank you."

"Congrats, Courtney," Jason called from the living room.

"Thanks." This time, she seemed too excited to be nervous.

Grace moved back to the sandwiches. "So, what's next?"

"Well, he said someone will come to Cradle Mountain, check everything out, and then I'll be placed. If I win, they do a big photo shoot and everything."

Grace popped some cheese onto the bread. "I'd wish you good luck, but I don't think you'll need it."

"Throw some this way anyway, though, would you?" They both chuckled. Courtney reached for the envelope she'd placed on the counter. "Oh, and before I forget, I found this on your driveway, beside the mailbox. I thought I'd grab it for you, seeing as the lazy fool didn't actually put it in the box."

Grace stilled, eyes on the unstamped envelope. "It's addressed to me."

"Yeah. Makes me think you're here to stay." Courtney waggled her brows suggestively, but all of Grace's attention was on the handwritten name.

The knife she'd been about to use on her sandwich slipped from her suddenly clammy fingers, falling to the counter with a clatter.

"McKenna," she whispered.

"I noticed that too. I assumed they made a mistake and meant to write Castle."

She held out the envelope, but Grace just stood there, too terrified to take it.

Suddenly, Jason was beside her, taking the envelope from Courtney's fingers. He gave Grace a questioning look, and she quickly nodded for him to open it. Honestly, all she wanted to do was throw the thing in the trash, but that wasn't smart. There was something in there that she needed to see.

With steady fingers, Jason tore the envelope carefully and pulled out a note. She almost relaxed—until she noticed something else in the envelope. Something red.

Taking the envelope from his fingers, she glanced inside.

Suddenly, her stomach dropped, the envelope tumbling from her shaking fingers.

Hair. Red hair. The exact color that hers used to be.

Grace quickly took the note from Jason, not missing his tight jaw or the angry narrowing of his eyes.

"Grace..." he growled in warning, but she was already reading it.

Red. Like the color of the sky at sunset when light has the furthest to travel through the atmosphere. A shade so pretty, I could never forget.

They all had your shading, Grace. She didn't. So I dyed her hair. It was my gift to her before she took her final breath.

She dropped the note like it was fire in her hands. Jason took it back quickly.

"Grace? Are you okay?" Courtney's voice sounded far away. "God, you're so pale! Sit down."

From her peripheral vision, she saw Jason pulling out his phone. Footsteps sounded, moving away from her. Courtney and Jason's voices were soft background noises.

The panic tried to pull her under, but she breathed in a long, deep breath. Held it. Breathed out. Grace repeated the action, vaguely aware of Jason returning to her side, talking.

Closing her eyes, she let the feel of the cool island counter pull her back to reality. Back to safety.

When she opened her eyes again, it was to see Jason's hands hovering, like he wanted to touch her, but they quickly fell again. "Are you okay?"

No. But she hadn't spiraled into a panic attack, at least. "Who did he take?"

"I don't know. But we'll find out."

His eyes shot to the front door seconds before it opened and Logan rushed in.

He went straight to her, taking her face in his hands. "Are you okay?"

She nodded, air whooshing out of her lungs. Just having him here took the edge off the panic. She heard Jason moving toward Courtney. A door opening and closing, leaving just her and Logan in the room. Several long minutes passed as Grace got her trembling under control.

It was even longer before either of them spoke, Logan continuing to study her.

Finally, her hands went to his forearms. "I need to know who the hair belongs to."

He nodded. He was just opening his mouth when he stopped. It was Logan's turn to shoot a glance toward the front door.

Oh, God, what now?

Reaching out, he took her hand, keeping her body firmly behind his as he moved forward. He looked through the peephole. "Stay back."

That was the only warning she got before he pulled the door open, jerking whoever it was inside before slamming the door shut and pushing their body against the wall. "Who the hell are you?"

Grace gasped. He had to be sixteen, maybe seventeen. His complexion had turned almost white. Her hands went to Logan's shoulder. "He's only a kid."

The teenager put his hands up in a defensive position. "I'm sorry! A guy paid me fifty bucks to drop the box off."

Box?

Shifting her gaze to the floor, she spotted the small gift-wrapped box that had slipped from his fingers when he'd been tugged inside. It had pink wrapping and a big black bow.

"What did he look like?" Logan just about growled to the boy.

The description they received fit Kieran exactly.

Logan asked the kid a few more questions, but it was clear he knew nothing else. When they let him go, Logan pulled out his phone, messaging someone. His team, maybe. Although, she was pretty sure Jason would have done that when he left.

Lifting the box, Logan took her hand and headed toward his office.

"Where are we opening it?" she asked.

Logan shook his head. "I'm not opening it in front of you."

What? "Yes, you are, Logan. I need to know what it is."

"No, you don't. I can open it and my team and I will deal with the contents." He stopped at his desk, carefully placing the box on the surface.

"Logan. This involves me, and I need to know what he left.

I'm strong enough to handle it." She hadn't fallen apart in the kitchen, and she wouldn't fall apart now.

"No."

Stepping closer, Grace touched his shoulders, waiting for him to look at her. "Remember those times you asked me to trust you? Well…now, I'm asking you to trust *me*."

His eyes closed. Brows tugging together. She knew the exact moment he gave in. His jaw clenched, eyes popping open. They were softer now. Like half of him had decided yes, and the other still insisted no.

Slowly, he tugged at the bow, then tore the paper off. He opened the box cautiously, almost seeming to expect a bomb or something.

Before he flipped it open, he looked her way. "Are you sure you want to see this?"

"Yes." She was proud that her voice was steady.

He sighed, opening the box. A note sat on top.

She was fun, but she wasn't you. Who do I need to take next while I wait?

Logan lifted the note, and that's when she saw what sat below.

A thumb with red nail polish.

CHAPTER 28

"*P*rints are in," Steve said, reentering Logan's living room while sliding his phone into his pocket. "It's Nicole Fleece."

Son of a bitch.

He hadn't liked the woman, but she sure as hell hadn't deserved *this*. Grace remained completely still beside him. Aidan, Jason, and Flynn were scattered around the room. The energy was low. Everyone was tense.

"Why her?" Aidan asked. "Just because she had a thin connection to us?"

Steve's gaze stopped on Grace for a beat before moving away again. "Young. Female. Attractive. Besides hair color—which he clearly took upon himself to change—she fits the MO of every other woman taken."

Grace shook her head, frowning. "No, not all the women have the same color hair."

"They all had red hair when they were taken," Steve said quietly. "Some weren't natural redheads. Over the course of their time at the compound, the color faded."

The sound of Grace's heart speeding up splintered through the room.

Dammit, he hadn't told her that part—and to be honest, he didn't know if he'd ever planned on it. Because none of the blame for these women being taken lay on her, and there was no way he wanted her to think it did.

A tense beat of silence passed. Steve shifted his weight from one foot to the other, looking uncomfortable.

Grace swung an accusatory look at Logan. "Why didn't you tell me?"

"I didn't want you thinking anything was your fault."

Beneath the hurt and the shock, he saw anger. He expected her to say more. Maybe even to yell at him—she sure looked mad enough—but she didn't. Instead, Grace turned back to Steve, her back unnaturally rigid.

Steve cleared his throat. "Grace, I know you have Logan and his team protecting you, but I feel obliged to let you know that I can organize a safe house if you'd pre—"

"She's staying here." Logan cut the man off before he could finish. Grace wasn't leaving his sight.

"That's a decision for Grace."

His stomach roiled as he looked at her. There was nowhere else she'd be safer. No one could protect her like him and his team. He was almost certain she would stay—but her prolonged silence had nervous tingles shooting up his spine.

"I'd like to stay here."

The nerves fizzled out of Logan. He placed a hand on her leg, not liking the invisible distance he felt between them.

Steve spent the next twenty minutes asking Grace questions about Kieran. Questions he was sure she'd answered eight years ago and were on file with the police who'd handled her case. He also spoke about safety measures that needed to be put in place, all of which Logan had already taken care of with his team.

He seemed to be about to leave when he stopped. "You're still counseling the women through Skype?"

"I gave them the option to continue seeing me online or finding a new therapist in the towns where they're located. All were okay with the online arrangement, bar Lizzie." A pained look crossed Grace's face. "I'm worried about her. She's struggling more than the others. She doesn't want to find a new therapist but doesn't want online sessions either."

Steve hadn't disclosed the locations of the safe houses. And he wouldn't. For the safety of the women. "Is there anything I can do to help?" he asked.

She shook her head. "I'll keep working with her. See if any progress can be made with our Skype sessions. Hopefully Kieran is found soon and she can return to her family."

Steve shoved a hand in his pocket. "I hope so, too."

After everyone said their goodbyes, Steve and Logan's team slowly made their way out. It wasn't until they were alone that Grace rose from the couch and left the room without a word.

GRACE WAS ANGRY. Angry at Logan for keeping something so important from her. Angry at the law enforcement agencies in the country for not being able to find Kieran. Lord knows, they'd had the time. And angry at Kieran for hurting her, and continuing to hurt other women.

She stepped into the bedroom and, without intending to, slammed the door with a bang.

It didn't remain closed for long. A second later, the sound of it popping open behind her echoed through the room.

Not sparing a glance over her shoulder, she headed into the adjoining bathroom, closing that door as well. This time, ensuring it didn't slam. She loved Logan, but she didn't feel like talking to him right now. She wasn't just angry; she was hurt. Hurt that he hadn't told her the whole truth.

Turning on the tap, she splashed some water on her face, letting it cool her warm cheeks.

Kieran had been watching her for about a month before he took her. Then he'd held her for a week. Did that *really* lead to eight years of taking women who looked just like her?

Knocking on the bathroom door cut through the sound of gushing water. "Can I come in?"

She closed her eyes, taking deep breaths. The rational part of her brain knew that Logan had just been trying to protect her. But the anger and hurt inside her was like a dark snake, slithering its way up her throat into her head, and there was no one else to project it on.

She opened her mouth to tell him no. To demand that he give her space. But the words didn't come. Because the truth was, she didn't want space from him.

"Yes." The word was barely a whisper.

A second later, Logan's heat pressed against her back, his arms surrounding her. Offering a cage of safety. "I'm sorry."

Two words. And some of the anger dissipated, giving way to the emotions she'd been trying to press down.

Sadness. Fear. Guilt.

Turning in his arms, she tilted her head up to look at him. "When did you figure it out?"

"The morning you told me that red was your natural color."

She nodded. That was before they'd seen Kieran on the hospital surveillance video. Before Grace had learned that Ice and Kieran were the same person.

It didn't matter. Nothing did, except bringing him down.

Logan stepped closer, his arms tightening around her. "I should have told you. That wasn't my information to keep."

It wasn't. But she understood why he did. The guy was too

protective. Too gentle. Shielding others against anything that could hurt them was ingrained in his nature.

"Thank you." She closed her eyes. Leaned into him. "I'm going to have a shower."

His forehead touched hers. "Would you like company?"

Yes. But instead of saying so, she shook her head. She wasn't entirely sure why. Maybe because she didn't feel deserving of his affection right now. The guilt was starting to drown the anger. All those women, taken because of *her.* Because of some loose resemblance.

It took a few seconds, but finally, Logan left the room. She instantly felt more alone than ever. But she couldn't call him back. Her voice was stuck in her throat.

Turning on the shower, Grace stripped, switched the lights off and stepped under the spray. The darkness was what she needed to allow her silent tears to fall. Guilt like she'd never felt tried to consume her. Suffocate her.

Closing her eyes, she let herself feel all of it. Her chest cracked wide open.

When warm hands eased around her body, Grace's eyes flew open. Even though she couldn't see anything in the dark bathroom, she could feel him. He was as naked as she was as he held her.

"I can't remain out there and listen to you cry."

Maybe her tears hadn't been so silent after all.

She lay her cheek on his chest. "I feel like it's my fault." Oddly, even more so because she'd *counseled* those carefully chosen women. Heard their heart-wrenching stories. Listened to their pain and trauma.

"It's not." His arms held her tighter, his chest vibrating with his words. "The only person at fault here is him. He gets all the blame, Grace." Logan's head lowered, his mouth beside her ear. "Even if he kept you, you wouldn't have been the last woman he took. Men like that don't stop until they're dead. You hold no responsibility here."

She nuzzled closer, his huge, powerful body a source of such incredible comfort.

"I *want* him to be dead." She didn't even care if that made her a terrible person. He'd hurt too many innocents.

His voice deepened, a dark undertone shading his words. "He will be."

She believed him.

Closing her eyes, she allowed herself to appreciate the powerful man who held her. Loved her.

That's when she finally heard the music. The soft lyrics of Ron Pope's "A Drop in the Ocean".

"This is one of my favorites," she said softly.

"And you're one of mine."

CHAPTER 29

$\mathcal{G}$race watched the trees pass outside the window. The soft rumble of the engine was background noise to the music playing through the speakers.

Logan's hand held hers tightly as they drove to The Grind. Two more days had passed since the notes from Kieran. Two more days of no progress on locating the guy. At least there'd been no more "gifts". A dose of Courtney was exactly what she needed.

But then, she was sure she would enjoy a dose of Courtney every day of the week.

Logan pulled into the parking lot. "Time for some coffee."

She nodded, stepping out of the car. "And a donut."

Sugar and caffeine sounded like a great combination right now.

Coming around, he took her hand as they headed inside. "Hm, I'll see how I feel after the coffee."

She just smiled. The guy didn't have a big, sweet tooth. That's something she'd learned over the last few weeks. Every time she'd offered him anything remotely sweet, he said no. She didn't try to understand that kind of bias.

Stepping inside, she smiled when she saw Courtney bending down to talk to a small girl. She only recognized her as Mila as she drew closer. A tall, slender brunette woman with long wavy brown hair stood beside them. Grace was guessing the mother.

She recognized her too. It was the woman who had been talking to Blake outside the shop that day.

She noticed Blake sitting at a booth, eyes on his daughter and her mother. There was a predatory protectiveness to the way he watched them.

"You sit with Blake, I'll wait for Courtney at the counter," Grace said to Logan.

He pressed a kiss to her temple before walking across to his friend.

Grace stopped at the counter, watching as Mila spoke to Courtney. "Thank you for my milkshake. I especially loved the sprinkles. Pink sprinkles are my favorite."

Courtney's smile was wide. "You are very welcome, Mila. Come back anytime. And pink sprinkles are my favorite too."

The girl beamed.

The lady placed a hand on the girl's back. Definitely the mother. "Thank you, Courtney. We'll see you next time." The woman spoke with a quiet confidence. When she looked at her daughter, all Grace saw was love.

It was beautiful.

When Willow and Mila walked away, Courtney looked up, her eyes widening slightly at the sight of Grace. She walked over, pulling Grace firmly into her arms and holding her.

When they parted, Courtney kept a hold of her shoulders, studying Grace's eyes. "I know you don't want to share the details just yet, which is completely fine, but just tell me one thing. Are you okay?"

"Yes." With Logan by her side, she was more than okay.

Courtney nodded. "Good."

Grace slid onto a stool while Courtney moved behind the counter.

"Coffee?" She was already grinding the beans.

"Please. And I'd love a donut."

"Coming right up." Courtney shot a quick look to the table where the guys were sitting. "You and Logan are looking very happy."

She couldn't stop the smile if she tried. "We are. The man just *makes* me happy." Even at a time when she should be stressed and anxious, he calmed her. Brought peace into a space where there shouldn't be room for any.

Courtney sighed. "So dang beautiful. He's one lucky man."

"No. I'm the lucky one."

Courtney finished the coffees and placed one in front of Grace before popping her elbows onto the counter. "You're both lucky."

Grace took a sip of the hot drink before lowering her voice. "Any progress with Jason?"

She rolled her eyes. "Girl, did you see me the other day when he opened the door? I was a mess and stuttering like heck. If I'm not a silent weirdo, then I'm a blabbering pelican."

"No." That was not the way Grace saw it at all. "You just need to spend more time with the guy."

"So I can embarrass myself further? The man probably thinks I belong in a loony house." Courtney nodded toward the mug. "What do you think of today's choice?"

Grace looked down, reading the mug.

Yes, I talk to myself. Sometimes I need expert advice.

Grace threw back her head and laughed. "Is this for me? Because I'm a therapist?"

Courtney pulled back. "No way. It's for me. I talk to myself so much I would have to be an expert by now."

Grace chuckled again. She was just about to take another sip when she noticed her throat felt funny. Tight, almost.

Frowning, she touched her neck.

"So, you've come in on a good day because I'm testing out a new donut supplier. We can try one of each flavor and call it 'research'."

Grace tried to listen to what Courtney was saying, but a faint buzzing had started in her ears.

What was that? It almost felt like—

Her hands released the mug so fast that coffee spilled over the edge. Rushing to her feet, Grace was immediately hit by a bout of dizziness that had her grabbing the counter edge.

"Whoa, are you okay?"

Placing a hand to her stomach, Grace frowned. "There wasn't any—"

Before she could finish the sentence, her stomach rolled with nausea. Grace doubled over. She was sure she would have tumbled to the floor if strong arms weren't suddenly around her waist.

She could hear Logan talking to her, but whatever he said was blocked out by the buzzing in her ears. It was getting progressively louder, like a plane landing right in her eardrum.

The tightness in her throat worsened.

Glancing up, she tried to focus on Logan, but he was a blur. She opened her mouth to tell him what she needed, but she was almost certain the words never reached the air.

Her breaths were now gasps, her stomach doing violent twists and turns while her skin felt hot and itchy.

Suddenly, she was lifted off her feet, and the air was moving around her.

～

"ANAPHYLACTIC SHOCK?" Logan just about shouted the words, trying and failing to make sense of what the doctor was telling him. They stood just inside her hospital room, Blake in the hall. "I

NYSSA KATHRYN

don't keep any sesame seeds in the house and all she had at The Grind was coffee."

The middle-aged doctor closed the folder in front of him. "She definitely had it in her system, Mr. Snyder. Remember, a single crumb is all it takes. The good news is, you got her here just in time. She should wake up soon and you can ask her if she consumed anything else. In the future, she needs to be more careful. And remind her to carry her EpiPen."

More careful? Grace *was* careful. Always. There was no point in telling that to the doctor though. The guy was already out of the room.

The door was only closed for a second before Blake walked inside, a phone to his ear. "Are you sure?" he asked.

Logan could hear Courtney's voice crystal clear from the phone. "None of my products have sesame seeds in them anymore. I don't even keep the stuff in the shop. All she had was a couple sips of her coffee."

"Okay. Thanks, Courtney."

"Send her my love," she said, voice worried, before hanging up. Courtney had wanted to come to the hospital, but Blake had convinced her to remain at work.

At the quiet rustling of sheets, Logan quickly returned to Grace's side. She blinked a couple of times before her eyes finally opened. When her gaze landed on him, confusion swirled in their depths.

"Hey there, honey. How are you feeling?"

She took two deep breaths. "Like someone's taken sandpaper to my throat." She tried to swallow but grimaced. Logan grabbed the glass of water a nurse had left, placing the straw at her lips. "Am I in the hospital?"

Once she'd had some water, he put it back and sat beside her bed, taking her hand in his. "You are. You had an anaphylactic reaction to sesame."

Her frown deepened. When she struggled to sit up, he took

her arm lightly and helped her. "No, that's not possible. I'm always careful. And all I had this morning was the coffee Courtney made me."

Exactly. It didn't make sense.

Her cell phone started to ring, cutting through the silence. They all ignored it.

"Are you sure you didn't have anything else?" he asked, trying to make sense of this.

She shook her head. "Nothing."

The phone stopped ringing, but almost immediately started up again. Clenching his jaw, he grabbed it from the bedside table, noticing it was a private number, before handing it to her.

"Maybe it's my dad," Grace said softly before answering. "Hello."

"Hello, darling."

All the color drained from her face.

Kieran. It had to be. Logan slid the cell from her fingers.

"What the hell do you want?"

The guy chuckled. "Logan, is it? Put me on loudspeaker, would you?"

"No." Hell no. "Tell me what the fuck you want."

"Logan." Grace's voice was soft but firm. "I need to hear what he has to say."

"You heard the woman."

At Kieran's condescending words, Logan gritted his teeth. But it was Grace's eyes that had him conceding. A mixture of strength and determination.

His muscles bunched as he pressed speaker.

Grace took a breath. "What do you want, Kieran?"

"Ah, there's my girl. How are you doing? Did the doctors give you something to make you feel better?"

What Logan wouldn't do to be able to reach into the phone and tear the guy's throat out.

"Was this you?" she asked, an edge of wrath to her voice.

"It was so easy. To sneak into the shop, throw some ground sesame seeds into their coffee machine. I knew you'd eventually visit that friend of yours again."

That son of a bitch.

"Why?" This time her anger was mixed with confusion. Logan took one of her hands in his own.

"Why have I done any of the things I've done? To prove how easy it is to get to you, darling. To fuck with you. You may think you're safe, holed up in that house with *him*. But you're not. Sooner or later, I'll get to you. And when I do, I'll kill that asshole for touching you."

Logan opened his mouth to correct the man. To tell him just how fucking wrong he was. But the line went dead.

Logan took both of Grace's hands in his. "Don't listen to a word he says. The numbers are in our favor. We *will* find him. And we will murder him."

She studied his face for a beat before nodding. "I want him so far underground that he can never hurt me or any other woman ever again, Logan."

"Already planning on it."

CHAPTER 30

Courtney popped the last chair on the table before doing a final wipe down of the counter.

Usually, she loved her job. No, correction—she freaking adored it. But today, she'd been counting down to her three p.m. finish. Counting down the minutes until she could go home, put on her comfiest never-be-caught-dead-in-these pants, and collapse on the sofa.

Shame she had a pile of paperwork to do before she left. Oh, and she needed to message Grace. Again.

It had been a few days since she'd been carried out of The Grind and rushed to the hospital. And Courtney had worried about her every minute since. Particularly because the reaction had occurred in *her* shop.

God, when Blake had told her the sesame seeds had been in the machine, she'd almost felt like she was in the twilight zone. He'd been light on the details. Something about a guy from Grace's past.

It had to be that guy Grace had mentioned the other week.

Argh, Courtney was furious just thinking about it.

She shot a quick glance out the window. Yep. Aidan was still there, parked right in front of the shop. It had been a different guy each day since the incident.

Was she in danger now? And why the heck weren't they sharing any details?

Dropping the cloth in the sink, Courtney headed outside, walking straight over to Aidan's car. He smiled as she bent down, elbows going to the open window. "Hey there, handsome, plan to watch me all night?"

A brow rose on his face. "You don't like being watched by handsome men?"

"Hm, probably depends on why the handsome man is watching me. Am I in danger?"

She said it with a smile and a hint of humor but, damn, she would like an honest answer.

Aidan gave her a knowing smile. "We're just being cautious. This guy from Grace's past is dangerous and we want everyone to remain safe."

So, *everyone* was in danger? Or just everyone who knew Grace? "Well, I hate to break it to you, but I'll be here for a tad longer doing paperwork. Possibly hours. Oh, and I'll be stuffing my face with comfort food. Aka, donuts."

The new supplier was amazing. Courtney had been eating the stuff like there was about to be a donut drought.

He chuckled. "That's okay. I'll be here. With no one else around, I can hear if you call for me."

Really? Lord, the man was a living, breathing superhero. "Want a donut to keep you occupied? A strudel? There's plenty left."

"Nah. But thanks for the offer."

Nodding, she headed back to the shop.

That man's smile could break a million hearts. But it didn't come close to making her own heart pound like Jason's. His smile. His dimples. Gah, Jason was gorgeous.

Moving to the door at the back of the shop, she walked

through the kitchen and into the connected office, grabbing a stack of paper.

Fun, fun, fun.

Her feet stopped halfway into the kitchen at the feel of a light breeze on her face. Then...what was that? It almost sounded like a slight shuffling.

She was turning her head even as someone suddenly shoved her from behind, right into the wall beside the walk-in freezer. The papers fell from her fingers, a hand coming over her mouth. Then something else pressed against her—something sharp, right against her side.

Ice shards ran up her spine. Her throat felt sealed, so much so that she could barely groan, let alone attempt to talk beneath his palm.

The knife pressed a little harder. For a second, her breath caught as she assumed he would pierce her skin. Panic bubbled to the surface, a lightheadedness almost blinding her.

He ground against her, his hardness pressing into her backside, his face nuzzling her hair. Oh, God, she thought she might be sick against his hand.

Then the knife disappeared.

She stood so still she barely breathed as his hand slid into her back pocket. She frowned as his fingers slipped around her phone, taking it out.

Was that all he wanted? The phone? God, she'd have handed it right to him if he'd asked. Heck, she'd have thrown in her credit card and the till.

The man stepped back, pulling her with him. Hand still covering her mouth. Then his hand went to the freezer door.

The second it opened, the light inside flicked on—and her stomach dropped. Her skin went clammy and her eyes grew wide.

Was that...a *woman*?

It took a moment for Courtney to recognize that not only was the woman totally still and lying on the floor of her freezer, but her open eyes were completely lifeless.

"I hear these are soundproof," he whispered so quietly, the words barely met her ears. Then he shoved her inside, where she tumbled on top of the dead body. The door closed with a resounding click and plunged Courtney into darkness.

That's when the scream released from her chest.

$\sim$

"GRACE, I don't want to be here."

Grace remained calm as she watched Lizzie on the screen. She sat in the conference room at Blue Halo while Logan worked in another room. Lizzie was her last patient for the day. "Why is that, Lizzie?"

"Because I only trust you. I wish you were here."

Their sessions had not been going well, and today was no exception. In fact, today, Lizzie seemed to be even worse than normal. "He doesn't know where you are. You're safe."

"I'm not just scared of him." Tears glistened her eyes. "I'm having these thoughts that just keep getting louder and more regular. This tingly numbness that creeps all over my skin and into my head. My mind fogs and my heart pounds so hard against my ribs it feels like my entire body is jolting. It doesn't matter how often I tell myself to calm down, my body doesn't listen! My brain and my body feel disconnected."

Grace's heart hurt for the broken woman in front of her. She was describing the beginnings of a panic attack. "Lizzie, when that happens, I want you to remember the coping strategies we've gone through. *You* are in control of you. Not the anxiety."

She nodded slowly. "The only good thing is that the panic always ends. But I know it will come back again."

"Are you keeping up with your medication?"

All the women had been prescribed medications for their anxiety, some on higher doses than others.

"Yes."

"That's good. And remember, you can call me as often as you need."

Lizzie nodded miserably. They talked for another half an hour. When they were done, Grace sighed, leaning back in her seat.

They needed Kieran caught *now*. The woman needed family support. She needed a therapist who could be there for her. With her. She needed more than Grace could give her at the moment.

Standing, she moved over to the window. From up here, she could see Cradle Mountain in all its beauty. She could also see almost the entire town. It wouldn't surprise her if the view was the reason the guys had chosen this location.

Hopefully, once this was all over, her father could come and see Cradle Mountain and meet Logan. She'd spoken to him only a few days ago. It had been a long chat. She'd told him about Logan. About her feelings for him. And also about Kieran.

Her dad was worried, but he was also relieved that she had Logan and his team protecting her. Hopeful about the possibility of Kieran being caught soon.

What happened to Grace had almost killed him. And she knew that Kieran still being out there weighed as heavily on him as it did on her. But if anyone could eliminate the guy once and for all, it was Logan and his team.

Grace turned and headed down the hall. She could hear Logan's deep voice from his office as he spoke to someone on the phone.

Shooting a look at the wall clock, she noticed it was just past three.

Stepping into the workout room, she ran her fingers along the punching bag. Once upon a time, she'd taken boxing lessons. That felt like ages ago. Back when she was almost a completely different person. She'd done the lessons at her therapist's recommendation. It had been one of many methods she'd tried on her path to healing.

She'd been terrible at it. Grace almost laughed at the thought. The experience had been very effective in helping her get the anger out, though. Some days, her rage had consumed her, taking all her energy and leaving her exhausted.

The boxing lessons had only lasted a couple months. When she'd discovered the power of music, that was it. Music had been her magic pill. Until Logan.

Like he'd heard her thinking about him, two strong arms wrapped around her waist.

She gave the smallest jolt of surprise.

"Sorry." Logan's mouth was close to her ear, grazing her skin. "I should have made a noise when I approached."

She leaned back into him. "You move very quietly for such a big guy." Silently, in fact.

"We were trained to be silent so that our enemies wouldn't hear us coming." He pressed a kiss to her neck. A shiver rocked her spine. "Have you hit a bag before?"

She was so focused on his lips that she had to replay his words in her head a couple times before they made sense. "A bag?"

He chuckled. It vibrated from her neck, right down to her toes. "A punching bag."

"Oh. Yes, I have. My therapist suggested I try it. I was...angry for a while. She thought it might help."

"Did it?"

Gosh, that breath on her neck...it had all her hairs standing on end. "At first, yes. But it didn't calm me. I needed peace, not exhaustion."

His hands trailed down her arms, fingers entwining with hers. "Maybe lessons with me would be different."

Oh, she was sure they'd be different.

Turning in his arms, she finally looked at the man, almost

getting lost in his magnetic gaze. "I suppose lessons with you don't sound terrible."

"Hm." Leaning down, he pressed his lips to hers. Even though he'd kissed her not that long ago, she craved it like she'd been away from the man for days.

When they eventually separated, they made their way down to his truck. It wasn't until they were partway home that Grace's phone rang. She frowned at the unknown number before answering.

"Grace speaking."

"Grace, it's Steve."

Steve? Why was he calling her? "Is it one of the women?"

"The guard I have on Lizzie just called. The woman's losing it. I put a female guard on her, but it doesn't seem to matter. She wants *you*."

Grace dropped her head into her hands. The poor woman. "I want to help her."

"Want" wasn't really the right word. She *needed* to help her in whatever way she could.

"Based on Lizzie's instability, we placed her safe house the closest to Cradle Mountain." Really? Grace had assumed all the women were at least a plane ride away. "She's not far. I'll send a car now—"

"I'm coming too," Logan interjected, loud enough for his voice to carry through to Steve.

Steve sighed. "I was counting on it." Then the phone went dead as he hung up.

CHAPTER 31

*L*ogan tightened his fingers around Grace's hand as the car pulled into a long driveway. Gray clouds covered the setting sun. Rain threatened at any moment, contributing to the ominous dread tugging at his gut. The feeling had started the second they'd been picked up at his home—and he didn't like it.

He'd been in the back seat with Grace the entire drive, but that hadn't stopped him from keeping his eyes peeled for any tail. There hadn't been one.

The only reason he was allowing this to happen was because Steve had assured him that outside of himself, the woman guarding Lizzie and the driver, a trusted agent, no one else knew about this location.

Luckily, no one had asked for Logan's or Grace's phone. If they had, it would have been a deal breaker. He needed his phone so he could contact his team if he needed them.

The gun in his holster helped calm him, too.

The driver stopped in front of an old wooden house. It was nestled amongst trees and, in the distance, Logan could hear the crashing of waves against rocks.

"I'll wait here," the driver, Trav, said from behind the wheel.

Logan climbed out of the car, going around to Grace's side and helping her to her feet. Small freckles of water dropped onto his jacket. Her gaze shot up. It would be bucketing soon.

"You doing okay?" he asked Grace, searching her face as they walked to the door.

She nodded, nibbling on her bottom lip. "I'm just worried about her. She's not in a good place, and I think moving her here has made her mental state worse."

Logan ran his hand up and down Grace's spine, trying to bring warmth and calm. Lifting his fist, he knocked on the wooden door. He could hear the sound of crying from inside the house. It was heavy and pained. Lizzie.

Trying the handle, he wasn't surprised to find it locked. Logan knocked again. The crying inside became louder.

After another beat, the sound of the car door opening echoed behind them. Then Trav was beside them, pulling a key from his pocket. "Steve warned that Sue, the guard, might have her hands full trying to calm Lizzie."

He unlocked the door, swinging it open, and stepped back.

Logan nodded his thanks, stepping into a well-lit living area, hand around Grace's. To the right was a kitchen, and up ahead was a closed door. It was behind the door where Lizzie's cries were coming from.

He walked forward slowly, hand going to the door and pushing open.

Lizzie sat on the bed, against the headboard, knees tugged up to her chest and head down. Her entire body was shaking.

Grace moved straight to the bed, sitting on the side but not reaching out. "Lizzie, it's Grace, can you hear me?"

The woman didn't move, cries continuing to cause her body to vibrate.

Grace continued to talk while Logan studied the room, listening in to how many heartbeats he could hear. He frowned.

There was just Grace's and Lizzie's...and the guard at the front of the house.

He frowned. Where was the female guard? She hadn't come to the door, and she wasn't in the room.

He moved to the window, not seeing a damn thing but trees. Then he crossed to the other side of the room, to a closed door that he assumed was a connected bathroom. As he drew closer, a light, acidic smell penetrated his nose.

His fingers wrapped around the handle and he tugged.

The second the door opened, he saw her. A woman lying on the white tiles, blood seeping from a bullet wound to the head.

Logan's hand went to his gun. He was mid-turn when the sound of a gun going off splintered the room. Pain laced his chest, sending him to the floor, and his vision went black.

GRACE SAT across the bed from Lizzie, trying and failing to calm her cries. Her heart hurt for the woman who looked so broken.

She vaguely heard Logan's footsteps behind her. But it wasn't until a door clicked open that Lizzie finally raised her head. And when she did—she withdrew something from her lap.

Grace barely had time to scream before the trigger was pulled, and Logan crumpled to the floor.

For a split second, Grace's world stopped. Then a buzzing started between her ears that had everything going silent around her. Crying out, she ran to Logan, hand going to his chest to stem the blood. Oh, God, there was so much, and he was so still! Was he even breathing?

She'd just lowered her head to listen for a heartbeat when another gunshot went off.

Grace jolted, eyes shooting up to see their driver, Trav, lying in the doorway, blood pouring from a bullet wound in his head.

She felt the blood drain from her face. When she looked back to Logan, she glimpsed the bathroom. Fear and panic washed over her like a tidal wave at the sight of a woman, eyes open, bullet wound to the head...just like Trav.

Lizzie rose to her feet, the desolation of moments ago wiped from her face, replaced with...nothing. Her expression was completely clear. The gun was still in her hand and pointed directly at Grace.

"Unlock your phone and slide it across the floor to me."

Grace's mouth dropped open. Who the hell was this woman? Her heart felt broken, *she* felt broken, and Lizzie wanted her phone?

A beat of complete silence and stillness passed before Lizzie huffed. "He's not dead, Grace. I shot the other two in the head. Kill shots. I shot Logan in the chest. The chest that's *still* moving."

Grace glanced back to Logan, noticing for the first time that, just as Lizzie said, his chest was rising and falling.

He wasn't dead. Not yet.

"Now give me your goddamn phone or I'll go against Kieran's orders and the next one *will* be a kill shot."

The name slivered into her ears. Her skin chilled, terror thundering through her chest. "Kieran?"

When the woman's eyes narrowed, flicking back to Logan, Grace cried out. "No!" With trembling fingers, she tugged the phone from her back pocket, unlocking it and sliding it across the floor.

Lizzie trained the gun on Grace once again as she bent down and lifted the phone. The gun remained pointed at her as Lizzie pressed some keys before putting it to her ear.

"It's done, and I've sent you our location."

When she hung up, she placed the phone on the floor and stomped on it. The thing shattered.

"Why?" The word tore from Grace's chest. She continued to

press against Logan's bullet wound, praying that he wouldn't lose too much blood.

"Why what? Why am I doing this?" She almost looked like she was going to smile. "Kieran and I love each other. He didn't treat me like the other women. We have a connection. A real relationship."

Grace just stopped the gasp from leaving her lips. Stockholm syndrome. Lizzie had developed a psychological bond to her captor.

How had she not seen it? But Grace already knew the answer to that. Lizzie's emotions had looked and felt real.

God, the woman was the best damn actress she'd ever seen.

"So everything you said to me was a lie." All their sessions together. The tears. The fear. The panic. Grace could barely believe it.

"Good, wasn't I?" She smiled.

"I don't..." Grace swallowed. "I don't understand." Anything. She didn't understand what the heck was going on.

"Then let me simplify this for you. Kieran watched those men destroy his compound through his surveillance footage. He went to Cradle Mountain for *them*, but it didn't take him long to find me. The first night, he came to my window..." She sighed. "I couldn't get the thing unlocked fast enough. Then each night after, I'd sneak outside to be with him."

"He's a rapist and a murderer, Lizzie."

A flicker of remorse flashed over her face. "We don't choose who we love."

Kieran must have seen her weakness and jumped on it. "If you wanted to be with him, why didn't you just leave with him that first night?"

Her eyes narrowed onto Logan, and Grace was a second away from leaping in front of him to save him from another bullet. "Kieran told me all about your history. He told me that as long as

Logan was alive, the asshole wouldn't stop until Kieran was dead."

That was true.

Logan's body twitched. Grace's eyes shot around to him. Was he waking? She knew that he healed faster than the average person, but would that still be the case with a bullet lodged in the wound? At least, she assumed it was lodged.

"Shit. Kieran better get here soon. If I need to shoot him a second time, there's a chance I could kill him. Kieran wants that honor."

Grace wouldn't be letting that happen. Rising to her feet, she positioned herself in front of Logan.

Lizzie scowled, following Grace's movement with her gun. "What are you doing? I told Kieran I wouldn't kill you either, but if I have to, I will."

"Lizzie, you need to listen to me. Kieran isn't going to kill me. He's infatuated with me. When he took me eight years ago, he was supposed to deliver me to the compound. He didn't. He kept me. It's exactly what he'll do again."

Lizzie shook her head, the gun lowering a fraction. "You're lying. He loves *me*. Everyone else is expendable. He told me so."

Grace took a small step forward, still blocking Logan's body with her own. "Do you know why he takes redheaded women? Because I'm a natural redhead. It began with me. Eight years later, and he's still as obsessed with me now as he was then."

Lizzie's chest rose and fell in quick succession. "*No.*"

A car engine sounded outside. Oh, God, was he here? "Lizzie, please believe me when I say, you *are* expendable to him. If you don't kill him, he'll kill you."

Anger marred her face. "No!" She raised the gun again.

Grace was readying herself to drop to the floor when another gunshot went off. She cried out...

Lizzie went limp, blood pouring from the side of her head.

Nausea rose in Grace's stomach. She looked across the room,

freezing at the sight of the man who had filled her nightmares for so long.

He smiled. "She always was a dumb bitch."

Grace dove for the gun that had dropped from Lizzie's fingers. She heard heavy footsteps seconds before a sharp pain burst through her head, sending her into darkness.

CHAPTER 32

Grace woke slowly, pain keeping her eyes closed. Her head throbbed at the back of her skull, and her skin was so chilled that goose bumps pebbled her skin.

She tried to move her arms, frowning when she couldn't. Something was stopping her. Something around her wrists.

Restraints. And she was sitting on a hard wooden chair. That's why her neck was sore. Her chin had been pressed to her chest.

Shuffling noises sounded around her. Slowly, she peeled her eyes open.

She was still in Lizzie's safe house, only now she sat in the living room. She swiveled her head around, ignoring the sharp pain in her skull, immediately spotting Logan in another chair, hands behind his back and feet bound with metal chains.

Her breaths sped up with panic. Blood no longer seeped from his chest, but there was something in his neck now. Wait...was that...the end of a dart? It almost looked like an animal tranquilizer.

Fear for Logan began to skitter over her skin. Her breaths whooshed in and out of her chest even harder, faster. His chest was still moving. Only slightly, but he was breathing. That was good.

Glancing down, she realized why she was so cold. Her top, pants and shoes had been removed, leaving her in just her bra and underwear.

She gave her restraints a small tug. Rope chafed against her wrists, digging into her flesh. She took more deep breaths, counting to five on each inhale, then holding the breath for another five.

More shuffling sounded from the other room. She steeled herself as footsteps drew closer, then Kieran moved from the bedroom into the living room.

Every step closer brought a new wave of fear. The man of her nightmares. The man who threw her into hell eight years ago. A hell she'd been clawing her way out of ever since.

Just like on the surveillance footage, his head was now shaved, his face thinner than she remembered. Something that had stayed the same, though, were his pale blue eyes. Eyes of pure evil.

"Hello, Grace." He studied her face. Her body. God, how she wanted to cover herself. Her skin crawled, having his eyes on her. "So many years have passed where I assumed I'd never have you again. Too many."

"What did you do to him?"

He cast a quick look at Logan before turning back to her. His smile reminded her of a lion as it hunted prey. "I shot him with a powerful tranquilizer created for large animals. I didn't know if the chains would hold him." If they were normal chains, they wouldn't. "Fortunately, it didn't kill him. I want you to watch that."

Grace couldn't allow herself to accept that would ever happen. No way. He wasn't going to die.

Kieran took slow, predatory steps forward. "Do you know how sad I was when I couldn't find you?" He gave her a hurt look.

"And *angry*? There was a lot of anger. I did a lot of terrible things before you. But after…"

When he stopped in front of her and lowered to his haunches, she tried to pull back but could barely move. Reaching out, he trailed a finger from the base of her neck, down to the top of her scar.

Revulsion mixed with fear throbbed inside her as he trailed his finger along the scar he'd created. His finger then continued over her stomach, her underwear, reaching the scar on her thigh.

"You're the only woman I've ever wanted to keep," he said quietly. "Since you, I've been searching for someone to take your place. Someone to chase away my demons and consume me the way you did. For a while, that woman was Lizzie. She *liked* being my favorite. A fucked-up upbringing will do that to a girl. But then I found you again."

"Don't. Touch me." The words sounded scratchy, even to her ears. But she was proud of herself for getting them out. For holding his gaze.

He almost looked like he wanted to smile. "You were so passive last time. I've been wondering if you'd grown some courage." His hand was now wrapped around her upper thigh in an almost intimate way…possessive. Her stomach churned with the need to be sick.

"And I was wondering if *you'd* grown a conscience." That, or died for his sins.

That same slight smile. "Afraid not. And now that I have you, I won't be letting you go." He squeezed her thigh so tightly she cringed. He leaned forward, whispering in her ear. "Ever."

The second he released her leg and stood, air rushed out of her chest. When the man touched her, she couldn't breathe. She could barely think.

"How did you find me?"

This time, his smile wasn't so small. "I'm sure you know by now that the security footage at my compound led me to Logan's boys. They'd just been all over the media, so identifying them wasn't hard. I flew out to Cradle Mountain to give them a taste of their own medicine."

Walking over to a kitchen drawer, he opened it, pulling out a knife. She tried not to react when he walked toward her, touching the sharp point with the tip of his finger.

"I intended to gut the whole team, one by one. Their enhanced abilities don't scare me. It's nothing a bullet or a bomb can't tame. Imagine my surprise, though, when instead of finding Logan in his kitchen—I find *you*. A woman who's disappeared off the face of the fucking planet for the last eight years. I thought I was seeing a ghost."

He shook his head like he still couldn't believe it.

"I turned off the power, wanting to see if you'd disappear along with the light, because surely you weren't real. But then the moon reflected off that delicate skin of yours that I've missed so much. Suddenly, I no longer cared about Lizzie, or any of the other bitches the Blue Halo guys stole from me. All I cared about was you."

"So you just used Lizzie until you didn't need her anymore? You always intended to kill her?"

He kept touching the knife like it was the sole focus of his attention. "Of course. I needed her to get you somewhere isolated. Everything I asked her to do, she did, like the pathetic bitch she was."

Grace tensed, forcing herself not to look into the other room and catch a glimpse of the now dead woman.

"Seeing that fear flash through your eyes as I waited for today, seeing your hands tremble and your body shake...it took me back. Back to eight years ago when I watched you in that bar. It was like my entrée before the main course. I also loved seeing those assholes get nervous. They knew I was close but they couldn't find me."

The guy was sick. "And now? What's your plan? To keep me indefinitely?"

"Of course. You belong to me, Grace."

He slid two phones out of his pocket, placing one on the kitchen counter and keeping the other in his grasp. Grace frowned, recognizing the one he held. "Is that...that's Courtney's." Ice trickled over her skin.

He chuckled. "It is. I never give anyone my contact details, not even Lizzie. It's how I've kept hidden all these years. That's why I took your friend's phone. Told Lizzie to call it with yours and send me your location."

He dropped the phone, stomping on it in much the same way Lizzie had to hers.

"Is she okay?"

"That'll depend on how long it takes for someone to find her. How long can a person survive in a freezer?"

Some of her fear fled, replaced by red-hot anger. Anger that he was hurting the people she cared about. That he had zero remorse. "I hope they find you and they gut you."

The smile left his lips. When he moved toward her this time, his steps were deliberate and powerful. Dropping down again, he wrapped his fingers around her neck, pressing the knife to her face. There wasn't enough pressure to cut her, but the threat was there.

"They won't. They'll be the ones gutted. You're mine, and what you did will *not* go unpunished. Just like Logan will be punished for touching you. And your father for hiding you from me."

She felt the color drain from her face. Her father? "What have you done?"

The knife was now moving down her chest, her stomach. "I took him."

No...

"But that's not the question you should be asking. Don't you want to know what I plan to do with him?"

A beat of silence passed. He was going to make her ask. Her words were spoken through gritted teeth. "What do you plan to do to him?"

The knife trailed back up her throat to sit just under her chin. She barely paid it any attention now.

"Instead of telling you, why don't I show you?"

Turning, Kieran walked out the door. The click of something opening, maybe the trunk of a car, sounded, then the bang as it was shut. Less than a minute later, he returned with her father slung over his shoulder.

Grace couldn't silence her cries any longer.

CHAPTER 33

*K*ieran dropped her father to the wooden floorboards with a heavy thud. His hands and feet were bound with rope. A myriad of purple and blue bruises covered his face and arms.

Her father groaned softly from the floor, rolling onto his back.

Tears filled Grace's eyes, threatening to overflow.

This was her fault.

Turning her attention back to Kieran, she chose anger over the million other emotions stirring inside her. "Leave him alone! It's me you want!"

"You're right. It *is* you I want." He marched up to her again, this time grabbing a handful of her hair and tugging it back. Pain seared the back of her skull, but she didn't make a sound, not wanting to give him the satisfaction. "I've wanted you for almost nine fucking years! But I haven't had you, have I? I've had to settle for shitty substitutes. Because of *him*. Because *he* hid you from me!"

She tried to shake her head, but his hold was too firm. "No. Because of me. I made him do it."

Kieran lowered his face to her neck. The sound was loud as he inhaled her. "Don't worry—you'll pay it back to me."

"Get away from her." Her father's voice was weak, but there was an undercurrent of strength.

When Kieran released her hair and walked toward her father, she immediately wanted his attention back on her. He kicked her father in the stomach, hard. Pain marred his brow, his groan loud.

"Stop!"

Kieran ignored her. Serving her father blow after blow. Grace screamed and begged. She promised the man anything she could think of, but he refused to so much as pause.

She yelled so much that her voice almost broke. Every blow to her father felt like a physical blow to her heart.

Finally, out of breath, Kieran turned toward her. "Are you ready to see what happens when people cross me?"

Her father wheezed on the floor. Kieran smirked when she remained silent, nodding toward the door.

"I'll need my tools, but don't worry, it won't take long. Once these two are dead, you and I are getting the hell out of here."

Tools?

When he disappeared, her gaze shifted to her father's still form. The normally strong man now lay bleeding on the floor.

"Dad..." God, if only she'd gotten out of Cradle Mountain sooner, like she was supposed to. Kieran never would have found her. And he never would have taken her father.

When her dad's eyes opened, she breathed a sigh of relief. A relief that he wasn't unconscious. He started shuffling toward her, his movements surprisingly quick, considering the way Kieran had just been beating the hell out of him.

"Dad, what are you—"

"Shh." He stopped behind her chair. She peered over her shoulder and caught him rising to his knees, turning so his back faced her own. Then his hands were brushing against her wrists as he began to work the ropes.

"I'm going to untie the rope around your wrists," he whispered. "Then I need you to do the same for me."

For a second, fear cramped her stomach. Fear of running out of time. Fear of Kieran catching them trying to escape. But she pushed it down. Kieran was already planning to do unspeakable things. They needed to try to get away.

Her dad was former military. He knew how to untie a rope quickly.

Suddenly, the material around her hands dropped, confirming her faith in her father.

She didn't stop to absorb her shock, instead twisting to work on the knots around her father's wrists. Her trembling fingers worked as fast as they could, but the knots were tight, her clammy fingers slipping more than they should have.

"When he comes back, put your hands back behind your back and hold the rope. I'll do the same. He'll think we're still bound. When I attack, you need to untie your ankles and run."

"No! I'm not leaving you and Logan."

The rope around her father's wrists finally gave way, and he leaned closer to her. "You *are*. Even if Logan were conscious, we don't have the keys for his chains. I saw the phone on the counter. You need to take it, run, and call for help. He'll expect you to go for the road, so go anywhere else. Run far enough that if he escapes from me, he won't be able to find you. When you're far enough, call for help. I'll do everything I can to keep him away from Logan."

Grace shook her head frantically, not wanting to put her father or Logan in such vulnerable positions. "No, Dad—"

"Gracie—please." His hands went to her cheeks. Tears filled her eyes, but she angrily brushed them away. "Logan would want you to do this. *I* need you to do this. I need you to be okay. You're all I have."

Suddenly, memories of her father in the hospital that day came back to her. His skin had been deathly pale, and he'd looked like he'd aged twenty years in a week. Grace's near death had almost destroyed him as much as it had her.

He had the training to beat Kieran in a fight. But he was older now. And he'd been working a desk job for years.

Everything in her told her not to leave. But the desperation in her father's eyes was something she hadn't seen since that day. Desperation for her to be okay. He needed her to live more than he needed to survive.

Slowly, she nodded. "Okay." One word, barely a whisper, but it tore her heart in two.

Some of the storm inside her calmed as he breathed out a sigh of relief.

Footsteps from the front of the house sounded as her father quickly grabbed both pieces of rope, pressing one into her hands before taking the other with him as he shuffled back to where he'd been lying.

Scrunching the rope between her fingers, Grace took a series of calming breaths as Kieran walked inside. A new fear now settled in her chest. Her heart pounded so hard she was almost sure he'd hear it.

Kieran dropped a large bag to the floor, the thump echoing through the room. "Who's ready to end this shit so we can get out of here? I know I am."

Bending down, he pulled something silver from his bag. Pliers.

Her stomach turned.

Kieran smiled at her. "Why don't we start with his teeth?"

God, she really was going to be sick.

He moved toward her father, his steps slow, like he was prolonging the moment. Grace could almost feel the excitement bouncing off him. He enjoyed inflicting pain. Enjoyed the power of having someone's life in his hands. The fear they exuded seconds before he hurt them.

Crouching down, he grabbed her father's chin.

Kieran never saw the fist coming.

Her father swung hard and fast, hitting the guy right in the face. The pliers flew out of his hand.

Shock transformed Kieran's features seconds before her father slammed him to the floor. Kieran's head bashed against the wood with a thud as her dad climbed on top of him.

"Now, Grace!"

Her dad's voice pulled her out of her shock. Leaning over, she started working the rope around her ankles. Her fingers still trembled, making the process take much longer than it should have.

Grunts and growls sounded through the room. Fists connecting violently with skin.

After what felt like endless minutes, the knots came apart, and Grace stood. Her knees threatened to buckle, but she refused to let them.

She shot a quick look at Logan. *Please, Logan. Wake up.*

Then her gaze shifted back to her father. She didn't want to leave them.

"No!" Kieran's roar had her breath catching in her throat. He attempted to lunge for her, but her father wrapped his arms around Kieran's waist, pulling him back.

Finally moving, Grace swiped the phone from the counter. For a split-second, she paused again, but when the grunts grew louder, all Grace could think of were the words from her father.

Run so far that if he escapes from me, he won't be able to find you.

Racing outside, Grace studied the road leading up to the house. Rain fell lightly from the sky and everything was wet.

He'll expect you to go for the road, so go anywhere else.

She didn't stop to think, just moved, her feet pounding the wet ground as she ran around the house and through the trees at the back. Fear stabbed at her chest. And guilt. So much guilt for leaving her father and Logan. It almost suffocated her.

She ignored it all, focusing instead on moving. Running. Escaping. She needed to call for help. She was the only person who could.

Branches scraped across her cheeks, the rain falling heavily on her shoulders, soaking the ground and trying to trip her up. Her skin was so cold that trembling had started to rock her limbs.

She didn't let it slow her down. Nothing could.

When her foot caught on a wet tree root, she went down, hitting the damp earth hard.

Grace didn't allow herself a chance to acknowledge the pain or recoup her breath. Every second could be the difference between capture and freedom. Life and death.

Her feet moved faster. The scent of rain and wet dirt filling her nose.

Minutes passed before she finally lifted the phone in her hand. She said a silent thank you to whoever was watching over her that the thing wasn't locked. She had two bars of signal. That had to be enough.

She slowed but didn't stop. She didn't dare.

FOOTSTEPS SOUNDED down the hall seconds before the knock came at Blake's office door. He looked up to see Jason and Flynn.

Jason leaned his shoulder against the doorway. "We're off."

Blake sighed, leaning back in his seat. He should really get going, too. But on nights when he didn't have Mila, the house was too damn quiet.

He ran a hand through his hair. "I'll be here for a bit longer."

Flynn tilted his head to the side. "No Mila tonight."

Ah, his team knew him too well. "Nope. Just me." He tapped his pen on the desk. "How's your mom doing?"

The team had chosen Cradle Mountain because Flynn's mom needed assistance. She'd recently been diagnosed with Alzheimer's disease.

"Honestly, man...it's hard. I hate that she got such a late diagnosis. I keep thinking, if I'd been here to notice the signs, she would have gotten the help she needed earlier."

As it stood, his mother had a caregiver who visited daily. Flynn was also there a lot.

Jason clenched his friend's shoulder. "You're here now."

He dipped his head in silent acknowledgment.

Yeah, Project Arma had taken a lot from them. In particular, time with loved ones.

The guys were just turning when the reception phone rang. They hadn't hired a receptionist yet, so it was usually up to one of them to divert the call.

Blake lifted the phone and did just that. "Blake speaking."

"Blake, it's Grace!"

Blake frowned, the men opposite him straightening. Her voice was trembling and out of breath, and a strong breeze sounded in the background.

"What's wrong, Grace?"

Heavy breathing came over the line. She was on the move. "Steve organized an agent to take us to see Lizzie. She was freaking out but it was a trap. She shot two agents and Logan. Then Kieran shot *her*. My dad's trying to hold him off, but I don't know how long he'll last!"

Blake's adrenaline spiked, his heart jackhammering in his chest. He called on his training to remain calm. "Where are you?"

"I don't know." A small sob sounded. More heavy wind. "I ran. I'm still running. I've just reached water."

"Just a second, Grace, we're going to figure out where you are."

He nodded to Flynn, who'd already pulled his phone from his pocket. He dialed Steve, who picked up on the first ring.

"Hey, everything okay?"

"Grace and Logan are in trouble. Lizzie was working with Kieran. We need her location *now*."

Steve cursed loudly across the line before quickly reciting the address. Blake rose from the chair, then they were all moving quickly, out of the office and down the stairs.

Blake sat in the passenger seat. "Stay on the line, Grace."

"I want to go back to the house! See if my dad and Logan are okay."

"Don't even think about it. You put as much distance between you and that asshole as possible!"

Her breaths were louder now, but the lack of footsteps told Blake she'd stopped. "Logan was unconscious and my dad's feet were bound together. He was injured. Kieran's younger and stronger—"

"And I'm still betting your dad told you to run. He would *not* want you going back there. Grace, listen to me. Stay away from him. Keep running." If Logan found out he let her go back, the guy would murder him. If someone had let Willow go back, he would do the same.

Silence.

Was she going to listen? Or was she going to return right to evil's doorstep?

As Blake waited, Jason's phone rang. He could just hear Aidan through the line. Jason cursed loudly.

"Okay. I'm running again," Grace said quietly.

Good. "We won't be long. You have my word."

CHAPTER 34

*G*race's teeth chattered loudly, her fingers so chilled she'd almost lost feeling. At this rate, if Kieran didn't kill her, the cold probably would. The sun had started to go down, and the wind had gained traction. Some gusts were so strong they felt like tiny shards of glass cutting into her skin.

Her fingers clenched the cell in her hand so tightly she was sure she was going to shatter the thing. She wouldn't let go. Couldn't. It was her one connection to safety.

She tried to move her legs faster, but her feet were numb. That was probably a good thing. She was sure there were enough cuts and scrapes from branches and pebbles that they were raw and bleeding.

She shot a quick look over her shoulder, guilt gnawing at her insides. Were they okay? Had her father been able to fight Kieran off, protect himself and Logan, even though his feet were bound?

The sound of waves crashing steadily grew louder as she moved. She was close to the water's edge.

When the tree line ended, Grace caught sight of rocks up ahead. Big rocks, presumably leading down to the water. Another gust of wind blew against her frosty skin. She wanted to groan out loud. She only just stopped herself. Everything in her was so cold she almost felt frozen.

Gritting her teeth, she kept moving. If her father could fight a man twenty years younger while injured and partially bound, she could continue moving even though her body begged her to collapse.

Lord, she hoped Blake and the guys were close. It hadn't taken them long to reach the house, so surely it wouldn't take Blake much longer.

She'd just taken another unsteady step when something sounded behind her—the distant crunching of leaves.

She stopped, almost stumbling in her angst.

A second passed, then more crunches. This time closer and in fast succession. Whoever it was...they were jogging.

Oh, God! She tried to move her feet faster. Reaching the rocks, she started climbing down. At the bottom of a steep decline, she saw water bordered by sand and more rock. It looked like the edge of a beach.

Now that the trees weren't covering so much of the sky, the rain hit her hard and fast. Blinding her. Her limbs trembled with a violent tenacity.

She was midway down when she heard the voice. "You fucking bitch!"

Her foot slipped on a wet rock. She fell, scraping her arm against a sharp edge, phone slipping from her fingers, tumbling down. She almost tumbled with it, only just stopping herself.

She cast a quick glance up, and her heart catapulted into her throat. Kieran stood at the top of the rocks, lips bleeding and both eyes almost black. There were bloodstains on his shirt. He looked very different from the way he had when she'd left him. But he was still here.

Where was her father? Where was Logan?

When Kieran started climbing the rocks, a small whimper escaped her lips as she turned, trying to move her body faster.

The sounds of him gaining on her had Grace's breath seizing in her chest. She pushed through it all. The fear. The panic. And moved.

She'd almost reached the sand when fingers tangled in her hair, pulling her back before slamming her head into the rocks.

White-hot pain blasted through her left cheek, all the way through to her skull.

Her hair was released, but almost immediately a foot hit her hard and fast in the ribs, sending her tumbling to the sand.

Her body wanted to shut down, her eyes already hedging with darkness. She forced herself to remain conscious. To move. To crawl through the sand in a weak attempt to put distance between herself and him.

Strong fingers suddenly wrapped around her throat, tugging her to her feet.

"You think you can run from me again?"

His lips were so close to her face that she felt his words like they were being seared into her skin, the heat of his breath burning her face.

"Fucking answer me, bitch!"

She could barely breathe with how tightly he held her neck, but if he wanted words, then she'd make herself speak. She was done being treated like his property. "I did it before!"

Rage contorted his face. His fingers left her throat. She barely saw the fist before it collided with her cheekbone, the same one he'd bashed against the rock. She hit the ground, but was only down for a second before he wrenched her back up, hand returning to her throat, stealing her air.

She grabbed at his fingers, clawed at his arm.

"You're *mine*!" Kieran yelled, his voice vibrating her eardrums. "Always have been. Always will be!"

Not...even...close.

Calling on all her strength, she brought up her knee, putting as much force behind the hit as she could, getting him right between his legs.

Kieran groaned. As he bent forward, she slammed a palm to his nose in an upward motion.

Both his hands went to his face, blood pouring between the seams of his fingers.

Then she ran. Moved her legs faster than she thought possible, each step sinking her into the wet sand. She still couldn't feel her feet, but somehow they were holding her up. That was enough.

Every step was a step away from him. If he chased her, she couldn't outrun him, she knew that, but she could buy herself time. Time for someone to find them.

On her next step, a heavy weight landed on her back, plunging her back to the sand. Shallow water pooled at her front. If her body wasn't so numb, she was sure it would feel like lying in a pool of ice.

Her body was immediately spun around. More water lapped around her. He reared his fist back, but before it could make contact, she shifted her head to the side. Shards of water splintered around her face and neck.

His face contorted. More anger. More spine-chilling rage.

She tried to dodge the next hit, but she was too slow. Pain cascaded through her head, blurring her vision.

She hadn't recovered when the next punch came, this one just as violent as the last. The metallic taste of blood filled her mouth and there was a sharp ringing in her ears.

"You should have been a good girl and done what you were told!"

"*Never.*" The word was wrenched from somewhere deep inside her, so quiet it was barely audible.

Kieran stood, pulling her to her feet with him. Then—his entire body went still.

Suddenly, he pulled a knife and pressed it to her throat. She could almost feel the fear bouncing off Kieran as his body shook.

It took every ounce of energy to peel her eyes open.

That's when she saw him. Logan. Moving down the rocks.

Her heart skidded in her chest. He was moving slower than normal, blood stains covering his shirt.

But he was alive.

Some of the suffocating weight on her chest lifted. Her body suddenly felt lethargic.

Kieran tugged her body tight to his. He took several steps backward, into the icy water. "*Fuck*. I should have let Lizzie kill that asshole!"

Yes, he should have. The guy's need for revenge, his need for her to suffer by watching Logan's death, would ultimately be his undoing.

Logan jumped from the last rock onto the sand and stalked toward them. His gaze deadly as it focused on Kieran. Dangerous.

"Let her go, Kieran." He growled the words, hard and menacing.

Kieran continued to move back. Every step plunged them deeper into the water. Her breaths were coming out in short gasps now. Her body was shutting down. She was so cold. *Had* been cold for too long.

"Stop, or I'll plunge this knife into her!"

Logan slowed. A ferocious anger radiated from his eyes.

"If I can't have her, no one can!"

The haze in her vision began to increase. She could only just make out Logan's outline as he continued to stalk toward them.

LOGAN'S WORLD slowed to pinpoint accuracy. The knife at Grace's neck, combined with the shaking in her limbs as Kieran pulled her deeper into the water, had his heart stopping in his chest. Her lips were blue. Her eyes glazed like she was seconds from losing consciousness.

Rage threatened to consume him. He needed to end this—and he needed to end this soon.

His next shift forward was a single step. He ignored the fire burning through his chest from the bullet wound. The exhaustion pulling at his limbs from the tranquilizer. "Is she worth dying for? Because if you kill her, I kill *you*."

Kieran smirked, moving back again. Then once more. He was almost chest deep. "You think I'm stupid? You're gonna kill me either way."

Yeah, he was a dead man. Logan couldn't let him live. Not after everything he'd done.

At the sight of Grace's eyes shuttering, Logan almost raced toward them full tilt. He just stopped himself. Such a move could cost Grace her life.

Instead, he took another small step forward, water soaking his ankles.

"You're right. But it can either be quick and painless, or I can draw it out. Make you scream and beg for the sweet release of death."

Kieran's chest was rising and falling rapidly. He was cold and angry, but he was also scared. He tried to hide it but Logan saw everything. The asshole knew these were his final minutes.

"Or I just kill us both." Kieran took a large step back, the knife pressing harder against her delicate skin—so hard, Logan saw a flash of red as the blade pierced her flesh. "I slice this knife right across her neck, then my own! I die knowing that no one else gets her!"

Logan's jaw clenched, his self-restraint waning.

He took another step forward. Water lapped around his knees, the cold barely registering. He was almost at the point where he could leap forward, clearing the distance to reach the weapon. Almost.

The hand holding the knife began to tremble. "All these years. She should have been with *me*! I never stopped thinking about her. Obsessing. I *deserve* her!"

"She doesn't want you." Another step forward. Then another.

"You think I fucking care what she wants?" The man was becoming more hysterical by the second. "Women are pawns in a man's world. They don't *get* to choose!"

God, he was a sick bastard. No one would mourn his death. Not a single soul.

When Kieran took another small step back, Logan's gaze zeroed in on the water pooling around Grace's chin. Her eyes finally closed. *Fuck.*

Scuffling sounded behind him. Feet against rock. People were here. His team. But they wouldn't make it in time. It was up to him.

Logan took another step forward. One to go.

"If I want her, I get her. And if I choose for her to die with me rather than live with you, then that's what's going to happen!"

Logan took his final step—then he leaped. Hand closing around Kieran's, tugging the knife from Grace's neck.

Kieran growled and thrashed, releasing Grace as he attempted to wrench the knife back and fend off Logan. But even injured, Logan was too strong. He plunged the blade straight into Kieran's neck.

Grace's body dropped below the surface of the water, but only for seconds before Logan released the knife and lifted her out, hurrying her to shore.

Blake made it to them first. "I can take her."

Flynn ran past them and dove into the water to get Kieran.

"No. I have her." And he wasn't letting go. Ever.

CHAPTER 35

*W*armth. It seeped from Logan's arm around her waist, right through her skin and into her heart. It was a warmth she'd been craving throughout the last week, ever since waking up in that hospital bed with hypothermia.

His thumb drew small circles against her ribs as Blake and Aidan spoke, sitting opposite them in a booth at The Grind.

She was still in shock about Lizzie. Never in her wildest imagination had she thought the woman's emotions hadn't been genuine.

Logan's head lowered, his mouth brushing against her ear as he whispered, "Stop beating yourself up."

She glanced at him, nodding. The man had been her everything over the last week. Not a day passed when she wasn't grateful for him. "It's hard."

His hand tightened. "I know. It will take us all a while to recover from everything."

Logan hadn't said the words out loud, but she knew he was shouldering a large chunk of the guilt. Guilt for letting himself get shot. For not being able to protect her from the start.

She shuffled closer. More beautiful warmth.

The low thrum of the coffee machine pulled her attention to the counter. Customers buzzed around the shop, their chatter echoing through the space.

"I'm just going to talk to Courtney." She leaned up, pressing a kiss to his lips before standing and walking across the room. She felt Logan's eyes on her the entire way. That had become her norm. Any time he wasn't by her side, he was watching.

She took a seat at the counter. She and Courtney had chatted a lot over the last few days. About Kieran. About her past. About what had happened on the beach.

And Courtney had spoken briefly about what happened here at The Grind, with Grace apologizing profusely for getting her entangled in it all.

Her friend's spine straightened as she made coffees. Suddenly, she turned, hands on hips, eyes narrowed. "Grace, *stop*. I'm fine."

Grace kept her voice gentle. "I know."

She'd already told Courtney that she was here if she needed to talk to someone. The woman had been locked in the freezer with Nicole's dead body for almost two hours before Aidan had found her. Nicole had been dead for over a week. The smell alone would have been unimaginable.

Now, Courtney gave her the same smile she'd been giving her since their rescue. The one that said, "Thank you for your concern but it's not necessary."

Guilt pressed on Grace's chest. She just didn't believe that Courtney was as "fine" as she claimed.

Her friend turned back to the coffee machine. "And having all those guys constantly checking on me in the hospital wasn't so bad. I swear I saw jealousy flick across every nurse's face."

Grace smiled. Courtney wasn't ready to *really* talk. But if the time came when she was, Grace would listen. "Well, I'm here for you, and I'm glad you're safe."

It could have been worse. So much worse. She only just

suppressed the shiver of unease that threatened to snake up her spine.

Courtney walked over to Joey, handing him two coffees before returning to Grace. "It's *you* that we should be worrying about. How are you doing?"

"Honestly, waking up and being told Kieran was dead...I was able to breathe my first easy breath in over eight years."

Well, maybe not "easy", not after becoming his victim again. But the relief had been overwhelming. It still was.

"And your dad?"

Grace swallowed. "Doctors want to keep him at the hospital a little longer for observation." He'd been unconscious when Logan had woken and broken out of his restraints, but his heart was still beating. The hospital had confirmed lots of bruising and a few broken bones, but the worst was the fracture to his skull.

Courtney reached across the counter, taking Grace's hand with her own. "But he'll be okay?"

"He should make a full recovery." *Thank God.*

He'd still been unconscious when Logan's team found him. If Grace had been the one to find him, out cold, bleeding on the floor...

She breathed through the pain of what had happened to him.

He'd only been kidnapped the day before. Returning home from work when he was hit on the back of the head, knocked out cold.

His work noticed his absence and tried calling, but her father hadn't been missing long enough for anyone to be overly worried.

Courtney squeezed her hand. "You and your dad are here, alive. Safe. If either of you need anything, even if it's just coffee and croissants expedited to his room, you let me know."

Grace smiled. "I'm sure he'll take you up on that offer when I mention it."

"Good. It will make me feel like I'm helping."

"Thank you. You've been such a good friend to me since I arrived in Cradle Mountain. You, Logan, and his entire team have made me feel so welcome."

Courtney smiled. "Does that mean you're here to stay?"

"Yep. For as long as Logan will have me."

Courtney squealed, clapping her hands. "Yay! The man is obsessed with you, so that's obviously going to be forever."

Sounded perfect to Grace.

When the door to the coffee shop opened, Courtney looked up, her cheeks immediately flushing. Grace didn't need to turn around to know who had entered.

Jason.

To confirm her thoughts anyway, Grace glanced over her shoulder and, sure enough, all six and a half feet of the man were heading toward Logan's booth.

He shot a quick look over to them, his gaze landing on Courtney before sending a wink her way.

Grace turned back to Courtney, noticing the red in her friend's cheeks had deepened.

Cute.

Courtney was just grabbing for a cloth when she paused, letting out a little squeak. Her eyes glowed with excitement. "They're here!"

Turning her head again, this time Grace saw a man and woman entering the shop. They held a big bag of what looked to be camera equipment.

Ah, it was time for the magazine photo shoot.

Grace wasn't surprised to hear her friend had won Most Unique Coffee Shop in Idaho. She'd been expecting it. But she was definitely proud.

"How do I look?" Courtney placed her hands on her hips and turned from side to side.

"Amazing." Her dress was bright pink with colorful polka

dots, and the streaks in her hair looked even more fluorescent than normal.

Courtney's smile widened. "Thanks. Time for me to dazzle!"

She watched her friend head down to the other end of the counter. Grace was barely alone for a second when a pair of large, muscular arms wrapped around her waist from behind. Warm breath brushed across her ear and neck, sending goose bumps racing along her skin.

"I think I should win an award too. For waiting so patiently over there."

Grace chuckled, spinning around on her barstool and placing her hands on his shoulders. "Hm, I agree. How about a kiss as a prize?"

"How about ten?"

"I can do that." She could do twenty.

Skimming her hands through his hair, she pulled his head down slowly, pressing her lips to his. Grace's heart drummed against her ribs. It always did with Logan.

"Mm." He eased back, but only a fraction. "I could kiss you all day."

When his gaze dropped to the bandage on her neck, his jaw visibly tensed. The tension only lasted for a second before he seemingly forced himself to calm.

He'd been doing that for days. Fire blooming in his eyes before he had a chance to mask it.

Grace took his face in her hands, letting the warmth of his skin penetrate her limbs once again. "I love you, and I'm okay."

Because of him. His strength. His courage. His love. She was okay.

GRACE's small hands on his cheeks brought him back to her. So did her words. She'd repeated that same sentence many times in the last few days. The woman knew he needed to hear them.

Kieran was dead. Grace was alive and safe. That's what he had to focus on.

She kissed him again. Just like always, it reached a part of his soul that no one had ever touched.

"I don't know if I'll ever be able to let you out of my sight again." He was a step away from signing himself up as her lifelong bodyguard.

She tilted her head to the side, a small smile stretching her lips. God, he loved that smile. "Well, you'll have to. Because I paid my deposit today."

Some of the tension eased from his shoulders, a smile stretching his lips. "You did?"

"Mm-hm. You are currently looking at Cradle Mountain's newest business owner. McKenna Counseling is one step closer to opening its doors."

His hands tightened on her waist. It was official. She was staying in Cradle Mountain. Staying with *him*. "Are you sure this is what you want?"

"Logan Snyder, I love you. *You* are what I want. So if you're here, I'm here."

His eyes shuttered, forehead touching hers. "You have no idea what those words do to me. I love you, too, Grace. Thank you."

Her fingers grazed the back of his neck. "Why are you thanking me?"

"For being so strong. For surviving. For loving me."

He was grateful for everything.

This woman had given him a peace like he'd never felt before, making everything he'd gone through in life up to this point feel worth it. Because it had all led him here. To her. And this was exactly where he wanted to be.

CHAPTER 36

*J*ason took a sip of his coffee, smiling at the sight of Logan at the counter. The man was so damn happy. And he deserved every second of it.

Hell, after everything the man had gone through, both before and after meeting Grace, he deserved peace.

"We're shortlisting applicants today, Jason. You still okay to train whoever we hire?"

Jason dragged his gaze across the table to his friends and teammates. It was Blake who'd asked the question, but Aidan sat beside him, also awaiting an answer.

"Yeah, that's fine. You guys are doing the searching and interviewing, so I'm happy to train."

Aidan lifted his brows suggestively. "Should we hire a single woman?"

Blake frowned. "Are we allowed to ask that in an interview?"

Jason tuned his friends out, instinctively searching for Courtney. He'd been finding himself doing that more often lately. She was behind the counter, a dozen of her mugs lined up in front of her as she smiled for the camera.

A matching smile that was impossible to stop stretched across his own lips.

The woman was cute. And quirky. And a hundred other things that commanded his attention.

There was just one problem.

"Looks like whoever the new receptionist is, she's all yours, Aidan," Blake said, pulling Jason's attention back to them. "Our brother over here has his eye on someone else." Blake grinned. "What are you waiting for, buddy? Ask her out."

When Courtney walked down the counter and slipped into the kitchen, Jason reluctantly focused on his friends. "I would, but..."

He stopped, not sure exactly how to explain it. Not when it barely made sense to him.

Aidan frowned. "What is it?"

"Sometimes it seems like she's interested." Like minutes ago, when he'd walked in and she'd blushed. "Then other times it's almost like she can't wait to get away from me."

Both his friends raised their brows.

Just like the rest of his team, Jason was tall, standing well over six feet. He was big, too. And the world knew what he'd gone through. What he was capable of.

Was she intimidated?

Blake shook his head. "Why would she want to get away from you? You're like a big teddy bear."

"Who knows how to kill people," Aidan scoffed

"*Has* killed people," Blake added.

Jesus Christ. "Not helping, guys."

Jason managed to turn the topic of conversation away from him and over to business. But when a few more minutes passed and Courtney still hadn't returned, he frowned. The people with the cameras were studying the door she'd disappeared through, seemingly also wondering where she'd gone.

Pushing to his feet, Jason excused himself from the table and headed toward the end of the counter nearest the kitchen. He stood there a moment, listening, trying to isolate what he hoped to hear. A few seconds passed, then he found it.

Her heartbeat. It was thumping in her chest, hard and fast.

Not caring that he was only a customer and not supposed to enter this part of the shop, Jason headed behind the counter and into the back room.

That's when he saw her. Standing in profile at the closed door of the small walk-in freezer. The freezer where Aidan had found her, trapped with Nicole's body.

She looked at it like it was some sort of puzzle she was trying to solve as she fiddled with her necklace, a small frown marring her brows.

Jason walked forward slowly. She didn't seem to see or hear him at all, confirming how intensely she was focusing.

"Courtney?"

Even though he tried to say her name as quietly as possible, she still jumped about a mile high before swinging her head around to face him.

For a moment, she seemed confused. Her mouth opened and closed multiple times, her eyes darting between his face, his chest, and the freezer.

"Are you okay?"

She wrapped her arms around her waist in a defensive gesture. "Yes. I mean, of course. I, um, just popped back here to grab some cakes we have in the freezer...for the shoot."

It was the first time she'd spoken to him without freezing or rambling. Something told him she was too distracted right now. He scanned the freezer door. "Do you want me to open it?"

When her gaze shot back to the freezer, she nibbled her bottom lip. He tried not to focus on her mouth, but that small gesture was doing crazy things to his insides.

"Yes, please."

He hated the fear mixed with frustration that coated her voice.

Moving forward, he tugged open the door. The freezer was narrow but deep, and he'd have to duck his head if he walked in. When she continued to stand there, not moving, he tilted his head. "Where are the cakes?"

Her relief was so thick he could almost feel it. Her body practically sagged. "At the back, on the top shelf."

Crouching slightly, Jason walked inside the cool room, grabbing the three cake boxes before heading out. She immediately closed the door after him.

For a moment, he stood there, wanting to talk to her about what had just happened. He was about to do just that, but she spoke before he could.

"Thank you. I, um...don't like the cold." Lie. "It's good to have another set of hands. I have Joey, but he's busy. I have a couple others on staff, but they usually work when I don't, mostly weekends."

"Anytime, Courtney."

She wet her lips. This time, his gaze zeroed in on her tongue as it swiped across her rosy-pink mouth.

His groin tightened. Fuck, but the woman affected him.

She took the boxes from his hands. For a brief second, their fingers touched, and a strange zing rushed through him.

Sighing quietly when she turned, Jason followed her out. They were just about to step back into the main shop when Courtney stopped and turned. "Is it okay if we keep this between us?"

His eyes softened at her vulnerability. "I won't say anything, Courtney."

Another visible wave of relief washed over her. Then she smiled. It was the first time she'd smiled directly at *him*—and it was radiant.

Damn, he needed to give her reason to smile at him more often. He made a mental note to do just that.

Order JASON today!

ALSO BY NYSSA KATHRYN

PROJECT ARMA SERIES

Uncovering Project Arma

Luca

Eden

Asher

Mason

Wyatt

Bodie

Oliver

Kye

BLUE HALO SERIES

(series ongoing)

Logan

Jason

Blake

JOIN my newsletter and be the first to find out about sales and new releases!

~ https://www.nyssakathryn.com/vip-newsletter~

ABOUT THE AUTHOR

Nyssa Kathryn is a romantic suspense author. She lives in South Australia with her daughter and hubby and takes every chance she can to be plotting and writing. Always an avid reader of romance novels, she considers alpha males and happily-ever-afters to be her jam.

Don't forget to follow Nyssa and never miss another release.

Facebook | Instagram | Amazon | Goodreads

JUN   2023

CPSIA information can be obtained
at www.ICGtesting.com
Printed in the USA
BVHW041652250423
663034BV00018B/252